THE FLATEY ENIGMA

Forthcoming from Viktor Arnar Ingolfsson:

House of Evidence

Day Break

THE FLATEY ENIGMA

VIKTOR ARNAR INGOLFSSON

Translated by Brian FitzGibbon

The characters and events portrayed in this book are fictitious. Any similarity to real persons, living or dead, is coincidental and not intended by the author.

Printed in the United States of America.

The Flatey Enigma was first published in 2002 by Forlagid as *Flateyjargáta*. Translated from Icelandic by Brian FitzGibbon. Published in English by AmazonCrossing in 2012.

Published by AmazonCrossing
P.O. Box 400818
Las Vegas, NV 89140

ISBN-13: 9781611090970
ISBN-10: 1611090970
Library of Congress Control Number: 2011963582

This book is dedicated to the memory of
my grandfather and grandmother,
Viktor Guðnason and Jónína Ólafsdóttir.

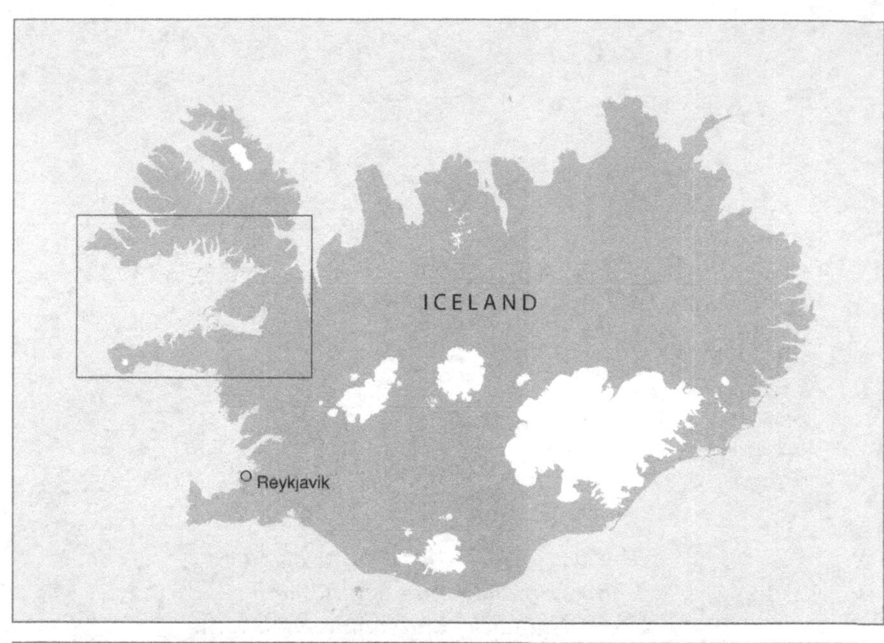
ICELAND
Reykjavik

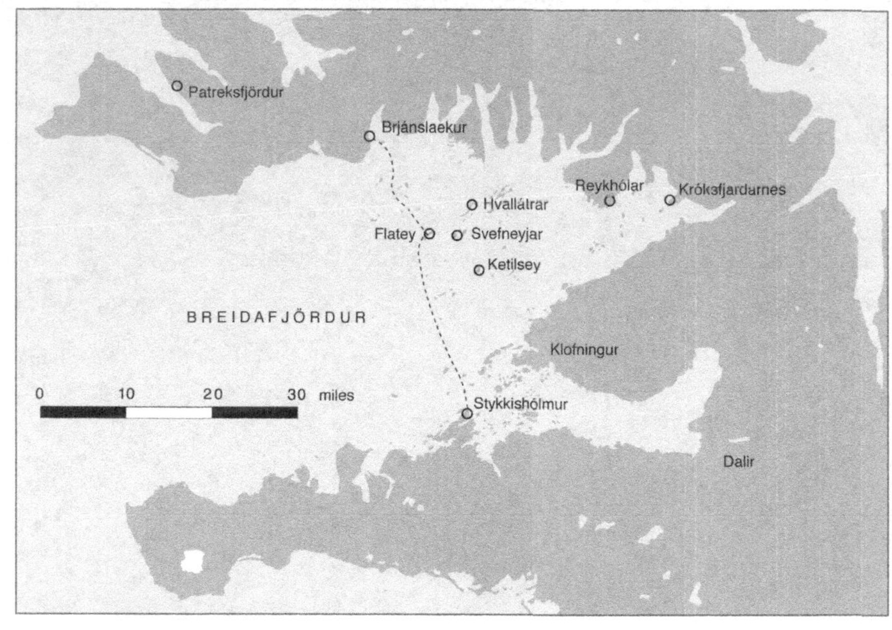
Patreksfjördur
Brjánslaekur
Reykhólar
Króksfjardarnes
Hvallátrar
Flatey
Svefneyjar
Ketilsey
BREIDAFJÖRDUR
Klofningur
0
10
20
30
miles
Stykkishólmur
Dalir

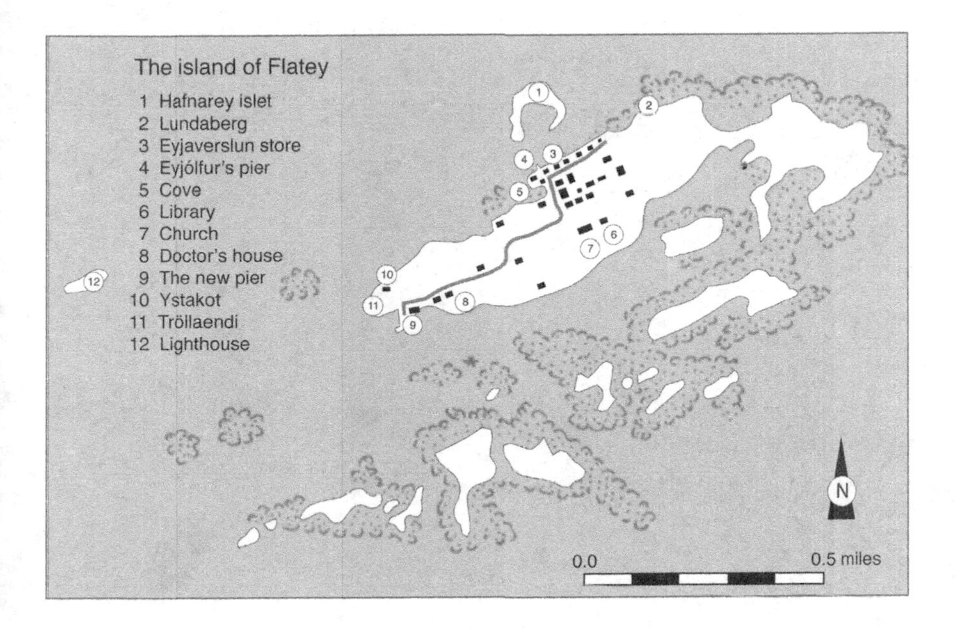

The island of Flatey
1 Hafnarey islet
2 Lundaberg
3 Eyjaverslun store
4 Eyjólfur's pier
5 Cove
6 Library
7 Church
8 Doctor's house
9 The new pier
10 Ystakot
11 Tröllaendi
12 Lighthouse
1
2
3
4
5
6
7
8
9
10
11
12
N
0.0
0.5 miles

The village on the island of Flatey in Breidafjördur has been used as a backdrop for several movies, but normally as a surrogate for some other place. On this occasion, the location is used to represent itself under its own name, since this story is set on the Breidafjördur islands in 1960.

The nature has been borrowed: its birds, seals, fish, winds, stillness, smells, and sounds. So too have its boats, piers, houses, hens, cows, and potato patches. But not its people. The characters who appear in this story are not based on any of the real people who inhabited those islands during those years. If anyone feels they see any similarities with actual people, they are purely coincidental. The events that are described here are pure fiction, but I would like to thank the islanders for lending me this setting for my story.

CHAPTER 1

Wednesday, June 1, 1960

An easterly wind swept across Breidafjördur with the break of dawn, and a sharp spring breeze intensified the foam of the waves breaking on the strait between the Western Isles. A determined puffin flew low, skimming the surface of the waves at high speed, and an inquisitive sea raven stretched its wings on a reef. Black guillemots plunged into the ocean, while knowing seagulls circled the air high above, scanning the horizon for food. The whole of creation in the fjord was ablaze with life and alertness in the glaring morning sun.

A small but sturdy motorboat tackled the choppy waves and moved away from the island of Flatey toward the south. The small vessel was a converted old rowboat and tarred in black, with its name painted on the stern in large white letters: *RAVEN*. It carried a crew of three: a young boy, a grown man, and another, who was considerably older. Three generations from a small croft called Ystakot, on the western corner of the island of Flatey.

Jón Ferdinand, the eldest, sat at the stern, steering. White stubble sprouted from his hollow face, and black snuff trickled out of his wide nostrils. Some tufts of gray hair spilled out of his old peaked cap, groping for his face in the wind. His big and rawboned hand held the tiller, as the old eyes under his bushy eyebrows searched for a little island in the south. It wasn't such an easy course to sail, even though visibility was good. Islets and skerries were scattered across the horizon before the mainland, beyond which lay the Dalafjoll mountains in the blue dusk.

Jón Ferdinand steered the boat head-on against the largest waves but held his course in the gaps between them. It was a small vessel, so it could be unpleasant if the waves hit the side of the boat directly. But the old man sailed by his instincts and seemed to enjoy this duel with the sea.

Gudvaldur, the steersman's son, sat down on the thwart in front of the engine bay, smoking a pipe and sharpening a large pocket-knife. Bareheaded, in a thick woolen sweater, he turned away with his pipe to avoid the spray of the waves that occasionally splashed over the gunwale. He had a weather-beaten face and a rugged expression and was blind in his left eye, following an injury to the eyeball that had whitened as it healed. The other eye was pitch black. Gudvaldur was named after a long-dead ancestor who had visited his mother in a dream, but locals normally just called him Valdi and associated him with the croft of Ystakot in Flatey.

A freak high wave broke over the boat, splashing the curly hair on the back of Valdi's neck. He looked up and scanned ahead. "Careful, Dad," he barked. "Don't forget it's Ketilsey were going to; you're heading too far south."

The old man smiled, flashing his few yellow teeth and raw gums.

"Too far south, too far south," he repeated in his husky voice, turning the boat against the wave, and Valdi resumed smoking his pipe and fiddling with his knife once he saw they were back on course again.

Little Nonni Gudvaldsson sat on a folded sail at the bow, clinging to the gunwale with both hands. He was feeling cold and seasick, and although he was well used to the sea and didn't normally allow the chill and queasiness to get to him, this was worse than usual because of his urgent, unseamanlike need to empty his bowels. Nonni had been late that morning and forgot to visit the outhouse before they left. He made no mention of this to his father because Valdi would just have told him to squat over the gunwale and do it right there. The boy didn't fancy that in these rough waters. Every now and then he stretched his head over the stern to see if they were drawing any closer to their destination, but the boat seemed to be taking forever. Then he lay on the folded sail again, pigheadedly bit his lip, and tried to contract the muscles of his anus. Shutting his eyes tight, he muttered to himself over and over: "For Christ's sake, Jesus, for Christ's sake, don't let me shit in my pants today."

He glanced toward the front of the boat again.

"Dad, Dad," he called out, "Grandpa's forgetting himself again."

Valdi looked up and turned to the old man. "You're veering too far east. We're going to Ketilsey, remember? Seal hunting."

The old man seemed bewildered a moment but then regained his focus. He wrestled with another wave and headed straight for the island, which was now just a short distance away. Then he looked at Valdi, muttering an old refrain: "To Ketilsey the men did row, to catch the sixteen seals."

Valdi didn't answer, stuck his knife back into his pocket, and emptied his pipe on the gunwale. Then he moved back to the stern.

The tide was out at the island, and the landing toward the south was well sheltered. Valdi took command of the boat now and Jón Ferdinand waited, ready with a small anchor dangling from a long chain. The boat broke a wave, which crashed on the rocks, and Valdi turned the engine off as the old man dropped the anchor. The chain slid overboard with a rattle, and shrieking birds shot into the air from the island. A seal surfaced a short distance away before suddenly vanishing into the depths again. Little Nonni stood ready at the stern, and as soon as the anchor had steadied the boat, he managed to grab a bulky, rusty iron ring hanging from the rock, and to slip the rope through it and fasten it. Hopping onto the boat again, he stretched over to grab a pile of old newspapers from the place where they were kept under the cover of the engine bay. Valdi watched the boy leap off the boat and disappear behind the rock.

"I've told you many times before not to shit on the island," he growled. "The seals will pick up your scent for weeks."

Little Nonni felt a tinge of guilt. This was one of the golden rules of seal hunting, but he couldn't help it. He ran up the island, found a good spot between the rocks, and yanked down his pants. The relief was immense, and he started to look around now. Natural monoliths formed a sheltered alcove, and two eider ducks lay brooding a short distance away. They were perfectly still, and only a trained eye would have been able to distinguish them from the turf. A sea pie perched on a rock and screeched loudly. His nest was probably close by on the edge of the shore. Further on, under a mighty boulder, lay the carcass of a large animal.

Nonni had often seen things like this on the shore, small whales, fat gray seals, or the bloated carcass of an old sheep. The novelty of this specimen, though, was that it was dressed in a green parka.

"Tell me about the Flatey Book,*" he asked.*

She pondered a moment. "Do you want to hear the long story or the short one?" she finally asked.

"The longer story if you have the time."

She gazed through the window where the sun was setting behind the mountains in the northwest and said in a soft voice, "I've got plenty of time now."

CHAPTER 2

Thursday, June 2, 1960

The mail boat sailed from Stykkishólmur to the island of Flatey once a week, on Saturdays, and then traveled on to Bardaströnd north of Breidafjördur. The wharf was in Brjánslækur, and it was there that the few farmers who inhabited the roadless fjords to the east of it came to collect their mail. Transport was limited in these parts, and the vast differences between the tides made sea travel there very difficult.

Once a road had been built over Kleifaheidi, there was far greater access to Patreksfjördur in the west and the villages to the north of it. A growing number of passengers started to travel on the mail boat, which increased its transportation of goods.

The boat followed the same route back from Brjánslækur, stopping off in Flatey on the way and terminating its journey in Stykkishólmur. The whole trip took an entire day, and it was often in the small hours that the boat was finally tied to the wharf of its home harbor.

Life was fairly uneventful in Brjánslækur when there was no mail boat on the way. On this particular Thursday, however, a young stranger stood on the wharf, watching an open motorboat approaching the shore, long in the distance from the south. The man was dressed in a coat tied with a belt at the waist. He was of average height, slim, and sported a conspicuous scar on his forehead. He squinted his gray eyes at the glaring sunlight, as if he were unaccustomed to light, and the cool breeze ruffled his thick, dark hair. A metallic oblong box with handles on the side lay at his feet.

The man stood alone on the wharf, watched from a short distance away by two old men under a shed who were intrigued by this unusual guest. A small truck was driving up the road, away from the wharf, and it soon vanished from sight to the west in a cloud of dust.

This was clearly an alien environment to the young man, and he anxiously scanned the broad fjord and islands in the distance. Two ravens hovered high above his head, croaking at each other. Down on the sea, some arctic terns fluttered and screeched. These riotous birds brought back memories, and they weren't good ones either, so he instinctively blocked his ears with his hands and closed his eyes a moment—until he realized that it was pointless trying to shut them off like that and decided to shrug off the feeling. He dug his hands deep into his pockets and clenched his fists.

The boat was pulling into shore now. The engine had been turned off, and the vessel was being steered toward the wharf. The stranger caught the rope tossed to him by the men on the boat and held onto it as the two men climbed onto the edge of the wharf.

"Hello there," said the man who stepped up first—a vigorous man in his sixties, chubby, with a round, ruddy face, a collar of white beard that lined his big cheeks, and a stubby nose. He was wearing thigh-high boots, an old woolen pinstriped cardigan, and a black cap on his head.

"I'm Ellidagrímur Einarsson, administrative officer of the district of Flatey; call me Grímur. I guess you must be the district magistrate's representative from Patreksfjördur?"

"Yes, I'm Kjartan," the man who had been waiting on the pier answered, taking the hand the officer was holding out to him. It felt thick and the skin was rough, but it was a warm and firm handshake.

"This is Högni, our teacher from the Flatey primary school and our church organist," said the local officer, indicating his partner, a tall, spare man in neat blue overalls and high Wellingtons. "Högni works with me during the seal-hunting season in the spring and helps out with the hay when the harvesting starts," the officer added.

Högni gave the young man an equally vigorous handshake. He had a large gray moustache, well-groomed to the sides, but otherwise clean-shaven cheeks. The teacher seemed to be of the same age of his companion but bore his age well. A bright peaked cap perched over the back of his head.

The local officer observed the district magistrate's man for a moment and took out a tin of snuff.

"So you've only just started to work for the magistrate, have you?" he asked, offering Kjartan some snuff.

"Yes, I took the coaster to Patreksfjördur the day before yesterday," said Kjartan, declining the offer with a wave of his hand.

"And they've thrown you straight into the deep end!" Grímur grinned roguishly, handing Högni the tin of snuff.

"Yes, this isn't exactly the kind of assignment I was expecting. They told me working for the district magistrate would be a clerical job, and that I'd be dealing with notarizations and things like that."

"So this isn't a long-term career move then?" Grímur asked.

"No, just until the autumn."

"Are you training to become a district magistrate?"

"No, I just graduated in law this summer, and I wasn't planning on any district commissioning job."

"So what are you going to do then?"

"Well, I might be able to join a lawyer's practice in the fall, so one of my tutors got me this summer job. I'd like to work in property law in the future, so it'll be good experience for me to audit some mortgage pledges this summer."

The local officer glanced at the box that lay at their feet. "Right then, let's just get this box on board and pick up the corpse. But let's stop off in Flatey to grab a bite to eat from my wife, Imba, on the way. She should have some lunch ready by one if I know her right."

"Have you identified the deceased yet?" Kjartan asked. He was hoping for a yes to make his job a little bit easier, but his wish wasn't to be granted.

"No, we haven't," Grímur answered. "The only thing that Valdi from Ystakot could tell us was that his boy found a dead man in Ketilsey and nothing more. Those lads sure talk a lot, not that they ever make much sense, and they normally repeat everything twice. As far as I can make out, though, the poor wretch had been dead for some time. Might have been shipwrecked or something in the winter and got washed up by the spring tide. As far as I can tell, it's basically just a heap of bones, and our job is just to collect them, though I guess we better be prepared for anything. Then we've got to log it all and file a report, of course. You must be pretty good at that."

Kjartan couldn't remember any part of his law education that covered chores of this kind, but he imagined he'd be able to throw something down on paper. He instinctively dug his hand into his coat pocket and fished out a notebook and pen. He tested the pen on a blank sheet, and it seemed to be working. The islanders watched with interest.

"Yes, I can write the report," said Kjartan awkwardly, shoving the notebook back into his pocket again.

The islanders stepped down onto the boat and grabbed the box that Kjartan eased over the side of the wharf. A small suitcase was passed down in the same way, and then finally Kjartan himself, once he had loosened the moorings. Högni tied the box tightly to the thwart with some old string while Grímur cranked the engine. Throwing the engine into reverse, they backed away from the wharf until they were out in the open sea. Then they pressed forward, heading south at full speed.

She browsed through some pages of the Munksgaard edition of the Flatey Book. *Occasionally, she would stop and read a sentence out loud. Every page of the book contained a facsimile photograph of a vellum leaf from the original manuscript. The images were clear and legible, even though the full coloring of the original was missing. The pages were white and well preserved.*

She finally closed the book, then opened it again to the front page and started to tell the story in a low, confident, and unwavering voice: "The Book of Flatey *contains a variety of writings: it starts with the Eddic and the Hyndla poems, the tales of King Sigurdur Slefa, and genealogies. All of these writings were probably set down at the end of the book but then moved to the front of the manuscript before it was bound. The history of Eirik Vidförull starts to take off on the fourth page, followed by the saga of the mighty King Ólaf Tryggvason. Ólaf ruled Norway from 995 to 1000, and his story forms a large part of the manuscript and is interwoven with many other accounts and tales, such as the Jomsvikings saga, the sagas of the Faroe Islands, sagas of the Orkneys, sagas of the Greenlanders, and many more..."*

CHAPTER 3

As soon as they had passed the skerry by Brjánslækur, Högni moved to the bow and lay down on a canvas bag that was spread over a pile of nets. He drew his peaked cap over his eyes, crossed his arms over his chest, and stretched out his legs. Kjartan sat on the thwart opposite Grímur, who was steering. The engine growled noisily, and the conversation was spasmodic.

"Not the most comfortable place to sleep," Kjartan said when Högni had settled down.

"The man's tired," Grímur answered, "and he likes to have a lie down on sea trips. The working hours in the hunting season are long, and he isn't used to hard labor. He's a boarder at my wife Imba's place and pays for it by working for me in the summer."

"Is he a bachelor then?"

"He's a widower; his wife died a few years ago. He sleeps in the school building and has two meals a day at our place."

The boat sailed smoothly along its journey. Grímur kept a sharp eye on the course he was steering because in many places their sailing path was strewn with rocks and reefs.

Kjartan felt he needed to keep the conversation going, without quite knowing where to start. He gazed across the bay. Everywhere he looked there seemed to be islands big and small.

"I've never been to Breidafjördur before," he said. And then, just for the sake of it, he added: "It must be true what they say then, that the islands in this fjord are countless?"

Grímur smiled and seemed to be willing to participate in the conversation. "They're certainly not easy to count with any exactitude," he answered, "and first you've got to decide on what you call an island. If we define an island as a piece of land that's surrounded by sea at high tide and has some vegetation on it, then maybe we can count them. By that criteria, there are about three thousand islands that have been counted in the whole fjord. But then you've got the barren skerries that no one's been able to count with any certainty, so they can be considered to be countless."

Kjartan nodded, trying to strike an interested air.

Grímur pointed at an island that rose high out of the sea: "That's Hergilsey, which was recently abandoned by the last farmer. It's named after Hergil Hnapprass. Have you read Gísli's saga?"

"Yes, but not recently," Kjartan answered.

"Hergil's son was Ingjaldur, a farmer in Hergilsey. The story goes that he sheltered the outlawed Gísli Súrsson. When Börkur Digri was going to kill Ingjaldur to punish him for hiding the convict, Ingjaldur the old uttered the following words..."

Grímur took a deep breath, altered his voice, and declaimed: "*My clothes are rags anyway, so little do I care if I won't be able to wear them down any further.*"

Grímur grinned and then added: "The people of Breidafjördur weren't bothered by trivialities."

Kjartan nodded and attempted a smile.

Grímur carried on pointing at the islands as they sailed, naming them and recounting their histories. To the west there was the skerry of Oddbjarnarsker, which had important fishing grounds that the poor traveled to in the days of the famine to survive. Then there were the isles of Skeley, Langey, Feigsey, and Sýrey. Each place name had its own story.

Högni woke up from his nap, moved over to them, and contributed his own anecdotes. As Flatey appeared on the horizon, he said, "One Christmastime, just before the turn of the century, a ship was sailing from the mainland with wood cuttings they were supposed to sell in Flatey as firewood. There were six men on board, but they ran into bad weather and got lost on the way. They finally reached the island of Feigsey, but the boat was wrecked."

Högni pointed Feigsey out to Kjartan and then continued: "The men were there for days on end, cold and without any food, but they could see people walking between the houses in Flatey when there was light during the day. Finally, their shouts were heard and they were rescued. They all survived the ordeal, which was quite a feat, because they'd had no food apart from a small ration of butter. A few decades ago a foreign freighter sank in the fjord here. It was carrying a cargo of telephone poles and barrels of thick motor lubricant. A rescue was launched, and some of the goods floated to shore. The men didn't really like the taste of what they took to be foreign butter, but it seemed to last forever."

Grímur laughed loudly at the story, even though he had definitely heard it often before and, in fact, had been one of the men who had tasted the motor grease.

Their chatter made time pass quickly, and they soon neared their destination.

As they drew closer, Kjartan was surprised to see how many houses there were on Flatey. First the church appeared, shimmering in a haze, since it stood at the top of the island, painted in white with a red roof. Then the village gradually started to take shape. The sun glared on the multicolored gables of the houses, and in many places laundry flapped on clotheslines.

Grímur slowed down the engine as they passed a small isle with high bird cliffs covered in white shells on its northern side but a well-sheltered bay that faced Flatey on its southern side. The strait between the island was no more than a hundred meters wide.

"We call that islet Hafnarey," Grímur announced. "Scientists say it's an ancient volcanic crater." He still needed to raise his voice because the screeching of the birds had now taken over from the noise produced by the boat's engine.

They sailed slowly into the strait and approached a small, dilapidated concrete pier below the village. Some kids were watching them with natural interest.

"This is called Eyjólfur's pier. The new pier is over by the fish factory at the southern end of the island," said Grímur. He steered the boat toward the mooring buoy floating in the strait and grabbed it with a short hook as they passed it. Högni tied the boat's stern to the anchored buoy and then moved to the bow to be ready for when they reached the pier. Kjartan sat on the thwart beside the casket and felt an urge to help them, but the crew seemed to be doing a good job and he would have undoubtedly just been in their way. Högni hopped onto the step below the pier with the rope and held the boat while Kjartan and Grímur clambered out after him. Högni then released the hawser and allowed the anchored buoy to drag the boat away from the pier again.

He scolded the children as he tightened the knot: “I strictly forbid you to go on that boat.” Then, to drive the point home, he added, “District Officer Grímur will stick you in that casket if you disobey!”

The kids recoiled slightly at the sound of this threat and stuck their heads together. A short and stocky man, dressed in dark Sunday clothes with a black hat and silver walking stick poised in his hand, elbowed his way through the throng of children and greeted Kjartan.

“Thormódur Krákur, I’m the deacon and the island’s eider-down tradesman,” he introduced himself in a loud voice, tilting on his toes and rocking to and fro.

“I’m Kjartan...the district magistrate’s assistant,” the new arrival said, hesitantly.

Thormódur Krákur bowed deeply. “Welcome to the district of Flatey, my good sir and officer. This is hardly the most felicitous of occasions, of course, but we islanders always welcome visitors from our most distinguished magistrature.”

“Thank you,” said Kjartan, transfixed by the medal that dangled from a threadbare ribbon on the deacon’s lapel.

Thormódur Krákur continued with his speech but lowered his voice now: “The church will, of course, be open for you when you return with the deceased. I’ll come down with a handcart to transport the casket when you arrive. Our pastor will find some appropriate words.”

“Yes...thank you,” said Kjartan. He hadn’t really thought about that aspect of the job. The district magistrate had only instructed him to collect the body from the island and to send it on the mail boat to Reykjavik, which was expected in two days’ time, and then write a report. After that his job was supposed to be done.

"But wouldn't it be possible to get a car for the casket?" Kjartan asked.

"The only possibility then would be to use the van from the fish factory, but it hasn't been started yet this spring. Krákur's cart is perfectly adequate," Grímur answered.

The deacon tilted on his toes again and said, "Yes, my cart is always used by the church for funerals here on Flatey."

"Very well," said Kjartan. "Thank you for taking care of that."

Grímur wavered impatiently. "My wife, Imba, is ready with the lunch," he said. "Let's not keep her waiting."

They walked across the village with Thormódur Krákur leading the way. Shouldering his walking stick like a rifle, he swung his other arm to the beat of a military march. Women were tending to their clotheslines in front of several houses and curiously observed the men as they walked by. Thormódur Krákur outlined the lay of the land for Kjartan in a lofty voice and pointed with his free hand: "That's the warehouse over there, and there's the telephone exchange, and there's the co-operative store," he announced, "and this is where our blessed priest lives, Reverend Hannes, and that's Gudjón's boy there tentering the seal fur."

They walked past three furs that had been stretched on the gable with the furry side facing the wall, and a young man was nailing up the fourth.

"And this is the cove and sea wall that was built and paid for in silver." Thormódur Krákur pointed at a long wall of piled stones that enclosed a narrow cove. They were being followed by a coil-tailed black dog, and a pack of cackling multicolored hens stepped out of their way on the road.

"And that up there is our church and graveyard, and behind the church there's the oldest library building in Iceland. It's not very big, but it contains various gems if you take a look. Even a perfect replica of the *Book of Flatey*, the most famous manuscript in Nordic history, the *Codex Flateyensis*, printed and bound by Munksgaard in Copenhagen and bequeathed to the library of Flatey as a gift to celebrate its hundredth anniversary."

The district officer's house was painted in white with a green roof and stood on the edge of the slope overlooking the village. The name of the house, *BAKKI*, was painted in big black letters on a sign over the door. Thormódur Krákur escorted the men to the entrance and then took off his hat to say good-bye with a handshake.

"I'll be at your disposal then when you come back," he said finally, tilting on his toes again. He then swirled on his heels and solemnly walked down to the village.

"Does the deacon always dress like that?" Kjartan asked Grímur as he watched the man walk away.

"No. Only on mass days and when he's receiving dignitaries," the district officer answered.

"He considers me to be a dignitary then, since this is hardly a mass day," said Kjartan awkwardly.

Grímur laughed. "Yes, my friend. Krákur has a deep reverence for authority figures, especially if they happen to be from the magistrate's office."

"What's that medal on his chest for?"

"That's the medal of honor from the parliamentary celebrations of 1930. Krákur received it for making a down quilt for the Danish king," Grímur answered.

"You've got to give it to him, though," Högni added, "he handles eiderdown better than most."

The mistress of the household welcomed them and ushered them into the living room where a small table had been laid for three.

"I'm Ingibjörg. I hope you'll be comfortable with us," she said when Kjartan greeted her and introduced himself. She was a thickset woman with a conspicuous birthmark on her right cheek, and she was dressed in traditional Icelandic clothes and a striped apron.

"I take it the magistrate's assistant will eat fresh seal meat, will he not?" Grímur asked as soon as he sat down.

Full of trepidation, Kjartan eyed several pieces of fat black meat steaming on a platter.

"Yes, maybe a little," he finally answered.

Högni also took a seat, since the woman of the house didn't seem to be expected to sit with them. She placed glasses on the table and a jug of water.

"We eat a lot of seal pup during the hunting season," said Grímur, stabbing a large piece. "And potatoes, too, if they're available."

Kjartan carved a tiny slice off one of the pieces and placed it on his plate. Then he stretched out for a potato.

The lady of the house reentered with a small simmering pot.

"Here's the melted sheep's fat. It's nice on top," said Grímur.

Kjartan could only bring himself to taste a morsel of the meat and then finished the potato.

Högni eyed him inquisitively and then said with a full mouth, "I once knew a man who wouldn't eat seal or sea raven either, but the funny thing was that he ate poultry and liked that."

Högni turned back to his plate and skillfully shoveled food into his mouth without soiling his distinguished moustache.

The lady of the house followed what was going on at the table from the kitchen doorway.

"Don't you like it, lad?" she asked when it was clear that Kjartan wasn't going to be having any seconds.

"I don't have much appetite after the crossing," he answered, taking a sip of water, although he felt that it, too, had a bizarre taste.

"You poor thing, what was I thinking? Let me see if I can find something gentler on the stomach after your sea journey." She vanished into the kitchen.

Grímur pointed through the west window of the living room.

"That's the doctor's house out there. We have a woman doctor now, and her name is Jóhanna. She lives there with her father, an old man, bedridden but very learned. He's far gone with cancer, poor man. Some people say he came here to die. Not the worst place to do that. It's a shorter distance to heaven from here, I mean. Our Jóhanna likes to keep to herself a bit, but she's a fine doctor. Behind the doctor's house there's our new fish factory. You can't see it from here. And beyond that there's the croft of Ystakot. It was the last croft to be built with turf walls on this island. That's where the clan who found the body live. There's no farming for them there, apart from their potato patch, but they go to Ketilsey and the skerries around there. They just about scrape by; it's a long way to go, and there aren't many eggs to be found. But they catch some seal and puffin there, too. They also do some line fishing and work at the fish factory when it's in operation."

For a brief moment the men focused on their meal until Ingibjörg reentered to place a bowl of soup in front of Kjartan.

"Here's some leftovers from yesterday's meat soup. I hope your stomach will find that more agreeable."

Kjartan tasted the soup and preferred it to the seal meat.

Grímur spoke again: "There are about sixty of us on the island right now. But people are leaving. It's mostly old folks that are left now. How many kids were there in the school this winter, Högni?"

Kjartan realized that the district officer knew exactly how many kids there were in the school and all their names, and that he undoubtedly knew more about their families than the kids did. The question had just been a ploy to draw the teacher into the conversation.

"There were fifteen, but many of them were from the inner islands," Högni answered punctiliously.

"Then they'll leave as soon as they can," Grímur continued. "There isn't much for youngsters to do around here the way things are right now. The catch is so meager, and the fish factory has never worked properly. Seventeen islands have been abandoned in this fjord over the past eighteen years, and now only eight of them are inhabited."

"How come?" Kjartan asked.

"The reason is simply that we don't have a sufficient work-force to be able to make full use of the resources this place has to offer. And young people are no longer content to be paid in food for their labor on the bigger farms. They want their wages in cash and to own their own houses. But Icelanders have yet to learn to appreciate these islands. With new farming equipment and good boats, there are many plots of land that could start yielding quite nicely here in the Western Isles, and that's something that'll happen with the coming generations. An area that can yield up to seventy pup seal furs every summer will always be considered to be a big asset in this country. The nation can't afford to allow resources like this go to waste, my friend."

Grímur looked at his plate and frowned. "The worst thing about this seal meat is that the fat cools off and hardens if you get carried away in conversation," he said and stood up. "But all you have to do is stick the plate on the stove to liven it up a bit again." He vanished into the kitchen with the plate in his hand.

Högni was full and stared inquisitively at Kjartan.

"Where are you from exactly?" he asked.

"I'm just from Reykjavik, from the east side," Kjartan answered politely.

"On both sides of the family?"

"Yes, Reykjavik on both sides."

"How old are you?"

"Thirty-two."

"So you started studying law a bit late then?"

"Yes."

"What delayed you? Lack of money, maybe?"

"You could say that."

"So I guess you must have worked to finance your studies before you started then?"

"You could say that."

"Where did you work?"

Kjartan hesitated before answering but was interrupted by Grímur, who returned with his plate and the melted fat simmering on the meat. "This is delicious," he said, smacking his lips. "Doesn't that soup go down nicely?" he asked Kjartan.

"Yes, thanks."

"That's good. You're welcome to stay in our loft until you've finished your business here. My sweet Imba will make sure you don't die of hunger."

"...This miscellany of episodes and sagas was characteristic of Icelandic literature in the fourteenth century. The objective was to collect related material from various sources in one book, and to compile and join stories about the same kings with the aim of forming a precise narrative, which was, broadly speaking, chronological,

even though the style could vary somewhat. The intention was more on collecting as much narrative material as possible than creating a structured whole. One could therefore say that the Flatey Book *is slightly chaotic when compared to Snorri Sturluson's* Chronicle of the Kings of Norway, *which deals with similar material. But thanks to this mania for collecting material, the* Flatey Book *contains many elements that cannot be found on vellum elsewhere, with countless episodes and verses. Ólaf Tryggvason's saga is followed by Helgi's saga, Sverrir Sigurdsson's saga, Hákon the Elderly's saga, and other tales. At the end of the book there is a set of annals that stretch from the origins of creation to the times in which the book was written...*"

CHAPTER 4

Lunch was now over in Flatey's district officer's home, and his wife placed a pot of coffee on the table. The men poured the boiling coffee into their empty glasses of water and snorted snuff. Kjartan also poured some coffee into his glass but declined Ingibjörg's offer of sugar and milk. The men sipped the hot coffee, sighed, and burped.

"I met a guy once who told me that coffee was God's gift to man to compensate for a long day's work," said Högni. "But I've always felt that there's no need for the good Lord to compensate man for the privilege of being able to work for his livelihood. But a drop of coffee is invigorating, and thank God for that."

Kjartan nodded approvingly.

"Now we're ready for anything," said Grímur, patting his potbelly and finishing the coffee in his glass. "Ghosts and specters won't bother you if you're on a full stomach," he added.

Högni laughed and said, "We call this the district officer's wisdom, and it's completely unproven."

Then they wandered outside, and the men grabbed two shovels from Grímur's barn. Kjartan asked why.

"You don't pick up a winter-old corpse with your bare hands. Not straight after lunch," Grímur answered, wiping a film of manure off the blade of the shovel with a tuft of grass he pulled up by the barn wall.

Kjartan followed the men, who walked off with the shovels on their shoulders, down to the village and across to the pier. Högni pulled the boat to the ledge, and they stepped on board. Grímur untied the moorings, turned on the engine, and headed off to the west of the island.

The district officer pointed out the Flatey lighthouse to Kjartan on a skerry a short distance away, and the croft of Ystakot soon appeared to the west of the tip of the island, half buried in the slope, just above sea level. A small, fenced-off patch of garden had newly been dug, and several neat-looking beds of dark brown soil could be seen. A young boy sat watching them on a rock on the shore.

"That's little Nonni," said Grímur. "He's just as peculiar as his dad and grandpa. He was in your school this winter, Högni, wasn't he?"

"Yes, and the kid can learn, but he only wants to do one thing at a time. He could spend days on end hunched over just one page of a botany book and then wouldn't talk about anything else. Then the next week it would be astronomy. He's become reasonably literate, though, and he's not bad at math either."

Högni gazed back at the land and then continued: "Valdi, little Nonni's dad, is also one hell of an eccentric. He's always scribbling worthless notes into a copybook. Details about the weather, who comes or goes on the mail boat, who attended mass and who didn't. And I think the old man, Jón Ferdinand, is going senile. He's also half deaf. Valdi's wife, Thóra, has given up on them all.

She works as a cook for a team of roadworks men on the mainland and never comes home. She just sends them money to buy some milk for little Nonni and some clothes."

Kjartan noticed that the boy was holding some glistening object to his eyes and that he watched their boat for a while until he suddenly stood up, ran to the croft, and disappeared inside.

Next the new pier and fish factory came into view. Three open motorboats were moored there, as well as a bigger boat with a pilot house. The smallest boat was black, and the others were painted white.

"Those fishing men haven't been able to catch anything recently," said Grímur. "They obviously didn't feel like going out this morning."

"They can't afford the fuel," said Högni. "I can't imagine the co-op giving them more of an overdraft."

"They should use their sail then," said Grímur. "The Ystakot clan still know how to do it. They can raise the sail if they can't afford the fuel for the engine. Their boat is that black one there. It's called *Raven*."

"Yeah, they sure know how to sail, those people," said Högni. "Old Jón Ferdinand was one of the most reliable foremen in Breidafjördur when he was still at the top of his game in the olden days. There weren't many who could steer sails better than he could. He could play ducks and drakes with those boats when the winds were good. They once sent him on a sailing boat to collect laborers in Króksfjardarnes. He had strong southeasterly winds in his sails on the way back and reached Flatey in only four hours. Even if the currents were with him, I don't think there are many people would have been able to handle it the way he did."

They soon reached Flatey's outermost reef and started to sail south toward a cluster of barely visible islands in the distance.

Kjartan dreaded reaching their destination. He had seen a dead person before, but it remained an uncomfortable memory. The task that awaited them was probably even grimmer. He nevertheless tried to feign interest as Grímur pointed out landmarks to him on their way—islands, skerries, and mountains in the distance, as well as the Svefneyjar islands behind them and Mount Klofningur on the mainland ahead.

As they approached Ketilsey, a great black-backed gull flew up and squawked. The sea splashed against the rocks as seals plunged into the ocean.

"They have this agreement between them," said Grímur. "The black-backed gull wakes up the seals when they're sleeping on the reefs. In return he'll get a good piece of the catch when the seal is fishing. His favorite part is the liver."

"...When ancient tales were written down on sheets of vellum, they were just one of many versions. Prior to that they had been passed down orally or written into older manuscripts. Each generation told the tales in their own way. My father told me stories from this book like fairy tales when I was a child. Since then I've trained my self to recount my favorite stories in my own way..."

CHAPTER 5

Ketilsey wasn't a big island, but finding the body wasn't easy. They had walked the full perimeter of its shore and then moved slightly higher. The district officer and the teacher were tired of searching.

"We should have taken Valdi with us and let him show us the spot," said Högni.

Grímur had his doubts. "Then the old man would've had to come along and probably the boy, too. They're practically inseparable."

He took off his cap and wiped the sweat from his brow with a red snuff handkerchief.

"Didn't the man say anything about where we should look?" Kjartan asked.

"No, damn it. I thought the corpse would just be lying there on the shore by the slip and that we would have been able to just follow the smell," Grímur answered.

"Could he have floated back into the sea?" Kjartan asked.

Grímur shook his head. "No, the tide is neap and the waves have barely moved since those men were here."

Högni glared at some of the black-backed gulls spiraling above them. "Do you think those bloody seagulls finished him off?" he asked.

Kjartan had almost given up on finding the body when he walked between some rocks. The green of the parka blended with the color of the patches of grass, and its hood was drawn over the skull so that only a portion of some bare facial bones were visible. Pants and shoes concealed the lower part of the body. A rotting stench lingered in the air, and a cluster of flies hovered above.

"He's here," Kjartan called out in a voice that he did not recognize as his own.

The men swiftly rushed to the scene, the district officer first.

"Not that I was expecting the smell to be pleasant," Grímur said, coughing.

"So this is where he was all along," Högni said in surprise, once he had examined the scene. "The sea must have been bloody wild this winter if it managed to chuck him all the way up here."

"No way," said Grímur. "There's no wreckage up here. The nearest pieces of driftwood and seaweed are thirty fathoms below."

Högni was taken aback. "Could it be that…" His voice trailed off.

Grímur looked around. "Yeah, he must have had some life left in him when he reached this island."

He scrutinized the man's body for a brief moment and then started to walk and look around.

"Look," he called out. Högni and Kjartan looked in the direction he was pointing.

It was a slanted crag against which several pieces of driftwood had been diagonally arranged. Stones and seaweed had then been piled onto the wood to create a small shelter. One man could have crawled into it and lain there lengthwise and been reasonably shielded.

"The man must have built this when he landed here. The Ystakot lads would never have done a botched job like this."

"Couldn't he have attracted someone's attention?" Kjartan asked. It was uncomfortable to think that the man could have been stranded there for some time, maybe in the heart of winter.

"No," Grímur answered, "that would have been difficult if he had nothing to make a fire with. The sailing routes are far west, and the next inhabited area is miles away. There are no fishing grounds around here, so no one comes until the Ystakot clan comes here to collect the eiderdown from the nests and hunt seal. There's nothing else that would draw anyone here."

"So did he starve to death?" Kjartan asked.

"Yeah, and froze. He wouldn't have been able to keep any heat in here without any fire. Especially if he crawled up here after being drenched in the sea."

"How the hell did he get all the way out here?" Högni asked. "There's no boat he could have come on. There's no regular sailing route that passes through here, so he could hardly have fallen off some ship."

"He must have come out here on a boat and lost it," Grímur answered. "Wouldn't be the first time."

"It would have been noticed if a man and his boat had gone missing from the fjord," said Högni.

"Unless he's from further afield," said Grímur.

"Doesn't matter. He still would've been missed," said Högni categorically.

"There was a shipwreck this winter in the distant west coast. Some men were presumed dead. Maybe one of them reached here on a lifeboat that drifted into the fjord and landed here."

"And the boat?"

"He could have lost it again."

"No," Högni disagreed. He stooped over the body and examined the clothes. "This is no sailor. Look at his shoes. These are the type of hiking shoes that tourists wear, leather."

"Right then," said Grímur, "this needs to be better investigated. Let's get him into the casket and head straight back to Flatey."

They fetched the casket and laid it by the side of the body. Next Grímur and Högni hoisted the body up with their shovels while Kjartan held the casket. Then they turned the casket so that the body rolled into it facedown. The patch of grass that appeared under the body was yellow and withered, apart from the swarm of maggots squirming in the roots of the grass.

"Shouldn't we turn him the right way around in the casket?" Kjartan asked.

"No," Grímur answered. "He won't be too bothered about which way he lies on such a short trip."

He took a glass receptacle out of his pocket, unscrewed the lid, and sprinkled it inside the casket. "I got this from the doctor," he said. "It'll reduce the smell and kill the flies and maggots."

The lid of the casket was lined with a rubber seal strip, designed to block out any air once it had been tightly screwed to the box.

They systematically combed the island for signs of the man's stay there. On a patch of grass at the tip of the isle, some flat stones had been arranged to clearly read as SOS, and each letter was about ten feet long. By the shelter they found an open plastic flask with a thin layer of water and some broken shells. There was nothing inside the shelter itself, however. Every possible crag was examined for any trace of information that the man might have scratched onto flat surfaces, but they found no marks that could have been left by a human. On one flat rock there were many small pebbles that seemed to form letters, although some of them had now been scattered by the forces of nature. Nevertheless, Kjartan drew a picture of them on a piece of paper, as precisely as he could, and readjusted two stones that seemed to have been thrown out of alignment and tried to form a word:

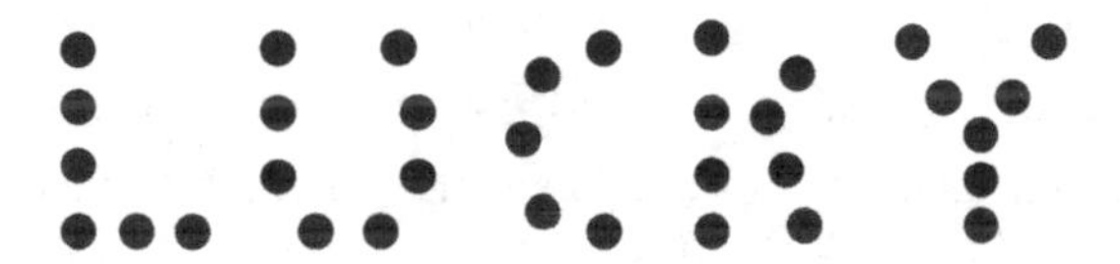

Grímur and Högni watched with interest. "Lucky? Does that have any special meaning around here?" Kjartan asked.

"No," Högni answered. "Although there's a stud bull in Hvallátrar called Lucky. The bull was given the name when he was young and got stranded on a skerry flooded at high water and had to swim to survive. It was a long way to land, and he probably wouldn't have survived if some people from Skáleyjar hadn't been passing there on their way to a dance in Flatey. At first they thought it was a seal that was swimming there, but then his ears popped up. They had never seen a seal with big ears in Breidafjördur before, so they swiftly hauled the calf on board. He got to travel with them to Flatey, and he was kept in a barn until he recovered from his ordeal."

Grímur and Högni fetched the casket and placed it on board the boat. Then they set off toward Flatey.

"Has anything like this ever happened on the islands before?" Kjartan asked as Högni was tying the casket to the thwart with some rope.

"There've been stories of people who were found frozen to death on the islands long after they were considered to have been lost at sea," Högni answered. "But they were known to be missing along with their boats and the rest of their crews. But this man was stranded on the island without anyone having the slightest idea that everything wasn't as it was supposed to be. I've never heard of anything like that in the fjord."

Although the casket had been painstakingly sealed, Kjartan could feel the stench clinging to him all the way at the back. He got very seasick, even though there was little movement from the waves, and repeatedly threw up over the gunwale. The islanders, on the other hand, snorted snuff with unusual frequency.

"…In the last decades of the fourteenth century there was a wealthy farmer in Vídidalstunga in the district of Húnavatnssýsla, who went by the name of Jón Hákonarson. We contemporaries know very little about this farmer, and he would, of course, have been forgotten today if he had never had the idea to create this majestic manuscript, which many years later came to be referred to as the Book of Flatey. *The writing of the manuscript took many years and was mostly completed in 1387. Some sections were then added in the years that followed, since the annals at the end of the book terminate in 1394.*

"It is impossible to say what led the farmer Jón Hákonarson to have these stories written down, but perhaps the manuscript was intended as a gift to a young man who at the time was taking over the kingdom of Norway, which at that time included Denmark and Sweden, and who bore the same name as two great kings who had reigned long before him—Ólaf. He was the third Norwegian king to bear that name, and the expectations that were placed on him were

clearly high. The vellum manuscript was also a veritable treasure that would have brought great honor at the royal court. But this Ólaf died or vanished in Denmark at around the time the book was being completed, and his death marked the end of Norwegian king Harald Fairhair's lineage. Ólaf's mother, Margrét Valdimarsdóttir, ascended to the throne and ruled until 1412..."

CHAPTER 6

It was close to seven o'clock by the time Grímur steered the boat toward Eyjólfur's pier in Flatey. Thormódur Krákur was standing on its edge, clutching his hat in his hands, with a large wooden cart by his side. Standing close to him was a priest in a cassock with a psalmbook in his hands. But apart from them there wasn't a soul in sight. The swarm of kids that had been so conspicuous earlier that day was nowhere to be seen, nor were there any curious faces peeping through the windows. The village seemed deserted.

Kjartan was stunned. "Where is everybody?" he asked Grímur. "Does everyone eat dinner at the same time around here or what?"

Grímur glanced across the village. "No, that's not the custom here. But people find events like these a bit disturbing. Death isn't much of an attraction around here, and people prefer to shun it."

"So people lock themselves inside then?" Kjartan asked.

"The adults avoid spectacles of this kind, and the children are kept indoors to avoid any inappropriate behavior," the district officer answered gravely.

Högni tied the boat to the pier, and Grímur and Kjartan carried the casket up the steps between them and placed it on the cart.

The priest, who was around seventy, possessed a solemn air, long gray sideburns, round glasses, and a bald head. He bowed and muttered something over the casket, which Kjartan neither heard nor understood. The priest then nodded at Thormódur Krákur, who put on his hat and started dragging the cart away. Grímur and Högni walked behind it, also helping to push it along. The priest followed behind, then finally Kjartan.

The path led up a slope, which proved to be no difficulty, because the load was light. Thormódur Krákur was obviously strong and capable of dragging the cart on his own without any great effort. The others nevertheless gently pushed behind as a token gesture. They took slow and dignified steps as the cartwheels screeched faintly to the rhythm of the silent march. It was a short distance to walk, but Kjartan felt it was taking them ages to reach their destination.

Thormódur Krákur opened the church doors with a large key, and the casket was borne inside. Two trestles has been prepared in the middle of the floor, and they lowered the casket onto them. Once this had been done, they walked outside again to breathe in some fresh air.

The village was suddenly bustling with life again. Children ran between houses. Three men were chatting at the bottom of the slope and occasionally glanced up at the church. Women unpegged their washing from the clotheslines. A young boy was escorting three cows at the bottom of the slope. The stillness had been magically dispelled.

"I asked Jóhanna, the doctor, to come over and take a look inside the casket," Grímur said. "She's more used to this kind of stuff than we are…I think."

The priest seemed eager to leave. "Remember to lock the door before you leave now, Krákur," he said over his shoulder as he rushed off.

"Reverend Hannes doesn't want to lose his appetite before dinner if he can avoid it," said Grímur, watching the priest speed away.

"I met a man once," said Högni, "who'd been sent to Oddbjarnarsker to fetch a body that had been washed up on the shore. It gave off such a terrible stench that he lost his appetite for three days, even though he felt hungry. He just couldn't keep the food down. Then they made him sniff some ammonia and he recovered."

"Does the doctor know we've arrived?" Kjartan asked.

"Everyone knows we've arrived," Grímur answered. "Jóhanna is bound to be here any second now."

"Isn't it difficult for a woman to be a doctor with transport being as difficult as it is on these islands?" Kjartan asked.

Grímur blew his nose before answering: "Hasn't been a problem so far. No one's had any sudden illnesses, and there are no pregnant women here. Anyone who's really sick gets sent to the hospital in Reykjavik. The main stuff she has to deal is arthritis, hemorrhoids, and toothaches. She's got strong hands and is quick at pulling out a tooth if she has to. She also learned how to drive a motorboat as soon as she moved to Flatey. She wants to be able to visit patients between the islands on her own if the weather's OK, without having to drag anyone away from their work."

"There's nothing new about a woman handling a boat on these islands," Högni added. "My great-grandmother, for example, used to be a foreman in the spring in Ólafsvík, so my grandfather was born in a fishing hut between trips."

"...In the decades before the manuscript was written, the black death had swept across Europe, and transport to Iceland was greatly reduced. The language of the Norse was changing, and they had probably lost the ability to be able to read the manuscripts that had previously been brought from Iceland. The sagas had largely been written to be exported and were obviously precious trading assets in the period in which the language spoken in Norway and Iceland remained the same. The Nordic countries were a single book market, as it were, and Snorri's Heimskringla, *or* History of the Kings, *was probably a best seller in Norway back then, just as much as it was after printing was invented. Jón Hákonarson's majestic manuscript was slow to get off the ground, on the other hand, because the Norse couldn't read their old language anymore, so it remained in Iceland for many centuries."*

CHAPTER 7

Grímur's predictions about the doctor's arrival proved to be correct. They did not have to wait long before a woman dressed in dark clothes appeared beyond the graveyard. She took the shortest route between the graves toward them.

"I knew we could count on her," Grímur said with a twinkle of admiration in his eyes. "Jóhanna Thorvald never keeps you waiting in this district if she can help it."

Jóhanna was around thirty, with a pale complexion and long dark hair tied at the back in a ponytail. She wore glasses, jeans, and a black coat, and she held a small briefcase in one hand and a paper bag in the other.

"Thank you for coming over, Jóhanna," said Grímur.

"What do you want me to do?" she asked, barely glancing at them.

The three men looked at each other. Finally Grímur answered: "You could maybe take a brief look at the man in the casket. See if he has anything in his pockets or whether he has any distinctive features. Anything that might give us some indication of who he is."

"I can do that if one of you is willing to write the notes."

Grímur looked at Kjartan. "Isn't that your job?"

"Yes, probably," Kjartan replied.

Jóhanna took a thin plastic coat out of the paper bag and put it on. It included a hat, which she placed and tightened around her head. Finally, she placed a white surgical mask over her face and slipped her hands into some rubber gloves.

"Ready?" she asked Kjartan.

"Yes."

"Then let's start."

They walked into the church. Kjartan stopped five steps away from the casket and took out his notebook and pen. Jóhanna placed her open briefcase on one of the pews and loosened the latches on the casket.

Some flies appeared as soon as she lifted the lid, but they didn't seem to have much life left in them and soon tumbled to the floor. The mixture Grímur had sprayed inside the casket had clearly done its job.

For a long moment Jóhanna stood motionless by the casket, staring at its contents in silence.

"A male judging by the clothes," she finally said.

"Yes, we know that much," Kjartan answered.

She glanced at him. "It doesn't matter what you know. You just write down everything I say. This will be my report to the Directorate of Health."

Kjartan seemed taken aback. He hadn't realized the investigation had actually started.

Her eyes continued to linger on Kjartan a moment.

"I remember you from high school," she said finally.

He gave a start and suddenly looked up, but he was unable to distinguish any expression behind her mask. He could not place her face. She must have been in a lower year, but he couldn't bring himself to ask her. They looked into each other's eyes for a moment and then gazed down into the casket.

"*Corpus decompositium*," she said.

"I'm sorry?" Kjartan didn't understand Latin.

"The body is decomposed," she said.

That's pretty obvious, Kjartan thought to himself, but he said nothing and just jotted it down on the page.

Jóhanna firmly gripped the parka and trousers and turned the body over in one swift move. A few additional flies woke up with the shift and flew out of the casket.

"No remains of skin or flesh on the face, nor in the eyes," said Jóhanna, taking some implement out of her bag, which she used to loosen the skull's clenched jaw.

"No cavities in the teeth, but worn. Some gold fillings. A man well into his middle age and wealthy enough to be able to afford a good dentist."

She examined the skull under the hood.

"Remnants of gray hair."

She walked to the other end of the casket and scrutinized the shoes. "Sturdy leather hiking shoes. Lace missing on right shoe."

Next she examined the hands. "No rings on his fingers."

She loosened the parka around his throat and unzipped it.

"Quality parka with a rust-free zipper. Seems to be a foreign label; color: dark green." She peered into one pocket and then fetched some tongs and a small envelope in her briefcase. "In the outer pocket there are several small shells, mussels, small starfish, remains of…sandworm, I think." She placed it all in the envelope as soon as she extracted it from the pocket.

"The deceased may have eaten some of this to stave off hunger. Need to examine this in the autopsy. Test for shellfish poisoning, if possible."

She examined the inside of the parka. "No internal pockets on the parka. Wearing a brown woolen cardigan under it. No visible labels on the cardigan. Side pockets. A leather wallet in the right pocket." She removed the wallet with her tongs, placed it in a small envelope, and took it over to Kjartan. "Here, take a look."

He opened the wallet and counted several banknotes and coins. He counted: "Seven thousand two hundred and fifty-two crowns and fifteen cents." There was nothing else in the wallet, and he left the money in it.

"That's a lot of money to be carrying around," he said.

Jóhanna looked into the other pocket of the cardigan. She took out a small folded piece of paper with her tongs and handed it to Kjartan. He unfolded the note and examined some words that had been written with a pencil, and then he read them out loud: "This book belongs to me, Jón Finnsson, and was a gift from my departed father's father, Jón Björnsson, as can be verified, and was personally given to me by my departed father and is cherished in their memory." The handwriting was clear and legible.

Kjartan pondered the note. Below it another hand had written "folio 1005." On the back of it thirty-nine letters were written out in three rows of meaningless text.

O S L E O Y I A R N R Y L
E M H O N E A E N W T L B
A U R M L E Q W T R O N E

The note had been ripped out of a perforated copybook, a small sheet with blue lines and narrow spacing. He placed the note in the envelope with the wallet, which he in turn slipped into his pocket.

"So we've got a name to go on, Jón Finnsson," Kjartan said. "This is some kind of a book inscription, but a rather old-fashioned use of words."

"Some of the islanders are a bit old-fashioned," said Jóhanna.

She finished searching through the pockets but could find nothing else.

"Under the cardigan a light brown cotton shirt and green foulard. Quality clothes, it seems."

"Could he be a local from these islands?" Kjartan asked.

"Very unlikely," she answered. "He would have been missed. No one's isolated enough here to be able to disappear without questions being asked after two or three days. Then there's the clothing that doesn't quite fit the islanders' style."

"A foreigner maybe?"

"I haven't the faintest idea about that," she said. "But this'll have to do for now. We'll send him to Reykjavik like this. They'll be able to investigate it better down there."

She placed the lid on the casket and locked it firmly. Then they walked outside.

"Is Jón Finnsson a name that rings any bells?" Kjartan asked the three men waiting outside.

"In what context?" Grímur asked.

Kjartan took out the note and read them the text.

Grímur and Högni stared blankly at each other, but Thormódur Krákur tilted on his toes and puffed up his chest. "I know who this Jón Finnsson is."

"Who is he?" Kjartan asked.

"That's Jón Finnsson, the farmer in Flatey, the one who delivered the *Flatey Book* to the bishop of Skálholt, Brynjólfur Sveinsson. It was the bishop who sent the book to the king, wasn't it?"

The deacon looked around with a triumphant air.

"But that was in the autumn of 1647," Grímur added.

Thormódur Krákur continued: "Those words are written at the beginning of the *Flatey Book* and were copied in that note. It's actually quite peculiar that the only person who inscribed this book was the person who allowed it to leave the family."

Thormódur Krákur gesticulated to add emphasis to his story.

"And the *Flatey Book* is now with the king in Copenhagen," said Grímur. "So this was hardly copied from the original source."

"What could have been the purpose of copying that text down on a piece of paper?" Kjartan asked. "And what does folio 1005 mean?"

The others looked at each other, but no one had an answer. Finally Grímur said, "Sometimes tourists who've read some of the *Flatey Book* come here and want to find out about the making and history of the manuscript."

"And who's the person who can tell them about it?" Kjartan asked.

"Various people here and there," said Grímur. "Most of the islanders can recount some of the sagas if they're asked. Sigurbjörn in Svalbard is pretty well read and often quotes the book, although Reverend Hannes speaks better Danish and talks to the foreigners."

As the men were chatting to each other, Jóhanna slipped out of her plastic coat and packed it back into her bag. Then she took Kjartan's notes.

"I'll copy these and bring them back to you tomorrow," she said before walking away without saying good-bye.

Thormódur Krákur turned the key in the lock of the church door and then vigorously shook the handle to convince himself that the door was definitely locked.

"No one goes in here without me, and no one goes out except in God's name," he said, drawing a cross in front of the door with his hand before sticking the key into his pocket. "Isn't that enough for this evening then, District Officer?"

"Yes. Thanks for all your help," said Grímur.

The deacon grabbed the cart and pushed it down the slope, allowing it to roll in front of him until he reached level ground, and then he turned it around again. He paused a moment and started to spin, first making three clockwise circles and then making three counterclockwise ones, blessing himself after each circle. Then, dragging the cart behind him, he headed home.

"He doesn't want any impure spirits to follow him home to his cottage tonight," Högni said with a smile.

"He's a bit special and holds some unconventional beliefs," Grímur explained to Kjartan.

"He's also a bit of a psychic," Högni added.

"In what way psychic?" Kjartan asked.

Grímur answered: "Krákur can catch glimpses of the supernatural, although he's useless when he's really needed." He smiled.

"A normal medium wouldn't have any problems communicating with that dead man in the box in there," Högni added. "For example, there was a man from a farm in Kjálkafjördur who could never shut up at funerals. He was always talking to ghosts."

Kjartan forced an awkward smile. "I don't expect the case to be solved that way," he said. And then, just to change subject, he asked, "Does Thormódur Krákur live off his eiderdown work?"

"Yes," Grímur answered, "and the odd little job here and there. He has two cows and makes hay for them in the patch of field behind my land. He can sell the milk. He also works in the slaughterhouse in the autumn and has rights to collect eiderdown and eggs on some of the islets up here to the north. But he farms out those rights to others and gets eiderdown in return. He had a shock when he was young, and he's been terrified of the sea ever since." Grímur gazed at the church door. "Plus he's incredibly superstitious," he added.

"What kind of shock?" Kjartan asked.

"Krákur was reared by a farmer on the island," Grímur answered, "and was considered to be a bit of a wild one and a boozer, so the farmer decided to teach him a lesson one day when they were out at sea and sent him up a crag to knock out a seal pup. But they didn't wait for the boy while he was doing it and went off to check on some nets. When they came back, the crag was submerged in water and the sea came right up to the boy's chin where he was standing on the rock."

"And ever since that day," Högni interjected, "Krákur prefers to stand on his toes."

"The boy was extremely well behaved after that," Grímur continued, "but hasn't had the guts to go back to sea ever since. Although he still doesn't say no to a drop of schnapps, if he's offered it."

"Does that mean he never leaves the island?" Kjartan asked.

The men exchanged pensive glances.

"Yes, I don't remember Krákur ever going anywhere," Grímur answered. "His wife Gudrídur was the one who traveled. She used to go to Reykjavik to visit her daughter before she developed her leg problem."

Kjartan turned the conversation to another subject: "So what do we do now? There's nothing to give us any indication of who the dead man is. We don't know of anyone being reported missing."

Grímur stroked the beard on his cheek. "We can write a description of the man. Describe how he was dressed. Then we can hang up a notice at the co-op. Maybe someone will come forward.

We can also talk to the people on the other islands over the radio and find out if any of the farmers remember this tourist."

"Where can I get to a typewriter to write a description?" Kjartan asked.

"I have a typewriter at home. Let's go back to the house. I think I'm getting hungry."

As they walked down the slope, Kjartan was still pondering what lay ahead.

"The district magistrate spoke about dispatching the body down south on the mail boat on Saturday. But how will it be transported from Stykkishólmur to Reykjavik? Does someone need to follow it maybe?" he asked.

"I guess so. The casket will go on the bus if there is room. Otherwise, there's the co-op van. The police officer in Stykkishólmur will take care of that for us somehow," Grímur answered.

Kjartan nodded. "That's probably the best thing. I'll also talk to the magistrate tomorrow about any further arrangements," he said.

Ingibjörg received them with a ready dinner: boiled puffin breast with potatoes and a knob of butter. Once again the table had been set for three in the dining room and the woman did not sit with them any more than she did at lunchtime. This time the meal was silent. It was eight o'clock and the radio was turned on. The evening news was being broadcast. The newsreader was giving an update of Soviet leader Khrushchev's latest disarmament proposals. Then there was a piece about an all-night session in the Icelandic parliament before the imminent summer recess.

Kjartan had gotten his appetite back and ate well. In fact, he'd never eaten puffin before and preferred it to the taste of the seal meat he'd had earlier that day. The news ended and Grímur turned off the radio.

"That's politics for you," he said. "You're better off being neutral when those superpowers are at each other's throats. But here in Iceland it's the Progressive Party you should be voting for," he said to Kjartan. "Young people tend to turn to socialism if someone doesn't set them straight. And the Conservatives are even worse."

Högni responded with an indulgent smile and gave Kjartan a furtive wink.

"I think Khrushchev is just a Progressist," said Högni. "There aren't any real communists left anymore, not since Comrade Stalin died."

"He's only kidding," Grímur said to Kjartan. "Högni is the biggest Progressive I know. He just hasn't realized it himself yet. It's the same story with a lot of people who waste their time trying to vote for other parties. Don't let it sway you, lad."

That was the end of the political debate, and the men walked out of the house with coffee in their glasses.

The sun was setting in the sky in the west, and there was a chill in the air.

"How many days do you reckon that man survived on that island?" Kjartan asked.

"Difficult to say," Grímur answered. "Maybe a few."

Högni sipped on his coffee and said, "There was once a woman who tended to her animals in the winter on a remote island out there in Skardsströnd. There were two laborers with her, a man and a woman. The man had run out of tobacco after the long period of isolation, and the girl had some boyfriend on the mainland. So they wanted the old woman to allow them to go home, but she wouldn't let them until they tricked her by extinguishing the fire in the hut. That way she had to send them to the mainland to fetch more fire. But when they left her, there was a cold northern wind one night, and the sea froze over so that the old bag couldn't be reached for the next eight weeks. She had something to eat on the island, even though it was raw, and she got a tiny bit of warmth from the animals, but she was always considered a bit weird after that."

Högni gave Kjartan a meaningful look.

"But the man in Ketilsey had neither food nor heat," said Kjartan.

"You're right there, lad," Grímur answered with a grave air. "I just hope the poor wretch didn't have to suffer long."

They walked inside, and the district officer showed Kjartan the old typewriter on the small standing writing table in the living room. It seemed to be in reasonable condition, and Kjartan placed two sheets in it with a carbon sheet in between and rolled it into place. He recalled the doctor's words from memory and then started to type. He was accustomed to using a typewriter and wrote texts with relative ease. The opening read as follows: "Notice to the inhabitants of the district of Flatey. The remains of a man's body were found on Ketilsey."

Once the description of the man's clothes had been written, he added the words of Jón Finnsson that had been found in the deceased's cardigan pocket. Finally, he wrote: "If anyone can provide any information on the man's journey to Ketilsey or knows of a missing person, they are asked to contact Grímur Einarsson, the district administrative officer of Flatey."

"...the characters in the sagas contained in the Flatey Book *are not my favorite people. If its accounts are accurate, these were some of the worst rogues, and few of them were honorable leaders. Ólaf Tryggvason's and Ólaf Haraldsson's relentless endeavors to convert*

the Norse to Christianity are of little credit to their religion. It can also be argued that the Viking raids delayed the advance of civilization in northern Europe for centuries. It is, however, the Icelandic record keepers that I admire. The people who passed the sagas down from one generation to the next, first orally and then from one vellum sheet to another. There are countless phrases in the Flatey Book *that have now become sayings that are quoted over and over again, without anyone being remotely aware of their origin. Sayings such as 'No one can stand against great odds,' 'Ale is another man,' and 'The one who yields is generally the wisest.' These are all sayings that Icelanders have become accustomed to using without thinking particularly about their origin. Few contemporary authors exhibit this kind of insight...*"

CHAPTER 8

The deacon's house was located in the island's interior, a small low cottage. Even though the man was not tall, he still had to stoop to get through the doorway, once he had parked his cart by the gable of the building. The place comprised a small hallway sectioned off by a partition of rough crate planks, a kitchen, and one room, which served both as a living room and bedroom. Pink floral wallpaper adorned the walls, and the ceiling was of dark wood.

Thormódur Krákur removed his Sunday best clothes, folded them neatly, and placed them in a green painted chest that stood at the foot of the bed. He then put on his work clothes: old gray overalls, woolen socks, and frayed rubber shoes.

Gudrídur, his wife, was boiling fermented ray and potatoes. She was a stout woman and even shorter than her husband. Because of her bad legs, she sat on a bench by the cooker and used both hands to shift her body to and fro. Her false teeth soaked in a glass of water on the kitchen table. They were a little too big, so Gudrídur only put them in when she really needed them at meals.

"The food smells great," said Thormódur Krákur as he sauntered into the kitchen and they sat at the table. They folded their hands as the husband intoned, "We thank you, our Lord and Savior, for this meal we are about to receive, in Jesus' name, amen."

As they were eating, Thormódur Krákur described the transportation of the corpse to his wife. Even though he hadn't actually looked into the casket himself, he could quote the words of the district officer and embellish the story with a few imaginative touches of his own. The topic did nothing to dampen their appetite, and the pieces of ray were rapidly devoured with smacking lips. Gudrídur pounded her fish and potatoes into a mush, because even though she had put her teeth in, she found it awkward to chew with them.

Thormódur Krákur waxed lyrical about the Ketilsey mystery in a long monologue. He couldn't recall any other event of this kind on the islands over the decades. Shipwrecks and sea accidents had been an inevitable part of the islanders' lives in his youth, but for a stranger to be stranded out on an island like that was completely new to him. Gudrídur concurred with a string of exclamations and finally asked, "Do you think you'd be able to communicate with your late foster father if we took out the Ouija board? Maybe he'd have a message from that stranger."

Thormódur Krákur shook his head. "No, not straightaway. My foster father is so unsociable. He'd never deliver a message just like that. Maybe he'll appear to me in a dream soon and give me some sign. Then we'll see. The danger with people who perish in a horrific way like that is that they can be troubled spirits."

The meal was over, and Gudrídur cleared the table and placed the dishes in the sink. It was a time-consuming task because she had to sit on the bench and shift back and forward, using her hands. Then she put some coffee beans into the grinder, while Thormódur Krákur fetched a pile of books in the living room. The pile was carefully wrapped in old newspapers and tied with string. He cautiously unwrapped the books and placed them on the kitchen table. The first book on the top of the pile was an old Bible, below which were four hefty tomes of the *Flatey Book*, volumes one, two, three, and four, printed in 1944.

Thormódur Krákur lit a stubbed candle and opened the Bible where a bookmark had been placed. He read a short passage from the fourth book of Genesis out loud, while Gudrídur put on the coffee, and then closed the Bible again and took out the second volume of the *Flatey Book*. He opened it at a bookmark in the middle of the Foster Brothers' saga and, as they drank their coffee, read a long chapter about Thorgeir Hávarsson and his namesake, Thormódur, Kolbrún's poet. When he had finished reading, he put the books back in their place. Then he went outside again to complete the day's work. The animals still needed to be tended to before nightfall.

He fetched the cows in the field and milked them in the shed. Little Nonni from Ystakot came to collect the half pot of milk his family bought from them every day, and Högni greeted him on his way from the district officer's house to the school. They chatted for a while, and then Thormódur Krákur filled several buckets of water from the well by the shed and emptied them into the cows' trough. Finally, he prepared for bed, and it was long past midnight when he turned in.

"... The Flatey Book *is the largest vellum manuscript known to have been written in Iceland. It contains a total of 225 sheets and therefore 450 pages. The book is so large that only two sheets could be obtained from each calfskin, and therefore 113 calfskins went into the making of the book. Of these, 101 went into the main section, which was written in Vídidalstunga, and then another twelve went*

into the additional material, which was written in Reykhólar nine decades later. This double-fold sheet is called a folio, but if the calf-skin is folded in four it is known as a quarto. The sheets are about forty-two centimeters long and twenty-nine centimeters wide. The preparation of the skin used in the Flatey Book *required a great deal of labor, tanning, shaving, and scraping for it to be turned into usable vellum. It can therefore be said that the book is the work of many hands. There are no accounts of this work, so the methods used are unknown. The technique used was probably similar to the one applied to tanning on the mainland, although less lime was probably used...*"

CHAPTER 9

Friday, June 3, 1960

Kjartan woke up to repeated cockcrows from the village below. It took him some time to remember where he was and identify the sound. The bed lay under a sloping ceiling, and opposite the headrest a color photograph had been blue-tacked to the wall. The picture was probably of a Norwegian fjord with a big modern ferry set against a backdrop of forested hills and cliffs.

He heard the cockcrow again and knew it was time to get up, but he was paralyzed by a heavy sense of dread. It was a familiar feeling that sometimes hit him at the beginning of a day, particularly when he was forced to venture into the unknown. But he tried to bite the bullet and shake it off. His shyness and social phobias were the two things that plagued him the most in life. He therefore did his utmost to avoid situations that brought him into too much contact with strangers. But now that he'd been saddled with this assignment that took him from one stranger to another, he had no say in the matter.

Three fat bluebottles buzzed against the windowpane by the top of his bed. He stood up and gazed through the glass. Two kids were rounding up a black sheep and a lamb in a field on the western side of the island. They were within earshot, and their voices could be heard calling when the ewe turned against them and refused to be led. The sky was slightly overcast but sunny.

Kjartan got dressed and climbed down the almost vertical staircase from the loft. A strong fragrance of coffee wafted through the kitchen, and the mistress of the household was hanging up washing on the line in the level yard in front of the house. She was dressed in the same woolen clothes she'd worn the day before and was wearing her striped apron. A girl of about eight years of age stood by her side and handed her pegs, which she fished out of an old can of paint.

Kjartan grabbed the pot of coffee on the stove and poured himself a cup. He then walked outside and looked down at the village. The tide was coming in, and the cluster of houses were reflected in the sea that was filling the cove below the embankment. A number of inhabitants could be seen wandering between the houses, and no one seemed to be in a hurry. Those whose paths crossed paused to chat, both young and old. It was more the hens that seemed to be in a hurry as they darted between the gardens of the houses. Despite the sunshine, there was a breeze and it was quite chilly.

"Good morning, young man," Ingibjörg said when she noticed Kjartan had come out.

"Good morning."

"We still have dry weather."

"Hmm, yeah."

Ingibjörg finished hanging up the last garment.

"We're still far from the haymaking season, of course, but it would be good to be able to dry the eiderdown in the sunshine," she said.

"Hmm, really? Where is Grímur anyway?" Kjartan asked.

"They went out at the crack of dawn to check on the seal nets. They should be back by noon."

"Right."

"Grímur put up your notice before he left."

"Good."

"And the telephone exchange will open at ten so you can ring your boss, the district magistrate."

She turned to the girl. "Thanks for your help, Rosa darling. Run along and play now."

The girl put the can down and skipped away.

Ingibjörg disappeared into the house with the empty washing basket in her hands.

Kjartan sat on an old whale bone that lay by the gable of the house and sipped on his coffee. Visibility was good in the clear weather, and he felt he could see a white painted house on the mainland to the north, although it could also have been the remains of some snow.

The screeching of cliff birds reached him from Hafnarey and fused with the surrounding bleating of sheep. The salted scent of the sea lingered in the breeze.

Ingibjörg came out again and had removed her apron now, put on a tasseled cap, and draped a knitted shawl over her shoulders.

"I'll walk you down to the telephone exchange now," she said cheerfully.

They followed the path to the road and headed down toward the village. Ingibjörg walked a lot slower than what he was used to and occasionally halted completely to look at something or chat with the people they bumped into. He waited patiently and responded to the greetings of the people Ingibjörg introduced him to. But he was slightly unnerved by the way people brazenly stared at him as soon as they started nattering with the district officer's wife.

Finally they reached the co-operative building. There was a space on one of the store's doors that was obviously regularly used as a notice board. Some rusty old drawing pins were stuck to it, and a notice advertising the Whitsunday mass next week had recently been put up. Beside it was the notice that Kjartan had typed and stuck up with four new drawing pins. Ingibjörg paused to read it and nodded with a smile, as if to confirm it was all in good order.

The telephone exchange was in a one-story building above a stone basement, directly opposite the co-op.

White letters on a blue sign over the door read *Post & Telegraph Office*, and inside there was a small hall, with coat hangers and a small bench, that led into a small reception room. A few gray radio receivers hung on one wall, while on the other there was a cabinet full of compartments for the sorting of mail. A bulky safe stood on a plinth in one corner.

A small, delicate woman welcomed them with a smile. She was wearing trousers and a sweater, with long hair woven into a thick braid.

"This is Stína; she's the head of the telephone exchange and the post office," Ingibjörg said to Kjartan. Then she explained the reason for their visit: "The assistant magistrate needs to phone his superiors. Are you open yet, Stína?"

Ingibjörg sat in front of the desk and signaled Kjartan to join her.

"I'm just opening now. I just have to turn on the generator and switch on the exchange," Stína answered, slipping on some old work gloves and disappearing behind the door.

"That's the only electricity we have here," Ingibjörg explained a bit further, "the energy this generator produces. There's actually another generator in the fish factory for the fish processing, but it's rarely used."

Within a few moments they heard the muffled murmur of an engine and the smiling lady reappeared. She slipped on a bulky set of black headphones with an attached microphone and turned on the contraption by flicking a few switches. She waited a moment for the lamps to warm up and then said loudly and clearly: "Stykkishólmur, Stykkishólmur, Flatey radio calling." She repeated this several times.

She then put down the headphones and said, "Stykkishólmur will answer in a moment. He sometimes likes to keep you waiting, just to give people the impression that he's really busy."

She turned out to be right. A blast of static soon erupted, and a male voice answered through the speaker on the wall: "Flatey radio, Stykkishólmur answering."

"Good morning, Stykkishólmur. We have a call for the district magistrate in Patreksfjördur."

"One moment," the voice answered, followed by a silence. Stína and Ingibjörg solemnly waited without saying a word.

Kjartan looked out the window facing the village and saw two men standing by the notice in the co-op store. They seemed to be reading it with great interest and then stuck their heads together and looked in the direction of the telephone exchange.

"Flatey radio, Stykkishólmur. We have the district magistrate of Patreksfjördur on the line."

"Go ahead," Stína said, pointing at a black receiver on the desk in front of Kjartan.

He picked up the phone. "Hello, hello. Kjartan in Flatey here."

The voice at the other end of the line was faint. "Yes, hello, how's the investigation going?"

"We've recovered the body," Kjartan answered, "but we still haven't identified it yet. It seems likely that he was alive when he reached the island but then died of fatigue. He seems to have been lying there for several months after he died."

There was a brief silence, after which the magistrate said, "That's odd. Doesn't anyone know who he is?"

"No. The body is unrecognizable."

There was another brief silence while the magistrate evaluated the situation.

"Right then, so you'll have to send the body to Reykjavik," he then said.

"Yes. The casket will be traveling on the mail boat tomorrow."

"Good."

"Should I come home today?"

"Today? No, hang on there for a bit and talk to some of the islanders. There must be some way of finding out who took that man to the island."

Kjartan wasn't happy. "I'm not used to this kind of investigative work," he said.

"No, but you'll have to do for now. I'm not going to call in the police from Reykjavik if we can solve this in the district ourselves. District Officer Grímur will help you with your inquiries."

"Right then, but what about the notarizations I was supposed to work on?"

"They can wait another two or three days. Don't you worry about them; just concentrate on this. Be in touch tomorrow. Good-bye and best of luck."

The phone call ended, and Stína let Stykkishólmur know that was enough for now.

Kjartan handed her a copy of the notice and asked her to read it out over the radio to the other islands.

"Skáleyjar, Svefneyjar, Látur," she called into the mouthpiece. "Flatey radio calling."

She repeated this three times until the islands answered, each in turn. She had started to read out the notice as they were walking outside.

"Grímur will be back at lunchtime and you can talk to him about how to proceed," Ingibjörg said when they were standing outside the telephone exchange. Then she added: "Maybe you should take a walk while you're waiting for Grímur. Take a look around the island. Visitors normally like to go up to Lundaberg to look at the birds." She gave him directions.

Kjartan nodded approvingly, and Ingibjörg said good-bye and walked toward her house at an even slower pace than before. Kjartan started his tour by taking a look around the village. The doors of the co-op were open, but there were no customers to be seen inside. A handcart loaded with several bags of cement was parked in front of the warehouse. The muffled murmur of the generator resounded from the basement, and the sound of a radio voice could be heard coming from the house next door. These sounds blended with the screeches of the birds on the rocks of Hafnarey.

An elderly woman in a canvas apron was spreading eiderdown on a concrete step above the pier, and an old man was painting a small boat that lay upturned on the edge of the cove. A face was watching him through the priest's house's window.

Kjartan sauntered off, following a narrow gravel path that meandered between the houses. There was a strong smell of chicken shit in the air that fused with the scent of the vegetation that had started to flourish nicely in the sunshine, sheltered by the walls of the houses. Garden dock, angelica, and long grass thrived on the fertilizer the hens dropped behind them wherever they went.

Thormódur Krákur stood in front of an open shed dressed in his work clothes, and some eiderdown had been left out to dry on a white piece of sailcloth at his feet. When he saw Kjartan, he greeted him heartily: "Good morning, Assistant Magistrate. Where are you off to today?"

Kjartan considered telling him not to call him Assistant Magistrate but then decided not to bother.

"I'm just taking a look around," he answered.

"Good idea," said Thormódur Krákur. "Can I offer you some fermented shark?"

"No thanks."

"How about some freshly laid arctic tern eggs then?"

"No thank you, I'm not hungry."

"As you wish then. Any news about that Ketilsey fellow?"

"No, nothing new."

"No, huh? Ah well. This doesn't bode well. I've had some bad dreams lately."

"Dreams?"

"Yes, I'm considered to be a bit of a visionary dreamer, my friend. Not that I'm particularly apt at deciphering what they mean, but there are some old women around here who can decipher them if the descriptions are clear enough."

Thormódur Krákur broke into a broad smile that exposed his crooked teeth.

"Sometimes the signs are so obscure that no one recognizes the context until afterwards," he added.

"What were the dreams about?" Kjartan asked.

Thormódur Krákur blew his nose into his red snuff handkerchief and walked into the shed. "They were bad dreams, my friend, bad dreams. Many of them would have been better off left undreamt," he said, beckoning Kjartan to follow him through the door. Kjartan had to stoop to get through the entrance, but as soon as he smelled the stench inside, he almost felt like turning around again. A variety of seasoned foods were stored there, some of it hanging from the turf ceiling or immersed in barrels in salt or sour whey. A number of hens dwelt at the other end of the shed, which was partitioned off with wire netting.

Thormódur Krákur sat on a box, reached out for a large wooden frame, and placed it on his knees. It was a harp-like contraption that was stringed lengthwise through perforations in the wood, with one-centimeter gaps between each string. There were two wooden barrels on either side of him.

"I dreamt I was making hay out in Langey and spending the night in a tent," said the deacon. "It was incredibly cold and shivery on the island, and I couldn't find any way to warm up, no matter how hard I swung the scythe."

Thormódur Krákur grabbed a pile of rough, uncleaned eiderdown from one of the barrels and placed it on the frame. Then he started shaking the down and stroking the strings, loosening the dirt, which fell to the floor.

"Then I saw a raven," he continued, "that came flying and perched right over my tent, which was just a few yards away. I was going to shoo him away, but then I couldn't walk because my legs were as heavy as lead. Then another raven appeared and sat beside the other one, and they were both sitting on the top of the tent when I woke up. I dreamed that every night for the whole of Eastertide. I call that the Langey dream."

Thormódur Krákur grew quiet, threw the roughly cleaned down into the empty barrel, and picked up a new bundle to clean.

"How was this dream interpreted?" Kjartan asked.

"Everyone could solve that one. Those are deaths, my friends, two deaths, the same number as the ravens. It couldn't be more obvious. A raven on a tent always means death, whether you see them when you're awake or in your sleep."

"Is someone else going to die then?" Kjartan asked.

"Not necessarily; a very old lady from the inner isles died on Ascension Thursday. Maybe it was her. Maybe not. We'll soon find out."

Thormódur Krákur lifted his index finger by way of emphasis.

"Have many of your dreams come true?" Kjartan asked.

"Yes, my friend. Some of them have even been recorded in annals. The most famous were the Sigrídur dream, the sail dream, and the ram's testicles dream. Then there are others that have remained unsolved, even though many have tried. Those are the dreams I had about Stagley, and the calves and Ash Wednesday dreams, for example. Do you want to have a crack at them?"

Kjartan shrugged.

"The calves dream goes like this. I sense I'm up by the church, and then I see three eagles flying over Múlanes. They form a circle over the graveyard, and one of them perches on a tombstone while the others fly back to the mainland the way they came. The eagle that is perching flaps its wings wildly, and I see that it is covered in blood and the blood is splattering off the feathers of his wings all around him. Finally, he rests his wings and looks toward the harbor. Then I see that there is a big sailing ship with two masts moored there, but a hoard of bullocks are being led up the road and people are walking behind them wearing crowns and majestic robes. That's when I wake up. What do you think it means?"

"I don't know. I'm no good at solving riddles," Kjartan answered.

"Dreams are no riddles. You just have to be able to read the signs right. The calf dream is about some major event, that's for sure. Three eagles always precede an event, but the blood is a bad omen."

Kjartan smiled. "Are there other signs you can interpret?" he asked.

"Oh yes, many: a swan stands for wealth, a bishop is a bad omen, a flower stands for happiness in the summer but sorrow in the winter, a king mean success and prestige. But it can all be turned on its head."

"Do people around here believe in all this stuff?" Kjartan asked.

"Of course—anyone who takes the trouble to think about it, that is. Do you think the Creator just created dreams for the fun of it? No, sir. These are messages that evolved minds gradually learn to decipher. Everything serves its purpose. Even the hidden people and elves in the hills are there to fulfill a function."

"The elves?" Kjartan asked skeptically.

"Yes. Have you never seen an elf?"

"No."

"You'll see an elf someday, my friend. But there's no certainty that you'll be able to recognize him when you see him."

"How can I recognize one?"

"Keep a pure heart and don't doubt unnecessarily. People doubt too much. One should believe the things that are in the Icelandic sagas and the Bible and the things that old people say. Then our dreams and wishes can come true."

Thormódur Krákur had ended his speech and continued sieving the down. He seemed to have had enough of the conversation, so Kjartan said good-bye and left the shed. The fresh air was welcome.

A young man was painting a window mullion on the next house green. He had a long, bright forehead that stretched down to his eyes, and Kjartan wondered whether this was an elf. Probably not, he thought, as the young man put down his paintbrush and lit a cigarette. Then he remembered seeing this same guy nail a sealskin to the gable of the outhouse. The house was clad in white painted corrugated iron and the roof was green. Over the door was a sign that read *Radagerdi* and below it the year of its construction—1927.

"Are you a cop?" the boy called out to Kjartan.

"No, I'm no policeman," Kjartan answered, drawing closer.

"Oh no? I was told you were a cop from Patreksfjördur."

"No, I'm just an assistant to the district magistrate."

"Yeah, isn't that some kind of cop?"

"Not really."

"Aren't you investigating the murder of that guy on the island?"

"Well, no, I'm trying to find out who he is. I doubt whether he was murdered."

"I thought you were a real cop," said the boy, disappointed. He tried to turn on a red transistor that stood on a windowsill inside an open window.

"Have you ever heard Elvis Presley?" he asked.

"No, I can't say that I have," Kjartan answered.

"Actually, they never play him on Icelandic radio. Sometimes I can hear him on foreign channels at night when the airways are clear. They play a lot of Elvis. I've put up an aerial." The boy pointed at some copper wire that dangled between the gable of the house and the shed. It was fastened to some glass insulation, but a wire traveled from the aerial in through the open window.

“There was also an article about Elvis in the *Falcon* magazine,” the boy added.

He turned to the transistor again, which emitted no sound despite his attempts to shake it vigorously.

“Battery’s finished,” he explained. “I might buy myself a record player this autumn and some records.”

“Do you live here?” Kjartan asked.

“Yeah, but I’m thinking of moving to Reykjavik…or to Stykkishólmur.”

“Right.”

“Yeah, I’m going to learn how to use a tractor and maybe get a driving license.”

“Is there a tractor on the island?”

“No, not yet, but the district officer might be buying one for all of us to share. Then they’ll need someone who can drive it.”

It dawned on Kjartan to try out some investigative work, so he asked, “Do you remember seeing a tourist here in a green parka and leather hiking shoes anytime over the past months?”

“Is that the dead man?” the boy asked.

“Yes. He was an elderly man with gray hair. Probably traveling alone.”

The boy scratched his head and seemed deep in thought. “He didn’t come here in the winter or spring. I would have seen him then if he had. But maybe last summer. There were quite a few tourists around that time. Some of them foreign.”

“Foreign?”

“Yeah, they like to gawk at the puffins all day long. Sometimes I sell them sea urchins and skulls.”

“Skulls?”

"Yeah, seal skulls. My gran sometimes sears seal pups' heads and then boils them to make broth. So I just let them rot and dry them for a few weeks."

"Do they sell well?"

"No, not unless the men are drunk; then they sometimes buy something."

"Well, I won't keep you from your work," Kjartan said. "What's your name anyway?"

"Benjamín Gudjónsson. They call me Benny, but I prefer Ben, like Ben Hur."

"OK...Ben."

Kjartan turned and walked back. When he reached the village, he saw Grímur's boat pulling in at the pier.

"...Jón, the farmer in Vídidalstunga, got two priests to work as scribes on the royal book, Jón Thórdarson and Magnús Thórhallsson. Nothing is known of these men apart from their names, but it can be assumed that they were educated and experienced scribes. The entire execution of the manuscript shows great skill. The calligraphy is firm and elegant. Capital letters are generally colored and decorated with pictures of men, animals, roses, or flourishes. It seems to have been Magnús who drew these adornments or illuminations, as we call them. This involved a great deal of work, since it can be estimated that each page represented a day's work. Perhaps it was thanks to these decorations that the Flatey Book *was so well preserved. It was from the beginning regarded as a treasure because of its appearance and craftsmanship. Readers clearly browsed through the pages of the manuscript with caution and respect. There was no danger that the book would be used to make*

shoe soles or articles of clothing, which was sometimes the fate suffered by other manuscripts that had been executed with less skill when they were written. Thus it was the craftsman's work that preserved the author's narrative…"

CHAPTER 10

Kjartan followed Grímur and Högni's approach, and then he walked down to the cove and along the embankment to them as they pulled into a small landing and dragged the boat onto a sandy beach where they tied it to an old mooring stone.

The two men were carrying a seal pup between them off the boat and up the ridge of the shore when Kjartan walked over to them. Then they carried two more pups. They were heavy carcasses, and the men had trouble standing on the wet, slippery seaweed that covered the rocks.

"They sure weigh a ton," said Högni as they dumped the last one on the gravel.

"They're still smaller than I expected," said Kjartan.

"These pups are just a few weeks old," Grímur answered.

"But they're in good shape, fat and beautiful."

Grímur snorted some snuff and lifted one of the pups onto a wooden rack.

"The magistrate wants me to find out if anyone knows who the dead man was," said Kjartan. "He expects you to help me."

"We can pay a few visits after work today," said Grímur, sharpening a small knife. "But there's no point in us starting until the locals have read our notice."

He brandished his knife and pierced the skin around the pup's head, exposing the fiery red ruff of its collar beneath the black fur.

"I think there'll be some news this evening," Grímur said before he cut around the front flippers and then over the hind flippers and scut. These cuts didn't bleed, but exposed the white fat and blood-red meat.

"What makes you think that?" Kjartan asked.

"Two porpoises followed us for most of the way from the seal skerries. It's often turned out to be an omen when whales follow in our wake like that."

Grímur drew the knife and in one movement sliced the length of the abdomen from the throat down to the tail. He then started to skin the seal so that it included a thick layer of fat.

"Do you believe in that stuff?" Kjartan asked.

Grímur looked up from his work and grinned. "There are other signs, too," he said, pointing his bloody knife at the village. "Do you see the vicarage on the other side of the cove? I saw little Svenni running out of there and sprinting up the road. Then he vanished for a while, but I can see him dashing down the embankment now as if the devil were on his heels." Grímur pointed at a little boy who came running toward them. "Reverend Hannes has sent him down with a message for me and told him to hurry."

Grímur carried on flaying the seal and didn't look up when the boy stood beside them. "Officer Grímur, Officer Grímur," he exclaimed breathlessly and wheezily. "Reverend Hannes really needs to talk to you."

"Did he give you some candy to come and fetch me?" Grímur asked.

"Yeah." The boy dug his hand into a pocket to produce the candy and stuck some into his mouth.

"How many pieces?"

"Three big ones."

"Oh, it must be important then. OK, I'll pop up to him as soon as I've finished skinning the seals."

"Shouldn't we go straightaway?" Kjartan asked. Grímur looked at Kjartan and pondered a moment.

"You go ahead," he then said. "I'll be up after you. I imagine he needs to talk to you just as much as he does to me. And you can deliver something to him from me."

"...It is not known how ink was made in Iceland in the Middle Ages. Early sources describe ink made out of bearberry, soil pigments, and willow. It may well be that these methods were known and used in the making of manuscripts. It is also possible that the ink may have been imported or made out of foreign raw materials that were not available in Iceland. Swan feathers were probably used as quills. They were considered better if they were from the left wing because the feathers curve out to the right, away from the hand holding the pen. Before the writing started, the columns and lines were marked on the vellum with a sharp edge..."

CHAPTER 11

Reverend Hannes stood by the living room window of the vicarage observing the movement of people beyond the cove. The boy he had sent down with the message had vanished from sight some time ago, and there was no sign of his request having been met.

"Maybe I should just go down and talk to Grímur myself," the priest said uneasily to his wife, Frída, who sat in a comfortable armchair behind him, embroidering a white tablecloth. She looked up from her sewing, peering over her glasses, and sternly shook her head.

Reverend Hannes shuffled on his feet. "I think the authorities should know about this as soon as possible," he said anxiously.

"No, you're not going anywhere," the priest's wife snapped sullenly. "There's no way you're going down to Grímur's filthy landing," she added.

"It's not so bad on the shore when it's not raining. I can go in my old galoshes," said the priest.

"Don't you remember when you slipped on that whale oil and ruined your pants?"

Reverend Hannes remembered and gave up. He could also now see that the man from the district magistrate's office was heading up the embankment beyond the cove with a heavy bucket in his hand and little Svenni following him at a short distance behind.

"Here comes that fellow from the magistrate's office. I just hope he's coming here, but I can't see the district officer anywhere. He must have been busy."

Frída shook her head again and muttered, "I think you're better off telling the magistrate's man about this. He's of a higher rank. Besides, you can't let Grímur into this house in his filthy working clothes. It's indecent for an official like the district administrative officer to be walking around looking like that."

Reverend Hannes decided not to comment. The woman was born and bred in Reykjavik and seemed to refuse to come to terms with the fact that on these islands men had to be jacks of all trades, and that they didn't wash until the end of the day when they'd produced enough food for their families. Personally, he happened to like Grímur and Högni, the teacher, and he tried to meet up with them as often as possible. There was always the hope of a good story or some fun conversation. Of course, the men sometimes gave off a bit of a smell after a day's work, but that was just the way things were out on the islands. Reverend Hannes had been brought up in the Dalir district but had never had the guts to tell his wife that he actually quite liked that cowshed smell.

"Yes, you're probably right," he finally said. "The magistrate's representative seems to be a responsible and well-educated man. He'll probably know what the best thing to do is. This is a deadly serious matter."

The priest stepped outside and waited for Kjartan to arrive under the gable of his house.

"I hope you're here to see me," said Reverend Hannes.

"Yes, the district officer sent me up and asked me to bring some fresh bits of seal to your wife while I was at it," said Kjartan, handing him an old white iron bucket full of raw meat.

"Bless you for that, and God be praised for the food that He and the sea provide to man," said Reverend Hannes, taking the bucket. He then invited Kjartan to step into the small room he reserved for receiving parishioners, but he deposited the bucket in a little pantry off the hall.

"I've just had quite a shock, yes, quite a shock." Reverend Hannes poured coffee out of a thermos into two ready cups on the desk.

"Oh?" said Kjartan, picking up one of the cups.

"Yes, I walked down to the co-op earlier and saw the notice from your office when I was checking to make sure my mass notice was in its right place."

"Yes?" said Kjartan.

"Yes and ahem...I think I know who the deceased is."

"Really?"

"Yes, it just has to be Professor Gaston Lund from Copenhagen."

"How do you know that?"

"It's a bit of a long story. The professor came here from Reykhólar at the beginning of September of last year with some of the women who had been to the mainland to pick berries. He sent me Reverend Veigar in Reykhólar's regards and asked me if we could put him up for two nights, which, of course, was fine. He was obviously quite a distinguished man."

The priest took the lid off a cake dish and handed it to Kjartan.

"Here, have a pancake with sugar."

"He was Danish, you were saying?" Kjartan asked, taking a pancake.

"Oh yes. He was a professor from the University of Copenhagen. He'd spent the summer following the saga trails in the *Flatey Book*, i.e., the saga of Ólaf Haraldsson and the saga of Ólaf Tryggvason, in Norway, of course, and then he came out here to Iceland on a short trip, as I understand it. First he went east to Skálholt, where Brynjólfur served as bishop. Then he traveled north to Vídidalstunga, where the manuscript was put together and written. After that he traveled west to Reykhólar, where the manuscript was preserved for some time, and then over here to Flatey. He realized, of course, that no one could call themselves experts on the *Flatey Book* without first visiting the place the manuscript derived its name from. He also wanted to try to solve the old Aenigma Flateyensis, which I only realized later. From here he traveled directly to Reykjavik to catch a flight to Copenhagen. He was due to attend a very important manuscript symposium in Copenhagen, and then, of course, he had to start lecturing at the university straight after that."

"But how did he end up in Ketilsey then?" Kjartan asked.

"It's totally incomprehensible to me. He said good-bye to me when the mail boat was about to come in and set off for the pier with plenty of time to spare."

"So how do you know it was him then?"

"I should have recognized him from the description of the clothes, but since I just assumed that he was in Copenhagen, it never occurred to me. But it was the note with the quotation from the Flatey Book that convinced me. It's probably written in my handwriting."

"Oh?" Kjartan pulled out the note that he had stuck into his wallet the night before and handed it to the priest.

Reverend Hannes took the note and nodded after glancing at it. "I've sometimes had to receive foreign visitors who come here on the *Flatey Book* trail," he said. "I've tried to acquaint myself with the history of the manuscript as well as I can and, in the process, formed my own ideas about its history. The theory has been advanced that Jón Finnsson of Flatey inscribed the manuscript with those words that are quoted on the note to dispel any ambiguities regarding heirship. I, on the other hand, believe that he wrote this in the manuscript when he once lent it in Skálholt, quite some time before it was finally handed over to Bishop Brynjólfur. And I'm also sure that Jón Finnsson only intended to lend Brynjólfur the manuscript when he came for a visit in the belief that it would return to him once it had been transcribed and researched. Otherwise, he would have forfeited his ownership by his own hand with some declaration of ownership in the manuscript. A man doesn't give away an inscribed book without transferring the ownership in writing first. That's how it worked back then, and that's how it works now. I explained all this to the professor and copied the text down on that note for him. We actually disagreed on whether the Danes should return the manuscript to Iceland or not. He was very opposed to the idea and was collecting material for a thesis to support his opinion. But I think I managed to get him to listen to my point of view. I believe that Jón Finnsson's descendants or the Icelandic nation own the *Flatey Book* by right."

Kjartan listened to the lecture but was still gnawed by doubt. "But the man must have been missed in Copenhagen. Why wasn't there a search for him?" he asked.

"That's what I simply don't get. He led me to understand that he wanted very little attention on this trip and avoided meeting up with Icelandic colleagues or anyone he knew. These manuscript issues are so sensitive that he wanted to avoid any public debates here. Professor Lund was obviously one of the most prominent opponents on this issue. It's also possible that no one in Copenhagen knew he was coming out here. He was a bachelor and didn't contact anyone back in Denmark during his trip here."

"Did he speak Icelandic?" Kjartan asked.

"Yes, yes. He could understand it quite well, and could read and write OK. But, as with most Danes, his spoken Icelandic was a bit ropey, of course, although he got by just fine."

"What's that thing he wanted to solve you just mentioned?" Kjartan asked.

"The Aenigma Flateyensis. It's a semi kind of crossword. It came with the facsimile version of the *Flatey Book* that was given to the library on the centenary in 1936. The pages are loose inside the book, and no one is allowed to take them out of the library building or to copy the key that solves it. Every now and then visitors come here and take the test. But no one has succeeded so far. Some of the clues are, of course, very unclear, and the key is incomprehensible."

"Why was this man trying to solve the enigma?"

Reverend Hannes smiled faintly. "The professor is—or *was*, should I say—a member of Copenhagen's Academy of Scholars. They meet once a week at a famous restaurant called Det lille Apotek. The group is divided into two sections. Those who've distinguished themselves in the field of humanities and received recognition for it get to sit on the bench by the wall that offers the best view. The others have to sit opposite the wall by the passageway and sometimes get splashed with beer. The professor was going to win himself a better seat by solving the enigma."

"Did he succeed?"

"I don't know. He didn't want to say, and he was very reticent on the subject. Although I suspect he intended to disclose it when he got back to Copenhagen. Who knows? He gave me a copy of his answers, but I don't know if they fit the key."

Reverend Hannes opened a drawer in his standing desk, took out a folded sheet of paper, and handed it to Kjartan. "There you go. I think you should keep this."

Kjartan took the sheet and examined it carefully. The sentences were in Danish and Icelandic, although the handwriting was barely legible.

"I need to call Reykjavik," Kjartan said, "to find out if the body could be the professor's. Then you'll need to look into the casket to confirm that the clothes are the same you saw him in the last time. The body itself is, of course, unrecognizable."

Reverend Hannes sipped his coffee with trembling hands. "Yes, I suppose I better do that," he said.

Kjartan continued: "But could it be that he fell overboard off the mail boat and swam to Ketilsey?"

"I would think that highly unlikely. The island is miles from the sailing route."

"Are there strong currents there?"

"Yes, I'm sure, although I'm no expert on the subject. You need to talk to the seamen about that."

"When was it he left you again?"

"It was on September fourth. I've checked it in my diary. I remember there was some news about the manuscript issue on the radio the same evening he left."

"Didn't he have any luggage?"

"He had a small traveling bag, enough for a few days, with a toiletries bag, change of underwear, and that kind of thing. A camera and small binoculars. I seem to remember him saying that his case was in storage in Reykjavik."

Kjartan picked up the note that lay on the table between them.

"What does this mean on the note: folio 1005?"

"That's the *Flatey Book*'s registration number in the Royal Library in Copenhagen. I remember Lund wrote that on the note I gave him and then stuck it in his pocket."

Kjartan turned the note around.

"Do you know what these letters on the back of the note stand for?" he asked.

The priest examined the note. "No. He must have written that on the note after he left here. That's not unlike the series of letters that are supposed to be the key to the Flatey enigma, but he knew he wasn't allowed to copy the key. And he didn't go back to the library after I gave him the note."

Kjartan wrote down: *Gaston Lund of Copenhagen, 4 September*. "I'm going to the telephone exchange to call the Danish Embassy," he said and stood up.

Reverend Hannes escorted him to the door, said good-bye, and walked back to his wife in the living room.

"The case is in good hands," he said. "What I'm dreading the most is having to look at that body in the casket. I always find these things so uncomfortable."

He looked out the window and gazed into the distance for a long time before saying, "I remember the day Lund left us as if it were yesterday. I walked him to the door and shook his hand. He promised to write to me. Was I suppose to guess that something was up when I never got a letter from him?"

The woman put down her handwork. "Did you ever write to him?" she asked.

"No, I didn't, in fact. I was more expecting the letter to come from him."

She reflected a moment. "Maybe he was on his way here on another visit when the Lord took him away?"

The priest shook his head. "I don't know, but I can still picture him walking down the road with that little case in his hand. He left for the boat with plenty of time to spare because he was going to drop by Doctor Jóhanna's to get some seasickness tablets. He was worried about a rough crossing because the weather was getting worse."

He stared through the window in silence and then muttered to himself: "But how on earth did he end up on Ketilsey?"

"...The medieval lettering used was Latin Carolingian script, which reached Iceland from Norway and England, albeit with a few additions to fulfill the needs of the Norse language. Accents were placed over long vowels, and new letters appeared. The þ and ð came from English, from which they later disappeared but survived in Icelandic. The writing of the Flatey Book *also bears the personal traits of its scribes, Jón and Magnús. Jón wrote most of the first part and Magnús the latter half. And the workmanship reveals more. An unknown person with rather poor handwriting seems to have gripped the pen in four places in the first half of the manuscript, probably when Jón was sharpening his quill, because his handwriting is generally slightly thinner after the unknown handwriting that precedes it. This was no cowshed boy in Vídidalstunga who had sneaked in to try his hand at writing. The priest would not have allowed that to happen. It is more likely to have been someone who had some authority over the priest, perhaps even Jón Hákon himself. I think that is quite possible.*

"Magnús Thórhallsson's calligraphy and illuminations in the Flatey Book *are among the most beautiful to be found in Icelandic medieval manuscripts. One can assume that this artist was a sought-after scribe and that he made several manuscripts. He was well trained by the time he came to the* Flatey Book. *However, his workmanship and handwriting can only be found in a few words in two other manuscripts. One can therefore assume that his life's work has been lost..."*

CHAPTER 12

When Kjartan returned from the telephone exchange, he found the district administrative officer by his storage hut by the landing. Grímur sat on a wooden crate and had spread a canvas bag over his knees. He had placed the seal fur over it and was scraping the layer of fat off it with a sharp knife. A large basin of red soapy water lay by his feet, and another fur was soaking inside it. The third had been nailed to the gable of the hut, freshly scraped and washed.

Högni was on the edge of the shore sorting the seal parts into barrels, although he occasionally chucked pieces of fat at a flock of seagulls that had gathered on the rim of the shore. He put down his machete and walked toward them when he saw Kjartan had arrived.

"So what kind of sermon did you get from the priest this morning?" Högni asked eagerly, sitting on a rusty wheelbarrow and stretching out for the coffee flask and tin of cookies.

Kjartan started telling them about his conversation with Reverend Hannes, while Grímur listened in silence, scraping the fur.

"No wonder the priest's in a state of shock to find out that his guest never made it home," Högni said. "I bet he'll be saying his 'Our Fathers' tonight, poor guy."

"I called the Danish Embassy in Reykjavik," Kjartan continued, "and they immediately knew about Professor Lund's disappearance. It was reported in the Danish press this winter. They've been searching for him all over Norway for months, but no one seems to have suspected that he went to Iceland. The Danish embassy is going to get more information. Then I phoned the district magistrate in Patreksfjördur, and he asked us to try to get more information. The detective force in Reykjavik is following the case and will step in if we run into any problems in the investigation. They'll also be gathering some information on Lund's movements in Reykjavik."

Grímur pondered. "We can contact the crew of the mail boat. They might remember this passenger. There can't have been that many passengers on these trips."

Kjartan nodded. "But what about the farmer in Ystakot? You said he was in the habit of keeping a record of everyone who comes and goes on the boats. Do you reckon he can help us?"

"Good point," said Grímur. "We can go over to Valdi after coffee."

"*...when the* Flatey Book *was written, the Icelandic language was undergoing considerable changes. However, the book was transcribed from various other manuscripts, both old and newer. It therefore contains a blend of old and new spelling, with many inconsistencies, as is the case in all Icelandic manuscripts, since the scribes neither had any spelling rules nor dictionaries. Each group* *of scribes followed their own methods, although at the beginning of the thirteenth century, one can see that the first grammatical treatise from the mid-twelfth century was beginning to have an impact. But everyone wrote in the way they were accustomed to, and that was to remain the practice in the centuries that followed...”*

CHAPTER 13

The news of the discovery of the remains of the body in Breidafjördur got more attention from the authorities in Reykjavik once it was announced that the deceased was more likely than not a Danish university professor who was highly regarded in his homeland. The case had, in fact, been immediately referred to the detective force when news of the discovery of the body first broke, but they were waiting for the outcome of the postmortem on the remains and for the locals to collect as much information as they could. Once the deceased had been identified, it was felt that someone needed to be assigned to the investigation. They were obliged to get to the bottom of this and write a report.

Dagbjartur Árnason wasn't exactly the smartest investigator in Reykjavik's detective force, and he knew it. He therefore didn't take it too badly when he got saddled with assignments that others found tedious and even insignificant. In fact, there was no shortage of menial cases of this kind. Small-time counterfeit checks, shoplifting, and other trivial transgressions of that ilk were considered to be his specialty and principal calling. Dagbjartur was regarded as being a bit lazy and slow, although he could also be patient and affable, which occasionally came in handy when there was a need to dig up information that wasn't always directly accessible. These qualities could also be useful when investigating bigger cases, even though he could sometimes be so inept at seeing the big picture. For this reason he was often assigned the role of assistant on cases of this kind. He was also incompetent when it came to questioning hardened criminals.

The duty officer called Dagbjartur in the afternoon and told him to investigate Gaston Lund's movements in the capital at the end of August of last year—to find out, for example, if he stayed in one of the city's hotels. Did anyone in town know him?

Dagbjartur was in a slight daze and tired. Not because he had been overdoing it at work over the past few days or anything like that, but simply because he'd eaten too much lamb meat soup for lunch. He'd also assumed it would be an easy day at work with a restful weekend ahead of him. He was going to give his wife a hand with the gardening, unless of course some work that couldn't wait cropped up. That meant overtime and a higher wage slip at the end of the month, which was welcomed.

Dagbjartur possessed an awkward build, with narrow shoulders but a body that widened the further down the eye traveled. His bloated belly, broad hips, and chubby ass gave him a slightly conical shape that he clearly had problems finding suits to match. This gave him a slightly odd appearance. His trousers had obviously been widened with little skill and poor material and were held up by a narrow pair of suspenders. His face sported a double chin, but he had a friendly and understanding air.

In addition to Dagbjartur, the district administrative officer in Flatey was working on the case, as well as the magistrate's representative in the Bardaströnd district. This obviously was not the best the police force could offer, but they were to be given a chance before more people were called into the investigation. Whitsunday was looming, and most people were on vacation. More likely than not there was a logical explanation to this whole case, which would soon come to light. Besides, the islanders on Flatey had already surpassed expectations by putting a name of the deceased, even though it wasn't obvious from the beginning.

Dagbjartur was also unusually fast in getting results from his preliminary enquiries. He had taken a cab straight to Hotel Borg and asked reception to show him the hotel's reservations book from August to September of last year. The staid, middle-aged male manager at reception took out a book that was marked 1959, placed it in front of the police officer, and opened it to the right place. Dagbjartur started his search from the beginning of August. Conscientiously reading every single name, he didn't stop until he reached the last guest on September 10. His search had yielded no results. Gaston Lund had not checked into this hotel. Not that Dagbjartur was too bothered. He still had to visit the other hotels in town and then also the guesthouses. If he was in any way lucky, this assignment could drag on for quite some time.

"Ahem, excuse me, but what name are you looking for?" the manager asked, as Dagbjartur was about to close the book.

"Professor Gaston Lund, a Danish national."

The reception manager nodded. "Yes. Mr. Lund stayed with us last year," he said.

"Really? Is his name in the book?"

"No, the man chose to register under a pseudonym."

"And you remember that after all these months?" Dagbjartur asked, surprised.

The manager gave him a faint smile. "Yes, it was certainly an unusual check-in. I remember things like that."

He turned the guestbook around and skimmed through it with his skilled fingers.

"There, that's how the professor checked in," he said, pointing at a line on August 24.

It started off with what looked like a *G* and an *a*, but had then been crossed out with two strokes and followed by "Egill Sturluson" in block letters.

"My name also happens to be Egill, so it drew my attention, especially to see it written that way," said the manager.

"Yes, I can see how this name would have attracted your attention," said Dagbjartur, nodding. He took out his notebook and scribbled down this information. "Didn't you have any remarks to make to him about this?" he then asked.

"No, he was a very respectable-looking man and immediately agreed to settle his bill in advance, as well as the deposit. I saw no reason to raise any objections about it. It was obvious that the man was Danish and also a bit of an eccentric. If he didn't want to use his real name, he must have had his reasons for it."

"How do you know his right name was Gaston Lund?"

"That's the name he used when he signed his bill in the restaurant. He obviously forgot himself. I was the one who processed the hotel bill, so I remember it. There was also a man who came here to ask if Professor Lund could possibly be staying here."

"What did you answer?"

"I told him there was no guest here under that name."

"Why?"

"Because our guest obviously wanted to keep a low profile and the hotel didn't want to complicate things for him; it was the least we could do. Besides, he'd already checked out of the hotel by the time the question was asked, so I wasn't lying."

"When did he move out?"

Egill examined the guestbook. "He stayed here for two nights and left here on August twenty-sixth. He left a case behind, which I kept in storage for him."

"Did he then claim the case?"

"I expect so, but not on my watch."

"Where was the case kept?"

"We have a storage room in the basement."

"Can I see it?"

"Yes. I'll take you down in a moment."

Egill vanished behind a door but swiftly returned, followed by a young man who took his place at the reception desk.

"Follow me please," he said to Dagbjartur.

They walked down some stairs into a dark corridor. There Egill opened the door to a small cell and turned on the light. A number of cases were stored there on racks.

"You keep a lot of cases in here," said Dagbjartur.

"This is mostly the lost property that has accumulated. Sometimes guests forget a whole case. Some of these belong to guests who've run away without settling their bills. I don't expect they'll ever be recovered."

"Can you see the Danish guest's case here anywhere?"

"I can't remember what it looks like. It was probably a quality case, though. He was a pretty refined kind of guest." Egill perused the cases, took several out, and opened them. One of them was considerably heavier than the others and turned out to contain folders of files when it was opened. Also some clothes.

Dagbjartur took one of the folders and browsed through the contents. It was full of pages crammed with text written in Danish, and there were a few Norwegian postcards at the back. Finally he found a tab that was stapled to the very last page: *G. Lund* was written on it.

"That's probably it," said Dagbjartur.

The manager seemed very taken aback. "That surprises me," he said. "I'd always assumed the guest had picked up his case as he said he would."

"I'll take it with me now," said Dagbjartur. "Who was it who asked you if he was staying here?"

"I don't know the man's name, but I'm sure I've seen pictures of him in the papers. He's obviously well known in his field."

Dagbjartur smiled amiably. "I hope you're not too busy these days because we obviously need to go through some old newspapers."

"*...The* Flatey Book *was based on many sources or older manuscripts, no less than forty. The Thingeyar monastery library was probably the main source since there was an ample selection of books there.*

"Scholars have noted that the priests who wrote out the Flatey Book *were not great poetry lovers. They copied verse word for word from older manuscripts mainly out of a sense of duty but with many mistakes and showing a poor understanding of poetry...*"

CHAPTER 14

The road to the Ystakot croft was a narrow, winding dirt track, and they walked in single file, Grímur first, followed by Högni and Kjartan behind. Little Nonni was sitting on a mound and spotted them as they approached. Springing to his feet, he dashed down to the farmhouse and vanished inside. The croft was divided into three little gables with turf rooftops and wooden panels in front. The back of the house was mostly built into the side of the slope. A chimney protruded from the gable, heaving black smoke. There was potato patch to the north of the building and beyond that a small hut, presumably a storeroom. In the yard there were a number of wooden frames, seed potatoes, an overturned wheelbarrow, and a large barrel of water with a lid on top.

Valdi appeared in the low doorway and had to stoop to come out to them.

"Hello there," Grímur greeted him.

Valdi nodded in silence, stuffed tobacco into his pipe, and stared at Kjartan with one inquisitory eye. Grímur got straight to the point. Could he have by any chance written down who was on the mail boat on Saturday September 4 last year?

Valdi pondered this a moment.

"Why do you want to know?" he asked.

"Reverend Hannes thinks he knows the man you found in Ketilsey but said that he was supposed to be traveling on the mail boat to Stykkishólmur that day."

Valdi went back into the croft and soon reappeared with a blue copybook in his hands. He skimmed through it, reading it in silence.

"No, Officer. I didn't write anything about who traveled south that day."

"Why not, Valdi?" Grímur asked, surprised.

"I can't remember offhand."

"Was it maybe because no one traveled on the boat?" Kjartan asked.

Valdi looked at him. "Could be."

"Could we maybe see that page?" Grímur asked.

Valdi looked at them alternately and then handed them the copybook and showed them the page. It was crammed with words written in pencil, and the entry beside the date September 4 read: "Drizzle, moderate breeze, temperature 4 degrees. Passengers from Stykkishólmur, Hákon, and Filippía. Was in Akranes getting new teeth. Gudrún's son in Innstibaer on visit." Then there was a small blank space.

They heard a screech from inside the house. Jón Ferdinand came limping outside clutching his mouth. "Ouch, ouch, ouch," he wailed. "I burned my mouth."

"What the hell happened?" Valdi gruffly snapped.

"I was just sipping the broth of the black-backed gull," said the crestfallen old man.

"Have you gone mad, tasting the broth when it's still boiling in the pot?" said Valdi, taking the lid off the barrel of water. He stuck a ladle inside and handed it to the old man.

"Here, drink something cold."

Jón Ferdinand sipped the water, and Valdi looked at the guests.

"I have to watch over this man like a little child," he said.

Grímur examined old Jón's lips. "He'll get some burn blisters," said Grímur. "Maybe you should take him to the doctor."

"I'd be doing little else if I had to take that old man to the doctor every time he burned his gob," Valdi grumbled.

"Mind if I take a little look at your book?" Kjartan asked.

Valdi looked at Kjartan. "Why?"

"The priest said the guest came over from Reykhólar on the second of September. Do you keep a record of the boats that come from over there in your book?"

"No, no. There's no way you can keep track of everyone who comes and goes from the village. Boats anchor all over the place, and there are so many things to do. I only follow the mail boat when it comes on Saturdays. I grab the ropes for them because it's such a short distance for me to go out to the pier. Then I write down who was on the boat, just for the information and fun of it. No one's ever asked to look at this before."

Grímur heaved a sigh. "Right then, Valdi. We'll take this no further then. Maybe you could try to remember why you didn't write about it in your book on that day and just let me know."

The three men said good-bye.

"...Vellum manuscripts in the Middle Ages were not all preserved with the same care. In the thirteenth century and the first half of

the fourteenth century, many manuscripts were probably exported to Norway as merchandise. Their value diminished, however, when the language rapidly changed at the end of the fourteenth century. People no longer cared about these vellum manuscripts that no one could read. In Iceland, on the other hand, it was probably overuse that damaged the books the most. Books were lent from person to person and read from cover to cover. Then new transcripts were made and the old shreds were lost. The Reformation also cast a bad light on anything written by the monks. It is not known who held the Flatey Book *after Jón Hákonarson in Vídidalstunga, but in the latter half of the fifteenth century it was in the hands of Thorleifur Björnsson, a seneschal in Reykhólar. It was then owned by Thorleifur's grandson, Jón Björnsson, in Flatey, and he gave the book to his grandson, Jón Finnsson, who also lived in Flatey; and it is after their home island that the book is named.*

"In the sixteenth century, national awareness was awakening in Europe. An emphasis was placed on the power of the nation and the strength of the kingdom. Interest in the history of nations grew, and in the Nordic countries, learned men knew that sources were to be found in Iceland. The Danish king sent manuscript collectors to Iceland in the seventeenth and eighteenth centuries, and Árni Magnússon was the most prominent of these. But there were other collectors, too. The bishop sagas refer to Jón the farmer in Flatey, saying that he had a big and thick vellum manuscript of monk writings containing the histories of the Norwegian kings and a lot more, and here it was generally referred to as the Flatey Book*..."*

CHAPTER 15

Kjartan and Grímur headed to the telephone exchange after their visit to Ystakot and made calls all over. They contacted the mail boat over the Gufunes radio, since it was positioned out in the bay of Faxaflói, on its way to Stykkishólmur with a cargo of cement from Akranes. The crew of the boat could offer them no information on the foreign passenger. He could well have been on board, but they had no specific recollection of him. It would mainly have been the cook who interacted with the passengers the most, but he had been on vacation for those weeks last year. A young girl, who had just graduated from the domestic college, had replaced him during his absence. She was now married to someone in the Westman Islands, as far as they knew.

Reverend Veigar in Reykhólar remembered Gaston Lund very well but had not heard from him, nor expected to hear from him. He had only stayed one night in Reykhólar. The hotel owner in Stykkishólmur confirmed that Lund had not stayed at the hotel overnight, after the boat arrived from Flatey. The bus for Reykjavik was leaving the following morning, so he assumed he must have stayed somewhere else in the village, if he had arrived on the boat.

The driver of the Stykkishólmur bus was at his home in Reykjavik. "I can't even remember who was on my bus yesterday," he answered when Grímur asked him whether he remembered a Danish passenger on September 4 last year.

Finally, there was a message from the detective division in Reykjavik. Gaston Lund had stayed in Hotel Borg for two nights when he came to Iceland and left his case in storage while he was traveling around the country. The case had been kept in a storage room in the hotel's basement and had been forgotten. This was why no one had wondered why it hadn't been collected.

Kjartan and Grímur sat at the telephone exchange until dinnertime, continuing with their enquiries. Stína, the head of the telephone exchange, and her colleague in Stykkishólmur stayed open long past their normal working hours, eavesdropping on the conversations with excitement.

More information arrived from the Danish embassy. Gaston Lund had traveled from Copenhagen to Norway in mid-July. He was single, somewhat eccentric in his habits, and apparently liked to keep to himself. His colleagues at the University of Copenhagen knew he intended to go to Bergen, Trondheim, and Stiklestad in Norway, but he had never mentioned any visit to Iceland. Questions soon began to be asked when he failed to turn up to deliver his lecture at the manuscript symposium and to teach at the university. An extensive search was then launched in Norway. There had been a ferry accident near Bergen at the beginning of September, and people were starting to wonder whether he might have been among the victims.

The fact that the professor had been found dead on a deserted in Iceland made headlines in Copenhagen.

On the state radio news there had been a long report on the case, and the district magistrate from Patreksfjördur was quoted as saying that there was an investigation underway.

"*...In 1647 Bishop Brynjólfur visited the West Fjörds and celebrated mass in the church of Flatey on the twelfth Sunday after trinity, which was the fifteenth of September. Brynjólfur then offered to buy the* Flatey Book, *first for money and then for land, but his offer was rejected. But when Jón Finnsson then followed the bishop to the ship, he handed him the good manuscript. One can assume that the bishop intended to print the book in Latin translation for learned men, but he did not have the king's authorization to run a printing press in Skálholt because the bishop of Hólar had exclusive printing rights in Iceland.*

"*The Danish king Fridrik III reigned between 1648 and 1670. He had a keen interest in ancient knowledge and in 1656 wrote to Bishop Brynjólfur, instructing him to send him any antiquities, old stories, and documents that could be found in Iceland to increase His Majesty's collection in the Royal Library. The bishop then communicated the king's request to the Court of Legislature of the Althing, and in the same year he dispatched the* Flatey Book *abroad and it has been in the Royal Library ever since. Fridrik III acquired the* Flatey Book *as the king of Iceland, and one therefore needs to regard it as belonging to the Icelandic state. These are the reasons why Icelanders are currently requesting the book to be returned to Iceland, and this concludes this history of the* Flatey Book."

CHAPTER 16

Högni continued working on the seal pups when Grímur and Kjartan went off to the telephone exchange. All of the fur had been pinned to the gable of the hut, but there was still a lot of meat left on the carcasses and the fat was meant to be melted into oil.

Little Nonni came walking down the shore with a dented milk canister in his hand and timidly greeted the teacher.

"Have you read that Indian story I lent you yet, Nonni my friend?" Högni asked.

"Yeah, twice."

"Twice? That was unnecessary. We can go to the library together and see if we can find another fun book that you haven't read yet."

"I'm reading *The Flying Dutchman*. Dad got a loan of it."

"That's not a nice book."

"I know. It's really spooky."

"Yes. It's got a lot of ghosts in it. I wouldn't lend that book to small children."

"I only read it during the day and at night keep it where the potatoes are stored. That way I don't get too scared."

"I see. Have you planted the potatoes yet?"

"Yeah, yeah, almost all of them."

"Have you caught any seal pups this spring?"

"No, none. Dad and Grandpa went out to check the net by Ketilsey this morning, but didn't catch anything. It's my fault, Dad says."

"Why is it your fault?"

"I shat on the island and the seals smell the smell, Dad says. But I'm sure it's more the dead man who's to blame. The smell off him was a lot worse."

Högni found an old washing bucket and chucked some pieces of seal meat into it.

"There you go, lad. Take that home to your dad. Bring the bucket back tomorrow. Then we can go to the library and find something fun to read. Remember that books are your best friend," he said, smiling.

Nonni took the bucket and placed it under his arm. Then, fully focused, he started walking toward home without saying thank you or good-bye.

"Can you help me to understand the questions and answers in the Flatey enigma?" he asked.

"I can try to," she answered.

Then she read out the questions one by one, looked at the answers that she had on the piece of paper, and then looked up the relevant chapter in the Munksgaard edition of the book, with well-trained fingers. She ran her finger along the text, maybe read a few lines out loud, but generally only vaguely explained what the chapter was about. He nodded silently if the answers were identical, but otherwise read out the alternative answers. In this manner they went through all of the forty questions, one after another...

CHAPTER 17

Saturday, June 4, 1960

The eastern winds subsided during the night, and when dawn broke, the sun shone and a stillness hung over Breidafjördur. The water in the strait was dark blue and as smooth as a mirror, except for those spots where the tide swirled between the islets and shallows.

Kjartan gazed out of his bedroom window and recalled the old proverb that said that sunshine was of little use to the man with no sun in his heart. He took a few deep breaths and then started to pick up his clothes.

Grímur and Högni had long left to go out and check on the seal nets by the time Kjartan finally stepped outside. Ingibjörg was in the kitchen stirring baking dough and listening to music on the radio. There was yellow dough in a large bowl, which she held firmly under her left arm as she stirred it vigorously with a big baking paddle in her right hand. In the shuffle some flour had been sprinkled over the table. Kjartan saw that the eggs she was using for the baking were big and had black spots on them.

"Those are great black-backed gull eggs from the spring," she said as he picked one up to examine it. "There's no need to spare any of those eggs in these recipes. There's plenty of them at this time of the year, and they're fine for baking, even if they're a bit old and have started to gestate," she added.

Kjartan drank his morning coffee and ate a slice of bread with lamb pâté. He was gradually starting to feel better and more comfortable about his stay with the district officer and his wife, although he was still plagued by worries about the investigation. For a moment he managed to forget himself, though, by staring out the kitchen window at two white wagtails that were hopping between stones on the embankment; he whistled a few notes to the radio.

To his relief, Ingibjörg continued with her kitchen work and did not initiate any conversation with him. It was good to sit like that and just think a little. He also feared that if they started talking together, the conversation would soon veer toward his personal affairs, and that was something he was eager to avoid. He didn't want to tell any lies, so it was best just to keep his mouth shut.

But he certainly had plenty of work to do. He intended to meet the islanders who had a motorboat at their disposal that would have been sturdy enough to make a journey to Ketilsey in the month of September, and he now asked Ingibjörg who they might be. She answered that there were only five, three once you excluded Valdi from Ystakot and Grímur, the district officer himself.

Ingibjörg listed the others as she broke another egg and added it to the baking dough: "There's Ásmundur, the storekeeper of the island store. He owns *Alda*, a beautiful white rowboat with a motor mounted on board. Then there's Gudjón, my brother in

Rádagerdi, who has *Ellidi*, a six-ton open motorboat with a little wheelhouse on it, and Sigurbjörn, the farmer in Svalbardi, who owns *Lucky*, an old-fashioned motorboat; it's green. They're all decent, sensible, honest, and honorable people."

Kjartan gave a start. *Lucky* could be the name of a boat. It had never occurred to him. There didn't have to be any connection with the message the man in Ketilsey tried to leave behind, but it needed to be borne in mind in the investigation.

Kjartan knew the way to Rádagerdi, and Benny was alone at home and still painting the window. He seemed to be glad of the interruption; he put down his brush and lit a cigarette.

"Mom and my sister Rósa are up in the shed milking the cows, and Dad's with Sigurbjörn in Svalbardi, cutting his hair for the mass tomorrow," he said when Kjartan inquired about the other members of the household.

"Cutting hair?" Kjartan wasn't sure he had heard right.

"Yeah, Dad can cut hair a bit. He cuts it quite short, though, and it can be quite sore because his clippers aren't as sharp as they used to be. That's why I don't want him to cut my hair. Sometimes a barber comes over from Stykkishólmur on the mail boat and cuts people's hair while the boat goes off to Brjánslækur. I prefer him. He knows how to cut hair with style. You can buy brilliantine from Ásmundur at the island store."

Benny stuck his smoldering cigarette into his mouth, took a comb out of his back pocket, and combed his blond hair back over his forehead.

"This is how Elvis combs his hair," he explained, losing his cigarette as he did.

Kjartan said good-bye and walked away toward Svalbardi while Benny was searching for his cigarette stub in the rhubarb patch that grew along the walls of the house.

As luck would have it, Kjartan bumped into the farmers Sigurbjörn and Gudjón together. Sigurbjörn was sitting on a stool in front of the entrance to the Svalbardi farmhouse with an old sheet over his shoulders that was tied around his neck. Gudjón stood over Sigurbjörn cutting his hair. In addition to them, there were two women in the yard, probably a mother and daughter, washing bedclothes in a large basin. The youngest, a pretty girl of about fifteen or sixteen, looked at Kjartan with curiosity but coyly averted her gaze when he returned the stare.

Gudjón in Rádagerdi was a well-groomed man in his forties, freshly shaven with dark hair, which was meticulously combed back with hair wax. He was wearing pressed beige pants and a checked cotton shirt with a red scarf around his neck. Sigurbjörn, on the other hand, was somewhat older with a choppy mop of gray hair on one side of his head that had not been cut yet. The other side was crew-cut, revealing bluish white skin underneath. His feet were clad in woolen socks and rubber shoes that protruded from under the sheet.

This method of cutting hair struck Kjartan as being closer to sheepshearing than hairdressing. The cutting was also proceeding slowly because the clippers were stiff and painful on Sigurbjörn's head.

Kjartan introduced himself, and the others greeted him.

"Mild weather," Kjartan then said, for the sake of saying something.

"Yes," Sigurbjörn answered, "it's been like this all spring. Better weather than any of the oldest women can remember, I think. The arctic terns have never come this early to nest; I think it can only end in disaster. Ouch, ouch, take it easy with those bloody clippers, Gutti pal."

"You mean you think the weather'll get worse?" Kjartan asked, scanning the air, unable to spot a single cloud. But then he got down to business: "But anyway, you know why I'm here on the island, don't you? Can I ask you a few questions?"

Gudjón stopped cutting and straightened a moment. "Yeah, sure, of course," he said, intrigued.

"It's been established that the body that was found on Ketilsey was that of a Danish man who stayed here with the priest last year, Professor Gaston Lund," said Kjartan.

"Yes. We heard that straightaway yesterday," Gudjón answered.

"Do either of you remember the man?"

Gudjón shook his head, but Sigurbjörn nodded and answered, "Yeah, yeah, I sure do. I remember the man very well. I had an argument with him."

"Oh?" Kjartan was all ears.

"Yeah, or as much as I could. He was trying to speak Icelandic, the poor lad, and it wasn't altogether easy to understand what he was saying."

"Could he make himself understood, though?"

"He could speak some old Icelandic and that kind of thing. He learned it from the manuscripts, he said. Then he'd practiced speaking modern Icelandic with Icelandic students in pubs in Copenhagen. They obviously taught him some swear words and curses."

"Did he curse a lot?" Kjartan asked.

Sigurbjörn smiled and shook his head. "No, no."

"What did you argue about?"

"I asked him when he was going to give us the *Flatey Book* back, and he said it was going to stay in Copenhagen. The best scholars were there, he said. Then I asked him some questions about Sverrir's saga to test his knowledge, but he couldn't answer much. We then tried to reason about it a little more, but I think it's fair to say that we were just unable to understand each other."

Sigurbjörn grinned at the memory of it, but then he turned serious and said, "Of course, it was terrible for him to perish out on Ketilsey like that."

Gudjón seconded this with a nod.

"Where did you meet?" Kjartan asked.

"In the library. Hallbjörg in Innstibaer let him in to look at our Munksgaard edition of the book. He was very impressed by how it was kept in a glass case. I don't think they treat the original manuscript any better. He took several photographs. Then he was going to have a crack at the old riddle. That was when I asked whether he was going to return the manuscript to us, but he wouldn't hear a word of it."

Kjartan said, "We know that the deceased left the priest on September fourth and intended to take the mail boat to Stykkishólmur. We don't know if he ever boarded the boat. If not, is it possible that he may have left the island on some other boat? Could he have gone on one of your boats?"

Gudjón and Sigurbjörn looked at each other and both shook their heads.

"We go out very little that early in September," Sigurbjörn said, "except maybe to collect the hay on the outer islands when it's been cut. Later we take a few trips to the mainland to collect the sheep from their summer grazing. We never sail south to Stykkishólmur or anywhere in that direction at that time of the year. Anyone who needs to travel south takes the mail boat."

Kjartan persisted: "Is it possible that someone would have taken him on one of your boats without you knowing?" he asked.

"Taken the boat in secret, you mean?" Gudjón asked.

"Yes."

"That would be a first on these islands."

"Could it have happened? There's a first time for everything."

Gudjón and Sigurbjörn looked at each other and both shook their heads again.

"No," they said in unison, and Sigurbjörn added: "I think I would notice it straightaway if someone else had landed my boat."

Gudjón seconded him with a nod.

"Have you any idea, then, of how he could have reached Ketilsey?"

"I'm sure he didn't fall off the mail boat on the way to Stykkishólmur," said Gudjón. "The crew would definitely have noticed it if a passenger they had picked up in Flatey failed to disembark in Stykkishólmur. Especially in September when there are normally very few passengers on the boat. They're very observant and conscientious."

Kjartan wondered whether he should also mention that the Danish man had probably written the word *Lucky* with pebbles on Ketilsey, but he decided against it. He had no way of knowing if it was connected to Sigurbjörn's boat and could not think of how to formulate his question. Feeling the farmers could be of no more use to him for the moment, Kjartan said good-bye and headed back toward the village. Glancing back, he could see that the men were deep in conversation and seemed to have forgotten about the haircut altogether.

She read, "Question one: It will come near when it is God's wish. First letter. King Sverrir was going to his ship on a small rowboat when an arrow struck the bow over his head and another one came close to his knee. The king sat there and did not flinch, and his companion said, 'Dangerous shot, sire.' The king answered, 'It will come near when it is God's wish.' The answer is 'dangerous shot,' and the first letter is d."

CHAPTER 18

Detective Dagbjartur sat at the National Library with Egill, the reception manager from Hotel Borg, who was skimming through the newspapers of the last months. Egill was supposed to try to recognize the man who had inquired about Professor Lund the previous autumn. The reception manager was sure he had seen pictures of the man in the papers, and now they had to flip through them until they found him. This was their second day on this task, and it was proceeding slowly. Egill carefully studied all the photographs of men and occasionally stumbled on snippets of articles that drew his attention. Dagbjartur just sat there patiently, yawning and cleaning his nails. He had set himself a very clear and delimited task, which at best could be stretched out for another day or two. This temporarily freed him of petty criminals and paperwork. A press release had been dispatched to the papers that morning requesting the man to come forward, and it read as follows: "The man who entered Hotel Borg at the end of August of last year and enquired about Gaston Lund from Denmark is asked to contact the police in Reykjavik." The notice would not be appearing before next Wednesday at the earliest. Whitsunday was upon them and no papers would be coming out.

Large, thick folders of newspapers lay on the table in front of the two men, and Dagbjartur ensured each pile was renewed as soon as it had been viewed. It was a moderate task to be performing on a beautiful June day, and it seemed to be proceeding nicely. It was also a quiet day at the library on that Saturday, and there was only a small group of regulars at work. Every now and then a smothered cough, sneeze, whisper, or shifting chair could be heard. Otherwise everything was as quiet as a morgue.

Dagbjartur was dozing off in his seat when the reception manager suddenly exclaimed, "There he is!"

Dagbjartur popped off his chair. "Are you sure?" he asked, disappointed.

"Yes, yes," he said, "absolutely sure."

Dagbjartur looked at the paper. The picture was of an amiable-looking silver-haired man, who was named underneath as Fridrik Einarsson. The title of the article was "Killing methods in the Orkneyinga saga."

Dagbjartur glanced at his watch. There was still plenty of time left in the day to find this man and talk to him. There was no way of avoiding it. Dagbjartur sighed wearily.

Question two: Most impudent. First letter. When they reached Reine, they spotted three longships rowing down the fjord. The third was a dragon ship. As the ships passed the merchant vessel, an imposing figure walked onto the deck of the dragon ship and said, "Who is the commander of this ship, and where did you first make land and camp last night?"

Sarcastic Halli replied, "We spent the winter in Iceland and sailed from Gasir, and our commander is called Bard. We made land at Hitra and camped at Agdanes."

The man, who in actual fact was King Harald Sigurdsson, then asked, "Didn't Agdi sodomize you?"

"Not yet," Halli answered.

The king smiled and said, "Have you made some arrangement for him to perform this service on you later then?"

Halli answered, "If you're curious to know, Agdi is saving that up for nobler people than us and is expecting you to arrive this evening so that he can pay you this debt in full."

"You're exceedingly impudent," said the king.

The answer is "sarcastic Halli," and the first letter is s.

CHAPTER 19

The island's store was a two-story building close to the co-op building. Its doors faced west, but on its eastern side there was an extension and other entrances. From there was a staircase to the top floor where Ásmundur, the storekeeper, lived with his wife in a small apartment. The store and stockroom were on the lower floor. When Kjartan opened the door into the store, a shrill bell resounded in the empty space. Kjartan looked around and took a deep breath. Strong and familiar odors lingered in the air. Wooden furnishings gave off a symphony of smells to the accompaniment of a broad range of products: candy, shoe polish, coffee, nails, books, oatmeal, hooks, potatoes, needles, baking powder, coffee jugs, raisins, scythes, brown sugar, paint, lemonade, grindstones, snuff, caps, peas, rubber shoes, vanilla drops, rakes, chocolate, and net buoys. These and many other products were crammed into cluttered piles on the shelves that covered all of the store's walls. Some categories of products simply lay in bundles on the floor or on the counter.

Ásmundur soon appeared in the store. He was a short, fat man, bald with a round jovial face, dressed in a white storekeeper's apron tied around his potbelly. In his breast pocket there were two pencils and a folding ruler. The storekeeper greeted him amiably: "Hello, young man. We've got special offers on penknives and vitamins this week, cattle feeding corn is back in stock, and we've got the latest fashion in shoes from Reykjavik."

"I'm not here to buy anything and I apologize for the intrusion, but I came for another reason," said Kjartan at the end of the storekeeper's sales pitch. He then asked him the same questions he had asked the farmers earlier. Ásmundur's answers were similar. He remembered the Danish visitor quite well. The man had come into the store to ask about film for his camera.

"Unfortunately, I didn't have any rolls of film. I order them especially from Reykjavik when someone requests it. Since the Dane was on his way south anyway, I didn't bother ordering any film for him," said Ásmundur. "I did, however, manage to sell him two pairs of woolen socks." Then he thought a moment and said, "My boat certainly wasn't moved during that time."

"What do you use the boat for?" Kjartan asked.

"Mainly for small deliveries from the store," the storekeeper answered. "Having a decent motorboat can come in quite handy when you need to pop over to the mainland or to the inner isles when the farmers are busy in the summer. The co-op doesn't offer a good service like that, and that's how you get customers. But I never go south to Stykkishólmur because the mail boat brings supplies over once a week. Then I always take my boat away after the slaughtering season and let it rest in the storehouse over the winter. I don't like traveling by sea in the winter, both because of the dark and the cold. Farmers also normally find they have more time on their hands in the winter and like the change of doing their shopping in town."

"Have you any idea how that Danish man could have ended up in Ketilsey?" Kjartan asked.

"It's all people can talk about in the village," the trader answered. "But nobody can figure it out. Who the hell could have left the man out there? I know every single person on these islands, and I can assure you there isn't an ounce of evil in any of them. Maybe there was an accident. Maybe the man boarded the mail boat without any of the crew really noticing him. Then maybe he was standing by the gunwale and fainted and fell into the sea. Then perhaps he regained consciousness and swam until he found something to hang onto. Or the current was really fast and carried him all the way to Ketilsey. But it's all so unlikely that one can barely believe it."

Kjartan was on the point of giving up on the investigation. He felt no closer to solving Gaston Lund's death.

"How much do you charge for these penknives of yours?" he asked.

Question three: The bad choice he made for me. Second letter. King Magnús said, "Many people can be grateful to their fathers, and so am I in many ways and more than most, but he made a bad choice in the mother he selected for me." So "mother" is the answer, and the second letter is o.

CHAPTER 20

Kjartan was on his way back to the district administrative officer's home when he suddenly remembered that a new name had cropped up in connection with the Danish visitor. The farmer Sigurbjörn had told him that Hallbjörg in Innstibaer had allowed the guest into the library. It could do no harm to hear more details about that side of the story. The young boy who had taken the priest's message down to Grímur was now on Kjartan's path and was able to direct him toward Innstibaer. It was easy enough. There was only one path in that direction, and Innstibaer was the last croft on the sea side of the path. Two amicable orphaned lambs greeted him with their bleating by a quaint little house. Two women were sitting on wooden footstools on the sidewalk, knitting woolen socks in the sunshine. One of them was in her seventies, tall and stout. The other might have been just over fifty and was small with delicate features.

Kjartan greeted them and introduced himself. The women returned the greeting, intrigued, but did not introduce themselves in return.

"Is one of you called Hallbjörg?" Kjartan then asked.

"Yes, that's good old me, young man," the eldest answered.

Kjartan recounted his conversation with Sigurbjörn to her and asked if she remembered the Danish visitor.

"Yes, that's my job in the village, to take care of the key to the library. Anyone who wants to borrow a book has to get the key from me first. But when strangers come and want to take a look at the library, I take them there myself. That's the general rule, dear."

"Do you remember this Danish man?" Kjartan asked.

"Yes, yes. He wanted to have a go at the old riddle."

"Do you mean the questions in the *Flatey Book*?"

"Yes, it's a terribly innocent little riddle, but they haven't managed to solve it yet."

"Who's they?"

"All kinds of bigheads who claim to know things about the *Flatey Book*."

"Do you know if Professor Lund was able to solve the riddle?"

"No. I don't think so. Not that I was peeping over his shoulder when he was having a go at it. He worked on it until the early hours."

"Can I get to see the list of questions?"

"Yes, I don't see any danger in that. I'll lend you the key and you can have a look yourself. My leg's bad today."

The woman stood up stiffly and vanished into the croft.

The other woman silently glanced at Kjartan but immediately averted her gaze and focused on her knitting when he returned her gaze. She must have been a pretty woman in her day, and even though age was clearly creeping up on her, she still possessed a graceful air.

Kjartan stooped over the lambs that had settled by his feet and patted them until Hallbjörg returned.

"Here," she said, handing him an old key, which Kjartan took.

"Will I be able to find it on my own?" he asked.

"Yes. The Munksgaard book is in a glass case against the northern wall. You can't miss it. It's not a big building. You can open the drawer, and the enigma sheets are slipped inside the beginning of the book. Just remember not to take the sheets out of the library. Misfortune and bad luck will follow anyone who takes those pages out or copies them."

"Why's that?"

"It's just a fact, everyone knows. An old curse, dear. There are ancient magical runes on the sheets, and no one knows what curse they unleash if they're not treated carefully. The key to the riddle can only be found on those sheets, and they can never be taken out of the library. Unless, of course, the riddle has been solved, in which case the winner can keep the sheets."

"Is that the winner's prize then?"

"Yes, and the honor, of course. The person who solves the enigma will become famous."

"Is it a very old enigma?"

"Not that old, but a good hundred years at least."

"Have the sheets been in the library all that time?"

"No, no. The old librarian who received the Munksgaard book for the library's centenary celebration received the riddle with it. Before that it had been kept by the king in Copenhagen. These are very important documents."

Kjartan was on the point of leaving when Hallbjörg beckoned him over and shoved something into the palm of his hand.

"Here's a piece of candy, dear. Something sweet'll do you good." She gave him a warm smile.

Kjartan looked at the dark piece of candy in his hand and thanked her. He then said good-bye, and the lambs followed him as he headed toward the village.

Question four: Who was the cruelest woman? First letter. The saga of the Greenlanders talks about Freydís, the daughter of Eirik the Red, and how she reached an agreement with the brothers Helgi and Finnbogi to travel with her to Vinland. But after they arrived, Freydís's real wickedness was revealed and she got her men to enter their lodge and kill them. When all the men were dead, there were five women left that no one wanted to kill. Then Freydís picked up an axe, struck the women, and killed them. The answer is "Freydís," and the first letter is f.

He said, "Here the guest writes the name Sigrid, the daughter of Skogul-Tosti."

She browsed through the book and said, "This one is also possible. Harald Grenski came to the estate of Queen Sigrid the daughter of Skogul-Tosti. That same evening another six kings had arrived there, and all proposed to Sigrid. The kings sat in the ancient hall. There was no shortage of drink, so everyone got very drunk and fell asleep. Then in the night Sigrid bade her men fall on them with fire and weapons. The hall was burned down with the seven kings and their men inside. Sigrid said that this would dissuade puny kings from other lands from coming to her and trying to woo her. The letter is therefore s."

CHAPTER 21

Inspector Dagbjartur found Fridrik Einarsson, a university lecturer in Icelandic philology, at home in his quaint bungalow in Aragata. It had been two hours since Dagbjartur had left Egill, his collaborator at the National Library. He had been allowed to use the library phone and had immediately been able to reach the man Egill had recognized from the newspaper photograph. They set an appointment, and Dagbjartur had a bite to eat at a diner while he was waiting. He then took a stroll by the pond in the mild weather and eventually waved down a cab that took him past the university to Aragata.

Dagbjartur was led into a living room and invited to sit in a deep armchair. The walls were lined with crammed bookshelves, and large, hand-carved chess pieces stood on a chessboard on a beautiful table. The inspector gazed at them, sensing there was something odd about them.

"That's Viking chess," said Fridrik, a tall thin man in his sixties. "In addition to the traditional chessmen, there are two Vikings on each team. The chessboard is therefore ten squares wide on each side, instead of the traditional eight."

Fridrik adjusted the chess parts on the board and patiently waited for Dagbjartur to come to the point.

The policeman gave himself plenty of time to study the chess set and finally said, "You went to Hotel Borg at the end of August last year and asked for Professor Gaston Lund of Copenhagen. Is that correct?"

Fridrik seemed startled. He thought a moment and then said, "Yes. That's absolutely right. How on earth do you know that?"

"It doesn't really matter, but why were you looking for him?"

"Is this investigation linked to Professor Lund's death on that island in the west? I heard about that."

"Yes, we're investigating his death," Dagbjartur answered. "Why were you trying to find the man?"

Fridrik needed to reflect on this a moment. "I was driving my car down Pósthússtræti," he finally said, "and I just happened to glance through the hotel's restaurant window as I was passing. I thought I'd spotted the professor sitting at a table. I knew him very well from the days when I worked in Copenhagen and thought it was incredible that he would come to Reykjavik without contacting me or even giving me a call. It was bugging me all day, so next morning I went to the hotel and asked them if he was staying there. It turned out to be a mirage."

Dagbjartur gave Fridrik an inquisitive look. "But now you know that he was here during that period, don't you?"

"Yes, like I said, I heard about that dreadful thing in the west. I must have had some kind of premonition. It's happened to me before. I think I recognize someone and it turns out to be a mistake. Then maybe a short while later I meet the same person in some other place. It's an inexplicable gift."

Dagbjartur shook his head. "This time you were probably seeing right. You just got the wrong information at the hotel."

"Really, did I? It had to be. I saw Lund so clearly."

"You said you would have expected him to visit you?"

"Yes, of course. We worked together for many years in Copenhagen and often chatted about what we were going to do when he came to Iceland. He came here twice in the twenties and thirties but traveled far too little. But he knew the historical spots so well that he could describe them in the minutest detail. He must have intended to surprise me with his visit when that terrible thing happened to him."

Fridrik stared down at the table.

Dagbjartur paused a moment and then said, "It looks as if no one knew about the professor's trip."

"Oh really? Not that there's anything strange about that."

"Oh?"

"Yes. The professor didn't have any family, and when I knew him best, he was used to taking summer vacations alone. He never let anyone know about them and just wandered around Europe, following his personal whims. He'd always have lots of fun stories to tell when he came back to Copenhagen, though. He felt he could establish better contact with the locals if he traveled alone."

Fridrik stood up and walked to the bookshelves.

"The priest in Flatey claims he avoided his acquaintances in Iceland because of some controversy over a manuscript. Do you reckon that's true?" Dagbjartur asked.

Fridrik smiled numbly. "Oh yeah? Is that what it was? He was certainly adamantly opposed to most of his Icelandic colleagues on the issue, but I can't think of anyone who would have tried to make him pay for it in any way, although I'm sure he would have been the toughest opponent to dissuade. He cared more about those manuscripts than any human being. And he knew all the arguments and legal loopholes to prevent them from being handed over."

As Fridrik spoke, he took a folder off the shelf, opened it, found a typed sheet, and said, "I've been collecting material on this manuscript issue. Here's a thesis by Gaston Lund that I translated. Listen to this extract: 'The international research that is being conducted on the basis of these manuscripts would be hindered if the collection were to be dispersed. The results of the studies that are being made in Copenhagen are published in all the major European languages, whereas in Reykjavik the results would only be published in modern Icelandic. The humanities departments of the University of Copenhagen would unanimously oppose any handing over of the manuscripts.'"

Fridrik slipped the sheet back into the folder and put it back in its place. Then he took out a photo album and placed in on the table beside the chess board.

"So didn't Gaston Lund have any enemies in this country then?" Dagbjartur asked.

"Some of our fellow countrymen might have let a few insults fly when he vented his opinions at meetings. Lund could also be rash and excitable, but it was never serious enough not to able to be solved with a good glass of schnapps. But I think I know the reason why he wanted to travel incognito."

"Oh yeah?"

"The first time Gaston Lund came here was in 1926 or 1927. He was a member of what was considered to be a very gifted group of young Danish scholars. The story goes that Lund became intimately acquainted with a pretty local girl somewhere down south and got her pregnant. The fact that he refused to have anything to do with the child says a lot about his lower nature. He didn't come back until he accompanied King Christian the tenth of Denmark on his official visit in 1936. The mother of the child planned to introduce him to his son, but Lund reacted badly to this reunion and washed his hands of them. The Icelanders in Copenhagen heard the story and weren't impressed. But personally I think his behavior was just something that was beyond his control. The whole concept of taking on a father's role was so overwhelming to him that he couldn't cope. He always treated women with great suspicion after that. I think he didn't dare go to Iceland because he was scared of bumping into the mother of his child. And now when he finally came back again, he tried to keep a low profile in this clumsy manner."

"Did he ever receive any threats from this woman?"

"No, definitely not. But he was so deeply intimidated by her that he didn't dare to come here for decades."

"Do you know her name?"

"No. I heard this story as a piece of gossip and never asked for any further details."

"And could you write me out a list of all the Icelanders that you know he knew personally?"

"I can do that, yes," said Fridrik, skimming through the album. "Here's a picture I took of Gaston Lund. On a short trip to Sweden."

Dagbjartur saw the proud figure of a man standing in front of a group of people.

Fridrik said, "If you're interested in the professor's other faults, I could tell you that he was incredibly domineering. He often took over on those trips, uninvited, and that could be tiring. To people who didn't know him, it came across as brashness and arrogance. He could also be quite vain and full of himself and his position. In most of his traits, he was unlike any of the Danes I've ever known. They're normally gentler and more easygoing than Professor Lund was."

"Could I borrow that picture?" Dagbjartur asked.

Fridrik carefully removed it from the photo album and handed it to Dagbjartur, who stuck it into his notebook.

"They say in Flatey that Gaston Lund traveled there to try his hand at some riddle connected to the *Flatey Book*. Are you familiar with that story?" Dagbjartur asked.

Fridrik smiled. "Aenigma Flateyensis. It would have given Professor Lund a great deal of prestige to be able to solve that enigma. He would have been quite happy to have that feather in his cap."

"What kind of an enigma is it?" Dagbjartur asked.

"It's just a few questions about the sagas contained in the *Flatey Book*, but I'm not the best man to tell you that story. Árni Sakarías, the poet and historian, is the man you need to talk to about that."

Question five: King Magnús's men. Second letter. King Sverrir Sigurdsson reigned in Norway from 1177 to 1202, and his men were the valiant Birkibeins. It had previously been considered shameful to be called a Birkibein, but following the fall of Earl Erling it was deemed an honor. There were then constant conflicts between King Magnús and his men. It happened that an old beggar woman died and left behind her a cowled garment, or a hekla, *as it was called. A large quantity of silver was found stitched up inside it. When King Magnús's men heard about this, they took and burned the garment, sharing the silver between them. This became known to the Birkibeins, who from that point onwards called them the Heklaufs, and the second letter is* e.

CHAPTER 22

The Flatey library stands at the top of the island, just a few yards beyond the church. Kjartan contemplated the building when he reached the gate of the low fence. It was a tiny little building, even smaller than it looked from down below in the village. Once he had let himself in with the key, he discovered a single narrow room lined with bookshelves. Grímur had told Kjartan that the lion's share of the library's collection—old parchment manuscripts, diaries, and files—had long ago been transferred south to Reykjavik where they were preserved in the national library. What remained was old popular literature that was borrowed and read by the parishioners. Kjartan glanced at the spines of various books and dipped into some of them. Titles included *The Treasure* by Selma Lagerlöf, *The Ship Sails* by Nordal Grieg, and *Anna of Heidarkot* by Elínborg Lárusdóttir. Not exactly the most contemporary of selections.

There was no mystery as to where the Munksgaard edition of the *Flatey Book* was kept. Wedged between two windows against the northern wall, there was a low table covered with a pane of glass, and in a drawer underneath it there was a large open book. Kjartan looked at the pages through the glass. These were black-and-white photographs of the original pages of the manuscript in the same scale. The lettering was clear and distinguishable, but Kjartan was unable to read it. He opened the drawer and turned the pages. At the front he found some old handwritten sheets that he could read. On the top of the first page the words *Aenigma Flateyensis* had been written, and below that there was a poem:

A black darkness looms over the land,
but the sailing carries on the distant trail
to death's cold shores.
The most valiant asks: Why?

A potent spell dictates our journey,
And we are rowing for our lives,
Futile to seek any answers,
In battle we must place our trust.

Heavy gray clouds of eerie pelting hail,
Demanding the magic words,
The world under a skull
storing thoughts for the winter.

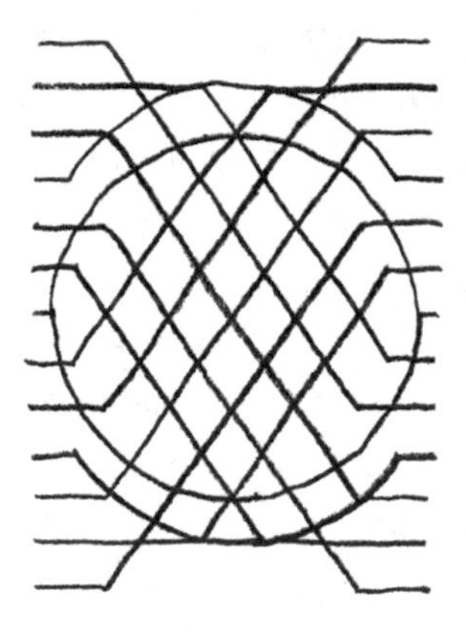

The bottom two lines were in a different handwriting than the other lines of the poem and were followed by these words: *This may be how the poet wanted it to end.*

Below it there was a bizarre drawing that had been executed with a rough pencil. Probably the magic rune that Hallbjörg had referred to, Kjartan thought to himself.

On the next sheet there were some kind of questions, forty in total, written in beautiful and perfectly legible handwriting:

1. It will come near when it is God's wish. 1st letter.
2. Most impudent. 1st letter.
3. The bad choice he made for me. 2nd letter.

Kjartan dug into his pocket and fished out the answers Professor Lund had given to the priest and compared the questions.

1. Dangerous shot—D
2. Sarcastic Halli—S
3. Mother—O

Kjartan felt no closer. The questions seemed odd, and the answers said nothing to him. The fortieth and last question read as follows: *Who spoke the wisest?* Following that there were three rows of letters.

O S L E O Y I A R N R Y L
E M H O N E A E N W T L B
A U R M L E Q W T R O N E

Kjartan took out the note that Jóhanna had found in Gaston Lund's pocket and which the priest had recognized. He examined the rows of letters written on its back and compared them with the three rows of letters written on the question sheet.

Professor Gaston Lund had clearly entered this library after he had said good-bye to the priest, and jotted down the key. And that was something he was forbidden to do and that would bring a curse on him, according to local belief. And he surely had been greatly cursed. The thought of it gave Kjartan a slight shudder. He refused to believe in curses of this kind, but there was no denying that it was very sinister nonetheless.

A note below the three rows explained that the thirty-nine correct answers should follow the same order as the thirty-nine letters in the answer to the fortieth question, and that this was how the poem should end.

Kjartan shoved the sheets back into the book. He stared at length at the note that had been found on the body, and then he decided that it was best to store that inside the manuscript as well. It was probably best to go along with the belief that the clues should be kept in the library and nowhere else. He wouldn't feel comfortable walking around with it in his pocket, now that he realized what it was. He left the book as he had found it. Then, after locking the drawer, he pensively stepped out into the sunshine.

What was it that had compelled Gaston Lund to come to the library and write down that key before going to the ship? Had he been so desperate to solve the riddle that he deliberately broke the strict ancient rules of the game? How had he gotten into the locked building?

Question six: Who could not hold back their tears? First letter. They dragged up the body, and King Sverrir said it was the body of King Magnús. They slid a shield under the body and lifted it onto the ship and rowed to land. The body was still recognizable because its complexion had not changed; it still had rosy cheeks and rigor mortis had not set in. Before the body was veiled with a shroud, the king allowed Magnús's men to file past it to identify it and bear witness. They filed past the body, and almost no one could hold back their tears. The answer is "Magnús's men," and the first letter is m.

CHAPTER 23

Thormódur Krákur stood watch on the flagpole stand in front of the church for two hours around lunchtime and finally rushed down to the village to ceremoniously announce that the mail boat was now visible on the southern horizon. Some men walked toward the shore, dragging two handcarts and preceded by a flock of running children.

Benny in Rádagerdi put down his paintbrush when he became aware of the gathering crowd and sauntered after them out of sheer habit, even though he had no errand there. Life was so drab for a young man on this island that even the weekly arrival of the mail boat was something of an event. Maybe he'd know some of the passengers, and there was also always the hope of some workers from the south who might be on their way to the inner isles.

By the time the kids came charging around the corner by the fish factory, the mail boat had reached the tip of the island. It was an old white oak boat that was heavy and sluggish, although the skipper managed to maneuver it with surprising agility toward the pier. Valdi caught the hawser that was thrown to him over the gunwale and looped it around the bollard. Then the boat was tied at the back. Little Nonni followed his father every step of the way and paid no heed to the other children on the pier.

Two young boys in their Sunday best stood by the gunwale of the mail boat and were soon lifted onto the edge of the pier and followed by a brown suitcase crisscrossed with strings. A woman welcomed them, enveloping them both in a simultaneous embrace and calling them her darling little sweethearts. Three sacks of mail were then hoisted off the boat and placed on one of the carts, followed by four crates of malt ale and two sacks of flour that went into the other cart. This seemed to be the sum total of the delivery from this trip. The load that needed to be sent south to Stykkishólmur would only be loaded on board when the boat was making its return journey later in the day.

The men on the boat were preparing to depart again when the weary face of a tall man in a dirty light trench coat with a brown peaked cap appeared out of the forecastle and stiffly stepped onto the deck. He held a heavy case and scanned the pier with his eyes.

"Young man," he shouted hoarsely at Benny, who was standing by the gunwale. "Would you grab this for me?" he asked, handing him the case. "But carefully now, carefully, I've got some fragile objects in there," he added as Benny stretched out to take the case. The man clambered onto the edge of the pier, but then wobbled a bit and grabbed Benny's arm for support.

"Bloody dizziness," he said. "I think I must have just dozed off on the way. The journey seemed endless." He looked toward the land and squinted his eyes at the fish factory on the embankment. "So this is the famous ancient island of Flatey in Breidafjördur. Is this it in all its glory then?"

"You can't see the village from here," Benny answered apologetically. "That's on the other side of the island. That's where all the houses are."

"Is that right, my friend? What's your name?"

"Benny...Ben."

"Benny Ben. I see. My name is Bryngeir, a poet and writer, even though I'm temporarily hacking for a Reykjavik rag."

"Just Ben...or Benny," Benny swiftly corrected him. He was almost on the point of giving up on the name that he'd decided to adopt after reading a book about Ben Hur over one whole night two weeks ago.

"Put the case down really gently, Benny Ben pal," said Bryngeir. "I have to check on its delicate contents."

There was a rattle of glass from the case as it knocked against the pier. Bryngeir crouched over it, unzipped it, and pulled out a half bottle of rum. He unscrewed the top, poured drink into it, and knocked it back. Then he had another swig, this time straight from the spout, and straightened up, propping himself up against the lamppost on the pier.

Benny tried to guess Bryngeir's age. His face looked rugged and gaunt, but something seemed to suggest that he wasn't quite as old as he first seemed. He was probably forty. His dark hair had started to gray and recede. But one of his eyebrows was as white as snow, as were his eyelashes on the other side.

Bryngeir refilled the tap of the bottle.

"Would you be partial to a drop of rum, young man?" he asked Benny.

Benny looked up at the pier where the islanders could be seen making their way to the interior. There was no one left but Valdi, who was loosening the moorings of the mail boat. It wouldn't do his reputation among the islanders any good to be seen boozing in the middle of the day, but he couldn't say no to some slight refreshment. Besides, it was Saturday, after all.

"Thanks," he said, taking a sip and coughing.

Bryngeir fished a half-smoked cigar out of his coat pocket and managed to light it after several attempts. "Is there any news about that dead man, the one they found here out on one of the islands?" he asked.

"He was Danish. They'll be taking him south when the boat sails back this evening," Benny answered, lighting himself a cigarette to keep Bryngeir company.

Bryngeir sipped on his bottle of rum and then said, "Yeah, I heard he was a Danish professor, the one and only Gaston Lund. Who was it that left him out there on the skerry?"

"No one knows. The guy from Patreksfjördur is investigating that."

"The guy from Patreksfjördur?"

"Yeah, he works for the district magistrate. His name is Kjartan."

"Kjartan? A lawyer?"

"Yeah. He's just started working for the magistrate."

Bryngeir puffed musingly on his cigar. "Tell me this, does this spy have a big scar on his forehead? From his left eyebrow up to his hairline?" Bryngeir pressed a finger against his forehead by way of illustration and drew an invisible line.

"Yeah, he has a scar like that."

"Well what do you know? I think I heard that in Reykjavik. That Kjartan was working in Patreksfjördur." Bryngeir took off his cap, shook it, and scratched his head before putting it back on again.

"Do you know him?" Benny asked, intrigued.

"Nah, not that much, but more than enough."

"How do you mean?"

Bryngeir declined to answer. "Where can a man find accommodation around here?" he asked.

"Accommodation?" said Benny. "Just need to find someone with a free bed."

Bryngeir broke into a grin. "Yes, of course. Guesthouses shouldn't even exist in a Christian country, some godly man who liked to travel cheap once said. OK, let's start walking and looking at the options. You can carry my case for me while I recover from the crossing." He took another sip from the bottle and shoved it into his trench coat pocket.

Valdi of Ystakot watched them walking up the pier and jotted something into his notebook. Little Nonni sat on the bollard and stared at the mail boat, which had by now reached the west of the island and was heading north.

Benny stared furtively at the newcomer's face as they walked. Finally, he just couldn't hold it in anymore and came straight out with it: "What happened to your eye? Why is your eyebrow so white?"

"It was a woman, young man," he answered without looking at Benny. "A woman did this to me after I seduced her one midsummer's night. She said that from now on I would be marked out from other men and that this would serve as a warning to all women. The next time I looked into the mirror that's what I saw. You better be wary of the female species, young man—you never know when you'll meet a witch."

The pair walked past the fish factory, and the doctor's house soon came into view.

"This looks like a nice home," said Bryngeir. "Reckon I might be able to crash here?"

Benny had his doubts. "I don't think so, not unless you're sick. The doctor lives here."

Bryngeir halted. "And what's his name? The doctor's?" he asked.

"The doctor's a woman. Her name is Jóhanna," Benny answered.

"Doctor Jóhanna? Not Jóhanna Thorvald, surely?"

"Yeah, exactly. Do you know everyone?"

"It's uncanny. My adversaries seem to be swelling around here," said Bryngeir pensively, seemingly oblivious to Benny's question. "No, we won't look for any accommodation here. On we go, my dear friend Benny Ben."

Bryngeir walked away from the doctor's house with long strides, while Benny traipsed behind him with the case.

"Hey," said Bryngeir. "Didn't he stay with the priest, the late Gaston Lund?"

"Yeah."

"Shouldn't I try to stay there then?"

Benny looked at the case he was holding. "That could be a problem. They're both teetotalers and they can't stand boozing."

"Good point, pal. Let's avoid any hassles. So what does that leave us with then, young man? Isn't there anyone around here who's partial to a drop of rum, is hospitable, has a free bed, and knows something about the old *Flatey Book*?"

Benny broke into a smile. "Yeah. Sigurbjörn in Svalbardi."

Question seven: What made it possible to ride around the coastline? First letter. That winter there was so much ice in Iceland than the sea froze all around the coastline so that it was possible to ride between the promontories of every fjord. The answer is "ice," and the first letter is i.

CHAPTER 24

A creaking sound penetrated the doctor's house from the road as the handcarts were dragged past the building on their way down to the village. Jóhanna peeped out the kitchen window and watched them moving away and eventually disappearing down the slope behind the graveyard. The mail would therefore soon be reaching the telephone exchange, and she would be able to collect her newspapers. It was best to wait a bit, though. Stína, the post-mistress, was pretty quick at sorting out the mail, but some of the islanders were bound to show up early to collect their mail and just have a chat. Jóhanna, on the other hand, was in no mood for socializing that afternoon. She heard more footsteps passing the house, and then silence descended on the neighborhood again. The redshank that nested on the edge of the road grew calmer and stopped twittering in alarm. Strange that it should have chosen to build itself a nest in such an inconvenient place when there was no shortage of undisturbed nesting ground nearby. And it had laid its eggs in the same place the spring before.

Half an hour later, Jóhanna looked up from the book that she was leafing through when she heard a faint moan from the next room. She stood up and walked in to her father.

"Are you in pain, Dad?" she asked.

"Not too much, but it would be good to get the afternoon dose now," her father answered. He lay under a white quilt in a high medical bed, looking shriveled and emaciated.

She glanced at her watch and fetched the dose from the pharmacy, which was a little room off the infirmary. He flinched slightly as she injected the dose into the intravenous drip connected to his arm, but he swiftly felt the effect of the opiate and closed his eyes again.

"Would you like me to read for you for a while?" she asked.

"No, I'm going to rest a bit."

"The mail boat has arrived. I'll go get the papers soon. We can read them when I come back. I won't be long."

He braved a smile and said, "I somehow feel I've read enough. I think I'll soon be meeting my namesake, the late Snorri Sturluson and the mysterious author of Njál's saga."

He closed his eyes and dozed off. She adjusted his quilt and gently kissed him on the cheek.

Question eight: Greatest skiing champion. First letter. They ended up on a big mountain. It was a steep, narrow slope, which ended abruptly in a precipice dropping to the sea. King Harald Sigurdsson said to Hemingur, "Entertain us now with your skiing."

Hemingur answered, "This isn't a good place for skiing because there is little snow now and it's stony and there is hard ice on the mountain."

The king answered that he would not really be putting his skills to the test if conditions were perfect. So Hemingur put on his skis and zigzagged down the slope. Everyone agreed that they had never seen anyone ski so well. He skied down the slope at such speed that it was a wonder he did not fall. The answer is "Hemingur," and the first letter is h.

CHAPTER 25

Bryngeir and Benny continued on their walk down the road toward the village. Benny was curious and asked the visitor what had brought him to Flatey, but Bryngeir was slow to answer and seemed to be more interested in taking in the surroundings. "Benny Ben, my friend," he finally replied, "the Reykjavik gutter press isn't in the habit of sending its best hacks out on long trips just because a heap of bones has been found on a deserted island. But as soon as it transpired that they were the bones of that Danish manuscript speculator who'd spent the winter in the remoteness of the fjord and forgotten to ask someone to pick him up, people started to sniff a story. And when I heard that the deceased was Gaston Lund and that this whole mystery was somehow connected to my old pet love, the *Flatey Book*, I immediately asked to be sent out here to solve the crime."

"What did you think was so significant about the *Flatey Book*?" Benny asked.

Bryngeir looked at his companion. "Have you read the book, young man?"

"No, it's too long. I started once, but I found it boring. And some of the words are written in a weird way."

Bryngeir shook his head. "Then I can't explain the magic of the *Flatey Book* to you, boy. No more than I could describe a Rembrandt painting to a blind old bag or a great Wagner opera to a deaf loan shark or a sexy young whore from Morocco to a eunuch. But I don't see why that jewel should be named after this pathetic dump of an island just because it was kept here under some lousy mattress for a few decades. It would have been more appropriate to call it the *Húnvetninga Book, Tunga Book*, or *Vídidalur Book* in honor of the men in Vídidalstunga who actually put the manuscript together and wrote it. They were geniuses, my boy, absolute geniuses. Let's drink to them, Mister Benny Ben!" Bryngeir took a swig from the bottle of rum.

Benny had no interest in the subject. "I don't give a damn about what they call the book. Maybe I'll just read it later sometime," he said, staring at the bottle with thirsty eyes.

They paused on the ridge overlooking the village, and Bryngeir scanned the houses below. He asked Benny about the crofts and the people who lived in them. Benny answered with some reluctance, since he found it a pretty unexciting topic for discussion.

Bryngeir was particularly interested in the district administrative officer.

"He's an OK guy, good at hunting seal and puffin but lazy when it comes to making hay," said Benny. "Högni, the teacher, normally cuts his share, and Grímur rakes. And then he reads the papers and argues about politics."

"Do you reckon he could have taken that dead man out to the island?" Bryngeir asked.

"No, definitely not, even though he has the best boat. The engine is brand-new. He normally doesn't take the boat out of the water in the autumn, unless the sailing route is completely frozen. But do you really think that someone from here would have deliberately left that Danish guy on the island?"

"In my experience as a reporter, everyone is guilty until proven innocent, lad. I've got to dig up some story because the only expenses my editor gave me on this trip were a bus ticket and a stingy traveling allowance that ran out at the beginning of the journey for some reason."

Bryngeir took another swig from the bottle and finally offered Benny some as well.

"Do you reckon I can get something decent to eat from any of these fine hosts?" he asked.

Benny seemed to think that was quite likely. They walked on down the pass and across the village to the house in Svalbardi.

The croft was a stately wooden house with a concrete basement, one story, and a loft. Close by were a storehouse, sheepcote, and barn. Sigurbjörn, the farmer, sat at a grindstone outside the barn, which he spun with a pedal, sharpening a big knife.

"I see you know how to make some sharp weapons around here," Bryngeir said to the farmer.

"This is just the missus's kitchen knife, but good to have close at hand if the farm needs protecting," Sigurbjörn said ironically.

"I come in peace," Bryngeir grinned. "I hear that the locals here will never turn away a traveler who needs a roof for the night."

Sigurbjörn put down his knife and eyed the man a moment. "A bed can normally be found for a decent guest," he said. Bryngeir took out his bottle of rum, took a sip, and then handed it to the farmer.

"And maybe even some food then if the guest makes a contribution?" he asked. Sigurbjörn took the bottle, sniffed its contents, and then downed it in a single gulp.

"Was that the sum total of the contribution?" he asked, handing the emptied bottle back to him. Bryngeir signaled Benny to approach with the case. "Here's a little extra." He took a full bottle out of the case and unscrewed the lid. Sigurbjörn stood up from the grindstone. "Let's go inside and look into the larder, lads."

Question nine: Small heart. First letter. Thorgeir Hávarsson went to Hvassafell and there were some men standing outside. The shepherd had come home from his sheep and stood there in the field, leaning forward on his staff. He was slightly hunched and had a long neck. When Thorgeir saw this, he drew his axe and let it fall on the man's neck. The axe cut very nicely, and the head came flying off, landing a short distance away. Thorgeir later said, "He never did anything wrong against me, but to be honest, he was so well positioned for the blow that I couldn't resist the temptation." When Thorgeir died some people say that they cut into his heart because they wanted to see what the heart of such an audacious man was like. People say that his heart was rather small; and some people believe that it is true that the heart of a courageous man is smaller than that of a coward. The answer is "Thorgeir," and the first letter is t.

CHAPTER 26

Author Árni Sakarías was not listed in the phonebook, so the only way Dagbjartur could meet the man was by going to his house and seeing if he was home. He lived in a small block of apartments, and the main entrance was unlocked. Dagbjartur found his place on the second floor, but the doorbell was broken. As he was knocking on the writer's door for the fourth time, a neighbor stuck his head out in the corridor and asked the policeman to cut out the racket. He said the author had gone up to the municipal pool for a swim, as he always did at this time of the day.

Dagbjartur found Árni Sakarías in the shallow pool where he was lethargically floating on his back with an inflated black cushion under his head, in the middle of a bunch of kids who were playing in the water. The policeman knew the author by sight; Árni Sakarías was a recognizable figure around the town, tall and chubby, with a shock of hair and a bushy beard.

It took Dagbjartur a few moments to attract the swimmer's attention. Once he had, he introduced himself and asked, "Are you familiar with some old riddle that's supposed to be connected to the *Book of Flatey*?"

The shortsighted Árni Sakarías peered at him through the thick and wet lenses of his glasses.

"The Flatey enigma, Aenigma Flateyensis. Yes, young man. I know the story quite well."

Dagbjartur wasn't used to being addressed like this anymore, not now that he was well into his forties, even though he looked older, but Árni Sakarías presumably didn't see too well, even with his glasses. But as it happened, Dagbjartur could still consider himself to be young when he compared himself to this author, who was well into his seventies.

"Mind if I ask you a few questions on the subject?"

The author took one stroke and allowed himself to float on his back again before answering. "Yes, you could certainly do that, but let me get out of the pool first, dry myself, and get dressed. I'm presuming the police will be happy to offer me a cup of coffee at the Austurbaer diner in gratitude for the information I'll be providing? Might help to trigger off my memory, you see. Useful thing at my age, young man."

Dagbjartur nodded, and half an hour later there were sitting at a table in the café on Laugavegur. They were the only customers, and Árni Sakarías asked the waitress to bring him the usual. She knew what that was and brought him a pot of coffee, a bread roll, and a Danish pastry. Dagbjartur asked for the same and the bill, which he paid.

As Árni Sakarías relished his pastry, he told Dagbjartur about the Flatey enigma.

"In the late summer of 1871, a group of Icelandic students were on a ship to Copenhagen where they were going to study over the winter. This was on the steamboat *Diana*, which operated as a mail boat to Iceland during those years. An excellent seafaring vessel, I've read, with first- and second-class cabins.

This was a few years after the *Flatey Book* had come out in print for the first time at the expense of the Norwegian state. Gudbrandur Vigfússon and Unger took care of the publishing, although the book was printed in Oslo, and the last volume was dated 1868. This edition became popular reading material among students in Copenhagen, and there was a copy in the possession of an Icelandic scholar who was a passenger on the mail boat. The students did a lot of things to entertain themselves on the *Diana* during the crossing, including quizzing each other about the stories contained in the *Flatey Book*. There's a whole gallery of characters that crop up in these stories, of course, and the students varied in their knowledge of them. This was their favorite pastime, though, and they decided to hold a formal quiz the following evening. A young man from the West Fjords, a budding poet and writer who also happened to be on board, was enlisted to set the quiz because he was known for his sound knowledge of ancient literature. He pored over the Oslo edition and by the following evening had completed his task. He hadn't slept a wink all night and kept himself awake with a bottle of schnapps. He produced a list of forty questions, the last of which depended on you getting the previous thirty-nine questions right. The solution was linked to an incomplete poem, and the right answer was supposed to complete the poem. One letter contained in the answers to each question formed the solution, and the last question revealed how the letters were supposed to be arranged to form it. The writer then proposed that if a solution could not be found to the riddle on this journey, the riddle had to be kept in the *Flatey Book* and could not be removed from it until the solution had been found. A peculiar picture was drawn on the first page, and the legend that developed around it was that it was a magical rune that protected the writer's instructions. The people of the West

Fjords have a reputation for knowing a thing or two about magic. The students brooded over the enigma that evening and tried to piece a solution together. The questions were considered rather odd, and many of them were open to a variety of possible answers that seemed to be based more on taste than logic. But although some of the boys managed to solve some of the questions and to produce thirty-nine letters, none could solve the key to the last question that was meant to complete the poem."

Once more Árni Sakarías became silent and for a moment stared out the window at the pedestrians on Laugavegur. Dagbjartur waited in a patient silence.

Finally, he resumed his narrative: "A tragic incident then occurred on the boat that night: the writer who had devised the enigma vanished from the ship without anyone noticing. Naturally, there was a great deal of commotion on board, and all interest in the riddle faded. There was one student, however, who held onto the papers and wrote about how the riddle was created, and then thought of taking it home to Flatey, as the poet had said. But that got delayed for some reason. The student died in Copenhagen that winter, and the sheets somehow found their way to the Royal Library. There they were placed in an archive with other material about the *Flatey Book* and were lost for many decades. The story of the Flatey enigma was well known, though, and was recounted in Copenhagen's student circles from one generation to the next. In the winter of 1935, a keen Icelandic scholar was looking through some material at the Royal Library when he stumbled on the sheets. The Icelander was pushy and insisted that the author's wishes be respected and the sheets sent to the Flatey library. It took several months to discuss this issue which, to be honest, was made in jest. Now it just so happened that they heard the Flatey library was celebrating its hundredth anniversary in 1936 and that the Munksgaard publishers were going to donate a facsimile copy of the *Flatey Book*, which had been published in 1930. The librarians at the Royal Library saw this as an opportunity to free themselves of the unwelcome document they considered the Flatey enigma to be, and were allowed to stick the sheets into the Munksgaard edition that was on its way to Flatey. The Icelandic scholar was then entrusted with the task of ensuring that this was all done. That smart aleck happened to be me, so I am considered to know more about this enigma than most. I can also be blamed or thanked for the fact that the sheets are now on the island. Someone at some stage wrote *Aenigma Flateyensis* on the sheet of riddles, which, of course, is Latin for the Flatey enigma. That was to harmonize it with the Latin title of the Munksgaard edition of the *Flatey Book*, which is *Codex Flateyensis*. The same person also had a stab at writing the last two lines of the poem, but no one has been able to verify it. So that's the story of the enigma."

Árni Sakarías shoved the last piece of Danish pastry into his mouth and poured himself some more coffee.

"So the enigma hasn't been solved yet?" Dagbjartur asked.

"Not that I've heard."

"Wouldn't it be possible to solve it without going to Flatey?"

"No, impossible. The key is there and nowhere else. The questions can be found in many places, but the key, which is the rows of letters, is only to be found on the sheet that lies in the Munksgaard edition in the Flatey library. That's where people have to go if they want to test their solutions."

"Why hasn't anyone just copied it?"

"It's a matter of simple decency. The librarians in the Flatey library have taken good care of the sheets, and those who want to test their answers have to swear they won't write the key down.

There's also a belief that anyone who breaks the rules will be cursed by a mishap. The fates of the poet and the young student in Copenhagen helped to propagate that myth. It is said that a powerful curse rests on the key to the enigma but that it won't be unleashed so long as the sheets remain within the four walls of the library."

"Have many people tried this?"

"No, I don't think so. Students who are completing their studies in Icelandic philology have been known to go on pilgrimages to Flatey to have a go at it. You have to be pretty well up on the subject to be able to hazard any guesses at the answers. This isn't a challenge for amateurs."

"Haven't you tried to solve the enigma yourself?"

"I just tried it once. The enigma is basically two riddles. I realized that you've got to solve the key to the fortieth question first. Without that, there's no way of verifying the answers to the other thirty-nine questions. I studied that for a while but found no solution."

"What happens if someone solves the enigma?"

"What happens? Well, nothing really. The winner savors the moment and gets to enjoy some recognition, as well as the admiration and envy of other scholars. I hope it doesn't happen anytime soon because many people secretly enjoy the failures of these whippersnappers in trying to find the key. Perhaps the enigma is unsolvable. Who knows?"

Question ten: The ice was slippery with...Third letter. The Birkibeins drove the fleet along the ice and killed many because most of them wore studded shoes, whereas the fugitives were on bare soles, and the ice was slippery with blood. The king rode close to them, and his task was to give one spear thrust to every man he attacked, and the Birkibeins then did whatever was necessary to finish them off and kill them. The answer is "blood," and the third letter is o.

CHAPTER 27

It was late in the day, and the mail boat from Brjánslækur was soon expected to reappear on its way back to Stykkishólmur. Thormódur Krákur arrived towing his handcart up to the doors of the church, where the three men—Grímur, Kjartan, and Högni—were waiting. The moment had come to transport the body down to the pier. Reverend Hannes arrived a short moment later, dressed in his robes. This time he was going to accompany his guest all the way to the ship. Grímur and Högni collected the casket in the church and placed it on the cart. There was also a sealed mail bag on the cart that looked virtually empty. Stína, the postmistress, wanted to take advantage of the trip down to the pier to get the mail onto the ship.

They set off. As had happened the last time the body was transported across the island, the village suddenly seemed deserted again. The inhabitants had all vanished. Kjartan wondered how it was possible for them all to be so synchronized. It was as if an invisible hand had swept over the village, ushering all the locals into their houses at the same time.

But there were two men standing on the embankment by the pass, and they were observing the procession. Kjartan recognized one of them, Benny from Rádagerdi, although he couldn't make out who the second person was because of the considerable distance.

"Who's that walking with the boy?" Kjartan nudged Grímur, throwing his head back.

Grímur looked back. "That's some reporter from Reykjavik. He was well oiled when he arrived on the boat today, and he hasn't sobered up. He seems to have found a drinking buddy."

"Do you think he's going to write something about Professor Lund in the papers?" Kjartan asked.

"He'll probably have to sleep it off first. I think Sigurbjörn in Svalbardi is going to be putting him up during his stay here."

The mail boat could be seen approaching from the north of the island, and the pallbearers quickened their pace. There was no point in keeping the boat waiting.

The Ystakot clan—Valdi, old Jón Ferdinand, and little Nonni—were alone on the pier when Thormódur Krákur drew the cart around the corner of the fish factory. The boat was pulling in, and now only one hawser came over the gunwale. The islanders had swift hands. The mail bag was thrown on board, and Reverend Hannes read some text while the other four men lifted the casket off the cart and started lowering it onto the boat. Two crew members then took it, while the heavy-browed skipper observed the proceedings through the bridge window with a pipe in his mouth.

"Who's paying for the freight then?" one of the sailors, who had grabbed the casket, called out.

All eyes were on Kjartan. "The district magistrate in Patreksfjördur will pay the bill," he answered after a moment's hesitation.

Then the boat slipped away from the pier, and Valdi loosened the moorings.

"May the grace and peace of our Lord Jesus Christ be with you," Reverend Hannes intoned, winding up his speech and blessing the mail boat with the sign of the cross.

It was as if a weight had lifted from the men's shoulders as they watched the boat sail south.

Benny and his drinking buddy had observed it all from the corner of the fish factory, but he swiftly turned around and vanished when the funeral cortege returned with an empty cart.

Grímur, the district officer, was in a more cheerful mood and suddenly talkative. Life on the island could get back to normal now. The reasons why Gaston Lund had ended up on Ketilsey were still shrouded in mystery, but that was still a triviality compared to the ordeal of having the corpse of a stranger lying in the church. "Right, lads," he said, wrapping his arms around Högni and Kjartan, "we're going to take the evening off now and play whist with my wife, and tomorrow we'll go to Reverend Hannes's Whitsunday mass."

He looked at Kjartan. "I hope you play whist?" he asked.

"Yeah, I suppose I do," Kjartan answered, smiling for the first time in many days.

A long telegram from the detective force in Reykjavik awaited the district officer when he got back to his house. It provided a detailed rundown of the day's investigation and contained nothing new, apart from the fact that Gaston Lund probably had a love child in Iceland in 1927, which he had been unwilling to acknowledge. The child's mother probably bore a grudge against him. Nothing else was known about this family, but the investigation was set to continue. The district officer was asked to look into it.

Question eleven: The severed head that killed a man. Second letter. A meeting was set up between a Scottish earl, Melbrigd Buck-tooth, and Earl Sigurdur to reach a settlement between them. Each earl was to be attended by a retinue of forty men, but Sigurdur got two men to mount each of the forty horses. When Earl Melbrigd saw this, he said to his men, "Earl Sigurdur has dealt us a treacherous hand, for I see two feet on each horse's side." A fierce battle ensued, and Earl Melbrigd and all his men were slain. Earl Sigurdur and his men fastened the heads of the dead to their saddle straps as they rode home rejoicing in their triumph. On the homeward ride, Sigurdur was spurring his horse when he hit his leg against a tooth protruding from the fallen Melbrigd's head, which made a slight incision that soon became swollen and painful, eventually resulting in his death. The answer is "Melbrigd," and the second letter is e.

CHAPTER 28

Bryngeir and Benny had watched the casket being lowered onto the mail boat. Bryngeir didn't want to draw any closer, but he got Benny to identify the men on the pier for him.

"The district officer, the teacher, the deacon, and the priest," said Benny. "The youngest guy is the magistrate's assistant," he added.

"Who owns these boats?" Bryngeir asked, pointing at the small boats moored at the pier.

"Some fishermen from other villages who were going to fish for the factory. But they haven't been able to catch anything, so they're moving to another village closer to better fishing grounds. Valdi from Ystakot owns the black one. He was the guy who found the dead man in Ketilsey," Benny answered.

"What boats were here last fall when the Dane came here?"

"Here by the pier, you mean?"

"Yeah."

"There were no fishing boats here last fall."

"Were there no boats at all then?"

"Maybe Valdi's boat, at the most. He stores it away in the heart of winter. I can't remember when he did that last year."

"Aren't there more boats on the island?"

"Yeah, but they're all stored in the cove in the fall. It's easier to keep an eye on them from the village that way, if the weather worsens."

The mail boat was now backing out of the pier, and the funeral cortege was dispersing. Bryngeir dragged Benny around the corner, and they rushed back to the eastern side of the fish factory. There were a few wooden barrels, which they hid behind as the others walked by. Benny was puzzled by this odd behavior but got a bit of a kick from hanging out with such a worldly-wise guy and actually found this touch of spying pretty exciting.

From their hiding place, they watched the five men walking on up the road past the doctor's house. Thormódur Krákur walked in front, towing the handcart, followed by the priest and finally Grímur, Kjartan, and Högni.

"What would you do if you needed to get to Stykkishólmur but couldn't wait for the mail boat?" Bryngeir asked Benny.

"I'd ask Dad to lend me his boat," Benny answered, omitting to say there was no way he would be lent the boat to take it to Stykkishólmur. It was too long a crossing, and he didn't know the sailing route on the southern side of the fjord.

"What about outsiders? How would they get to the mainland? What would I do if I needed to get to the mainland this evening?"

Benny thought a moment. He found it difficult to imagine why anyone would be in such a hurry.

"Well, of course, you could always get Dad to take you over to Brjánslækur. Or Sigurbjörn in Svalbardi, or maybe Ásmundur, the storekeeper. From there you can walk up to the road where the Ísafjördur bus passes. You can also sail to the mainland in Vatnsfjördur if the tide is high. That's a shorter walk."

Bryngeir grew impatient. “But south to Stykkishólmur, lad?”

“Yeah, maybe you could get someone to take you there if the weather isn’t too bad. It’s just a bit far to go on an open boat in the dark.”

Bryngeir walked past the fish factory and onto the deserted pier. He stared at the boats that were moored there.

“But the guy who owns the black boat?” he asked. “Could he take me to Stykkishólmur?”

“No, not very likely,” said Benny. “Valdi never has money to buy enough fuel. He also gets to travel free on the mail boat because he always grabs the rope when they’re pulling into the pier.”

“Let’s pay him a visit in his croft. Show me the way.”

Benny walked ahead of him off the pier and up the path toward Ystakot. They spotted little Nonni on the shore, and he spotted them.

“Dad, Dad,” Nonni yelled back toward Ystakot. “Two big men are coming, Benny from Rádagerdi and the boozer.”

Valdi had stepped out into the yard by the time Bryngeir and Benny arrived. Bryngeir eyed Valdi in silence. Benny kept his distance.

“What do you want?” Valdi finally asked.

“Can you take me to Stykkishólmur this evening?” Bryngeir asked.

“Why didn’t you take the mail boat?” Valdi asked.

“I was too late and missed it.”

Jón Ferdinand stepped into the yard as Valdi was thinking.

“I can’t see anything, I can’t see anything!” the old man shrieked.

“Open your eyes and then you’ll see, you fool!” said Valdi.

“Yeah, now I see the light, Valdi dear. You’re so good to me,” said Jón Ferdinand joyfully.

"You're so full of crap, Dad. You're a disgrace to us," Valdi snapped angrily, and turned to Bryngeir. "You can get a farmer from one of the inner isles to take you over to the mainland after mass tomorrow. They're all bound to come over for Whitsunday," he said.

"But I need to get to Stykkishólmur tonight. How much do I have to pay you?"

Valdi shook his head. "I can't leave the house. I've got to take care of my boy and my dad. He's completely lost it."

"What if I pay you three thousand krónur?"

"Three thousand krónur?"

"Yeah."

"That's a lot of money." Valdi calculated in his head. "That's almost five finished seal pup furs."

"Yes, that's quite a sum, but I'm in a hurry." Bryngeir pulled a wallet out of the pocket of his trousers.

Valdi stuffed his pipe and lit it. "Then I'll have to take my dad with us," he finally said, "and I've also got to buy fuel first. You've got to pay up front."

Bryngeir turned to Benny with a grin. "You see, it's just a question of the right price." Then, addressing Valdi, he said, "Hey listen, I think Stykkishólmur can wait."

Valdi winced. "Were you just bluffing with me?"

Bryngeir laughed. "I was just trying to establish the price of a ticket, my friend."

"Get the hell out of here," Valdi barked in a rage and stepped menacingly toward Bryngeir, who grinningly backed off but then tripped on a tussock and fell on his ass.

Benny stepped between them. "I'll take him with me," he said to Valdi, "and make sure he doesn't come back again." He then helped Bryngeir to his feet and led him away. When they had walked a few yards away from the croft, Benny said, "You better not make Valdi angry. He gets totally out of control. Once in the olden days he almost strangled a stranger in a fight. The man only saved himself by sticking a finger in Valdi's eye. That's why he's blind in one eye."

Bryngeir didn't seem to be too happy about his awkward retreat. "Then he can lose his other eye if he has to," he said, vexed.

Question twelve: Who cut King Sverrir's ear? Third letter. A man lay seriously wounded close by. His name was Brynjólfur, the son of Kalf of the Faroes. He hoisted himself to his knees and struck the king with his sword, aiming at his neck. The king deflected the blow with the rim of his steel helmet, which the edge of the sword struck, but his ear was grazed, and his neck was seriously wounded. In the same instant, swords and halberds fell so heavily on Brynjólfur that he could barely sink to the ground. The answer is "Brynjólfur," and the third letter is y.

CHAPTER 29

After dinner and the radio news, Grímur fetched a deck of cards and dealt them on the dining table where Högni and Kjartan were seated with cups of coffee. He then called Ingibjörg, who was clearing up in the kitchen, and the game of whist began. Kjartan enjoyed watching the islanders, who mostly played in silence, apart from their bidding and moderate exclamations according to how the game was going. There were all kinds of facial expressions and glances. Grímur was a zealous player and a poor loser. Ingibjörg, on the other hand, was cunning and knew how to handle her husband.

"Do people play a lot in Flatey?" Kjartan asked.

"Not in the summer," said Grímur, peering at his cards. "But a lot in the winter. Passes the time."

When there was a break in the game, Kjartan told them about the discovery he had made in the library earlier that day. Professor Lund had cheated in his struggle with the Flatey enigma and had written the clue down on a piece of paper and took it out of the building. And then Kjartan remembered the library key, which he still had in his pocket.

"I'll pass it on to Hallbjörg," said Ingibjörg. "I'll be going to Innstibaer later on to give the ladies some cookies to have with their coffee on Whitsunday."

"Do they live alone?" Kjartan asked.

"Neither of them ever married," Grímur answered, "but Gudrún has a son out of wedlock. The boy is a sailor now in Akranes and occasionally comes over on visits. Gudrún is slightly mentally unstable and not always the full shilling. Hallbjörg took her in out of kinship and takes good care of her. And the islanders are fond of those good-hearted women and slip them little treats every now and then. They knit nonstop, and that helps them to get by. Hallbjörg also takes good care of our library and gets a fee from the municipal fund for that. I think it was the price of two lambs this year. On top of that they've got Hallbjörg's pension. Gudrún and Sigurbjörn in Svalbardi are closely related. He also keeps a good eye on them."

After two hours of playing, Grímur and Kjartan walked across the island to fetch the cows. Temperatures would drop during the night, and it was therefore best to bring them into the cowshed. But that wouldn't be for long now. The nights were bright and the summer would soon be here to stay. Then the milking could be done in the pastures and the cows would be kept outside.

On their way to the pastures, Grímur lectured Kjartan on cattle breeding in Flatey, both now and in the future. The problem today was the shortage of good breeding bulls. No bullocks had been bred on Flatey for quite some years now, and bulls had to be brought in from the inner isles. Transporting them in little boats could be a tricky business, although they generally managed to do it without any mishaps. The bull just needed a bit of time to recover after the sea journey before he could be of any service to the cows.

"The farmers are thinking of pooling together to buy some good bullocks on the mainland this summer. No harm in improving the stock a bit," said Grímur.

The cows expected to be rounded up and waited mooing by the gate to the pastures. Thormódur Krákur had already collected his two, although Gudjón of Rádagerdi's cows were still grazing.

"We'll take them all with us," said Grímur. "We take it in turns to collect them, my brother-in-law Gudjón and I."

On the way home, they crossed the Ystakot clan on the road. Valdi was pushing an old wheelbarrow, and as they drew closer, they saw that it contained a dead sheep. Its angular head dangled over the rim of the wheelbarrow, and its gray wool was completely drenched and smudged in sand and seaweed. Valdi gave way to the cows that filed down the road and then put the wheelbarrow down when the men met.

"Grímur," said Valdi, taking out his pipe.

"Yes, Valdi?" said Grímur, pausing.

"Listen to me. I remember now why I didn't write it into my book when the mail boat sailed south on September the fourth last year. And you should have remembered why, too."

"Oh?"

"Yeah, because on that day I took the mail boat myself over to Brjánslækur to meet my wife, Thóra. So I wasn't on the island when the boat sailed back south that day. I asked Dad to keep an eye on who was traveling on the boat, but of course he forgot to and didn't write anything down."

"Oh," said Grímur. "And why should I have remembered that you went to the mainland?"

Valdi lit his pipe with a match and answered: "When I came back a week later, all of the fuel had been stolen from my boat. I reported it, don't you remember?"

"Yes." Grímur looked apologetically at Kjartan. "I remember that now. I never found the thief."

Valdi stuck his notebook back into his pocket, picked up the wheelbarrow, and with his smoldering pipe clenched between his teeth, walked off without saying good-bye. Little Nonni and Jón Ferdinand walked after him.

"Oh, we're always in such a rush," they heard the old man muttering.

"Those were memorable days," Grímur said, once the family was out of earshot. "Valdi went over to the mainland to collect his wife, Thóra, from her roadworks job, but she categorically refused to come home with him. She can't take them anymore. She could just about put up with it when the old lady, Valdi's mother, was still alive. She was a wonderful person and good to everyone, but after she died the men turned into semi-ogres. You can't expect a young woman to live with that. Valdi, of course, was completely crushed when he came back with no woman, and he felt ashamed in front of everyone. He hit the bottle in the end and was drunk for days. To be honest, I didn't take that fuel theft story very seriously, but it's obviously still bugging him."

"What are they doing with the carcass of that sheep?" Kjartan asked.

"Sigurbjörn of Svalbardi lost that sheep and two lambs on a skerry in the high tide on Monday," Grímur answered. "The sheep was washed ashore in Sund this morning. That's one of the disadvantages of farming on an island; so many ewes get lost in the sea. In one high tide many years ago, a hundred sheep were lost in Eyjahreppur. That was a lot of damage for small farms to have sustain."

"But what will they do with it?" Kjartan asked again, glancing toward the men over his shoulder.

"They're allowed to keep the carcass. They're going to make some sea stew with it," Grímur answered.

Kjartan wasn't sure he had heard right. "Sea stew?"

"Yeah. They boil the meat and the fat. It'll be well salted and tender after marinating in the sea and can taste quite good. There aren't many people around who'll do this kind of thing, but it makes a big difference to the Ystakot men."

Question thirteen: Drank from the keel. First letter. Egill, Ragnar's son, fought against the Wends on ships. At the end of the battle, Egill jumped onto the Wends' ship and axed the chieftain, dealing him a deadly blow. After that the Wends fled. Egill asked his servant to fetch him a drink. The servant answered, "There has been so much commotion on the ship today. The barrels are all broken and the drink has flowed down to the keel."

Egill said, "But I must have a drink."

The servant answered, "Please don't, sire. Most of it is blood and bodily fluids."

Egill stood up and removed the helmet from his head and dipped it into the keel and had three large drinks. After this Egill came to be known as Blood Egill. The answer is "Blood Egill," and the first letter is b.

He said, "Here the guest just wrote 'Egill,' *and the first letter is* e."

CHAPTER 30

The couple in Rádagerdi sat playing chess in the kitchen when they heard Benny coming in late at night. It was warm and cozy by the stove, and the scent of coffee wafted in the air.

"Is there anything to eat?" he asked.

"There are boiled puffin breasts in the larder," his mother Hildur answered.

"Were you hanging out with that guy from Reykjavik?" Gudjón, the farmer, asked when Benny reappeared with the puffin breast, which he had sliced and was feeding to himself with a penknife.

"Yeah, I'd had enough. He wouldn't share any of his rum. He drank it all himself."

"You're too young to be boozing with a grown-up man, Benny dear," said his mother.

"I'm not too young just to have a taste. There's never any fun around here," Benny said before disappearing from the kitchen. They heard him going up to the loft and turning on his transistor radio.

"I think that boy's going to move away from us if we continue living here," said Hildur. "He would have left ages ago if he didn't have that crush on little Hafdís in Svalbardi."

Gudjón nodded and moved the bishop two squares on the chessboard.

They were silent a moment as they focused on the game. Finally Gudjón said, "Högni, the teacher, mentioned that he's interested in buying the house if we move. He's tired of living in the school."

Hildur answered him, after giving it some thought: "If we sell the house, we could settle our debt with the co-op and maybe cover our trip to Stykkishólmur, but not a lot more than that. Check!"

"Check? Hmm, we'd also get something for our land. Sigurbjörn could do with more grassland. He has some money in the savings bank to pay for that. If we could rent land on the mainland, we could take the cattle and sheep with us. Otherwise, we could slaughter the livestock to pay off the co-op debt."

Gudjón hid his king behind his rook.

"But what if we don't get any land?" said Hildur.

Gudjón smiled reassuringly. "You're pretty good at filleting fish, and I can do some manual labor. And I can always take the boat out to sea and fish if I can fix the engine."

"It won't be easy to go away and leave all our friends behind," said Hildur, moving her knight.

"We can come here in the spring and work for the other farmers. But we can't hang around here in the winter without a bigger farm."

"Do you really think Högni can buy the house?"

"Yes, yes. He can also take out a loan," said Gudjón, moving his bishop.

“We can think about it over the summer and decide in the fall,” said the housewife, and then she concentrated on the game.

“Yes, but I think we should go for it,” said Gudjón. He found it difficult to focus on the chess and conduct a conversation at the same time. He looked at the board in confusion and finally played his knight.

Hildur promptly slid her rook down the board: “Checkmate!”

Question fourteen: They chose the spots to fall on. Seventh letter. The Baglar were being besieged by King Sverrir at the rock of Túnsberg. The Baglar saw banners from two armies. One came from Frod’s Ridge, the other from the town. They fought when they met; some fell and others fled. The Baglar then urged Hreidar to abandon the rock and assist their men. Hreidar answered, “Let’s see what they do first and if the Birkibeins are chased to the trench.” And then he added, “There is something odd about the way they are fleeing. It seems to me that they’re playing a trick on us. Do you notice how they choose dry spots to fall on or else fall on their shields? And do you see any sign of blood on their weapons or garments? No! Neither do I,” he said. “This must be one of Sverrir’s ruses.” The answer is “Birkibeins,” and the seventh letter is e.

CHAPTER 31

Sunday, June 5, 1960

The state radio made sure all Icelanders realized Whitsunday was on its way. Psalms bellowed out of Ingibjörg's radio, filling the district officer's home. The radio choir was singing Icelandic Whitsunday psalms.

It was still bright and slightly cloudy over Breidafjördur, and the wind had subsided and seemed to be turning. The farmers scrutinized the sky above and forecast good weather for the day and then rain in the evening. That wasn't such a bad thing, since the fields needed a sprinkle. The wells were also running low. But it would be good if the dry weather could hold up during the day while the church guests were walking about.

A festive atmosphere had spread across the village by the time Kjartan descended from the loft at around ten and peered outside. Grímur had put on his dark Sunday best, and he looked washed and shaven. His mop of hair was combed back, and he had brushed his bushy beard. Ingibjörg was wearing a pretty bodice and had sprayed herself with perfume. Pastries were served with the morning coffee.

The national flag had been hoisted on the high flagpole in front of the church and flapped gently in the warm breeze. Here and there people could be seen strolling about, but no one was working. Days of rest were sacred, especially Whitsundays.

Through the kitchen window, Grímur watched motorboats loaded with church guests from the inner isles approaching the strait between Hafnarey and Flatey.

"It used to be a more impressive sight back in the days when the island boats came to mass under lily-white sails. I think the good Lord probably preferred that," he said wistfully in between the names of the boats he was rattling off, as well as the names of those who were probably on board. Every now and then he lifted an old pair of binoculars to his eyes to confirm the identity of a person he had already guessed.

"Yes, yes, I knew it, that's the Skáley boat," he said smugly.

The travelers made the crossings in the boats in their everyday clothes, but carried church clothes with them in suitcases, as well as picnics in chests and flasks of coffee. People stepped ashore on Eyjólfur's pier and vanished into the houses of friends and relatives only to reappear in the village again a short time later, dressed in their festive clothes. Some knocked stealthily on Ásmundur the storekeeper's window, and he ushered them into the store through the back door on the eastern side of the building. The store was naturally closed on holy mass days, but he could always make an exception for people in dire need. The co-op, on the other hand, was firmly locked since it was next door to the vicarage and the priest himself was a member of the company's board.

Högni, the organist, rounded up all the choir members once all the boats had arrived and walked ahead of the group up to the church. They were supposed to rehearse before the mass.

At one thirty, the deacon, Thormódur Krákur, left his home in his Sunday best and crossed the village towing his cart with his wife, Gudrídur, sitting flat out on top of it. When they reached the vicarage, the priest and his wife appeared ready for the mass, and the four of them went to the church.

Ingibjörg was a member of the church choir and had vanished with the organist as soon as she had finished washing up after lunch. Grímur and Kjartan sat in the living room, drinking coffee in silence. Grímur was perusing through the weekly supply of newspapers that had arrived on the mail boat the day before, while Kjartan tackled a puzzle in a Danish weekly and thought of Gaston Lund. He was trying to form a picture of him from the few fragments of information they had gathered.

"Tell me something," he said to attract Grímur's attention. "Does anyone know who the father of Gudrún in Innstibaer's child was?"

Grímur was taken aback. "No. The boy was grown up and had gone off to sea by the time Gudrún moved here to live with Hallbjörg. I've never heard the father mentioned."

"Valdi in Ystakot wrote in his diary that Gudrún's son came on a boat the day before Gaston Lund went missing."

Grímur cleared his throat and shook his head. "You're taking this a bit too far now, pal," he said.

"And then there's that word—*lucky*," Kjartan said, growing more excited. "That's the word we think Lund tried to write with the pebbles in Ketilsey, and it also happens to be the name of Sigurbjörn of Svalbardi's boat. Isn't he related to Gudrún somehow?"

Grímur seemed apprehensive. "I hadn't really made that connection, but we should tread very carefully with this and not go blabbing about it to the Reykjavik police."

"Why not?" Kjartan asked.

"It's all so far-fetched, and it would go down very badly with the locals here if that kind of gossip were to get around. False accusations can do so much damage."

Kjartan suddenly shut up. The district officer's words hit him hard. He should have known.

A second round of church bells prompted the district officer to put down his papers and stand. Clearing his throat again, he said it was time to go. Kjartan followed him. The assumption had been that he would attend the mass like everyone else, and he saw no reason to fuel any controversy by declining to go, although he wasn't too keen on the idea. He hadn't been to any masses since his confirmation, apart from some funerals. Maybe this would give him a good opportunity to observe the islanders without being the center of attention.

He walked toward the church with Grímur in a slow and dignified stride, in unison with other groups that were heading the same way. People then huddled around the church entrance and greeted each other on both sides with handshakes and kisses.

Immaculately dressed children were playing on the slope below the church when the Ystakot clan came strolling over. They showed no signs of having dressed up for the occasion. Two boys broke out of the scrum and yelled out, "Nonni dung boy! Nonni dung boy!"

Their fun came to an abrupt end, though, because Högni, who had just stepped out of the church to catch a breath of fresh air after the choir practice and was standing a short distance away, angrily snapped at them and they fell into a shamed silence.

"What was that they called the boy?" Kjartan asked.

"Dung boy," Grímur answered.

"What do they mean?"

"Cow dung is an excellent fuel that used to be used as tinder for fires with dry bird skin. Nowadays most houses use paraffin oil, but not so long ago dung was the most common local tinder. They still use the old method in Ystakot, and little Nonni's job in the spring is to go around the sheds collecting cow dung to make tinder. He leaves it out in the fields in small cakes and allows it to dry. Everyone of my generation did the same as kids, and it was regarded as a perfectly respectable task. But now they've nicknamed him 'dung boy.' Hardly what you'd call progress."

The church bells rang again, and people squeezed through the narrow doors. Kjartan felt this was a completely different building to the one that he and Jóhanna had stepped into to examine the body in the casket just a few days ago. He hadn't taken the time to look around it back then. There were many candles glowing here now, and the altarpiece had come to life—a beautiful fresco of Jesus and two of his disciples painted in the same style as the picture cards he used to get at Sunday school when he was a kid. Grímur ushered him onto a pew where he sat beside Sigurbjörn the farmer. Gudjón had obviously finished cutting his hair after Kjartan had left them, but it was still a bit uneven over his cheeks. Kjartan involuntarily started to study the necks of the people sitting in front of him. A gallery of heads extended before him. Different stages of baldness and hairdos had been executed with varying degrees of success, and most of the women had plaits. Everyone was spic-and-span, and a strong scent of soap fused with the faintly stale air of the church. Sigurbjörn gave off a faint odor of alcohol and seemed to be half hungover.

The organ now sounded from the balcony, and the choir launched into the psalm. Kjartan listened and found the music strangely soothing. This might not have been the best choir in the land, but there was a pleasant harmony between the singing and the organ.

Reverend Hannes emerged from the sacristy and turned to the congregation. He coughed twice and said, "Dear parishioners, brothers and sisters, I would like to start this holy ceremony by giving you the sad news that Björn Snorri Thorvald, the father of our good doctor, Jóhanna, passed away in his sleep last night. As you all know, the old man had been very ill for some time, and now the good Lord has called him back to Himself and put an end to his suffering. His loving daughter was sitting by his side when the call came, and I went there this morning to commend his spirit to God. The removal will be on Tuesday and the funeral on Wednesday. Let us join our hands in prayer."

The congregation bowed their heads, and the priest led the prayer. Kjartan wondered whether the doctor was at the mass. The entire population of the islands seemed to have crammed into the church. He swiftly scanned the congregation but could see no sign of Jóhanna anywhere. At the very back of the church, however, he saw little Nonni of Ystakot standing up and sneaking out through the open church door. Yes, he probably would have done the same himself if he'd been given half a chance. It was swiftly getting hot and stuffy in there.

The organ erupted, and another psalm was sung.

Question fifteen: Cut in two by the prow of a ship. First letter. Sorli's Tale narrates how Hedin, the king's son, was slain by a spell. Blinded by magic, he allowed King Högni's queen, Hervor, to be taken and placed in front of the prow of his ship, so that she was cut in two when the ship was launched. Hedin and Högni then fought in a duel. It is said that there was so much evil attached to this curse that even when they had sliced each other in two from the shoulder down, they were able to stand up again and fight as before. A hundred and forty years were to pass before one of King Ólaf's courtiers broke this pitiful spell. The answer is "Hervor," and the first letter is h.

CHAPTER 32

Fridrik Einarsson didn't seem particularly pleased to be visited by Detective Dagbjartur on a Whitsunday afternoon for the second time in two days. Nevertheless, he invited him in and offered him a seat, but he anxiously glanced at his watch.

"My wife and I are off to a wedding. I don't want to be late," he said.

Dagbjartur tried to keep it brief: "We compared the list you made of Gaston Lund's Icelandic acquaintances and another list of the inhabitants of Flatey, which we got back from them yesterday. Björn Snorri Thorvald's name appears on both lists."

"Yes," Fridrik answered. "I could have told you that straightaway yesterday. I knew that Björn Snorri and his daughter Jóhanna were there on the island, but I couldn't see how that was relevant. I heard on the radio at lunchtime that Björn Snorri just passed away. My old colleagues seem to be fading."

"Did Björn Snorri and Gaston Lund get along?"

Fridrik looked at Dagbjartur in bewilderment. "How do you mean?"

"You said that the professor sometimes got into arguments about manuscripts with his Icelandic acquaintances."

Fridrik smiled. "Björn Snorri didn't argue about the manuscripts. He was one of the few Icelanders who was virtually indifferent to where the manuscripts should be preserved. He just wanted to know they were in a good place and that there was easy access to them..."

Fridrik suddenly shut up and frowned. "Easy access to them," he repeated hesitantly, lost in some thought.

Dagbjartur sensed there was more to this and calmly waited for Fridrik to continue. "But that was the problem. Björn Snorri lost his job in Copenhagen at the end of the war and was barred from accessing the manuscripts after that. I remember very well how unhappy he was with his Danish colleagues, including Lund. He'd been thrown out of the house with unnecessary force. But those were special times at the end of the war, and a lot of errors were made as a result of pent-up anger. My family and I took the father and daughter in some days after he was fired, and they came home with us to Iceland a few weeks later. Jóhanna and Einar, my youngest son, were half engaged in high school until Einar died in a sudden accident."

Fridrik's voice faltered a moment before continuing: "I think Björn Snorri must have gotten over his misfortune in Copenhagen, but he was ill for many years. I imagine it's the cancer that finally crushed him."

"Can you describe Björn Snorri a little bit better for me?" Dagbjartur asked.

Fridrik reflected a moment before starting: "Björn Snorri had a particularly sharp mind. He was a great scholar, and few contemporaries could stand up to him when it came to his knowledge of Icelandic manuscripts. Instead of focusing on the text, he started off by forming a picture of the scribes. By placing himself in their shoes, he could guess which manuscripts they were copying. Was the scribe in the habit of cutting his quill as he was leafing through a manuscript? When was the scribe in the best form, at the beginning of the work or later? Was there a greater danger of making mistakes at certain times? Did he think the text was fun and did this make him rush the work so that he could swiftly move on? Or was the text boring and did that give him cause to labor on the calligraphy and adorn the letters? In what environment did he learn his craft, and what were his specialized skills? Björn Snorri tried to form a picture of these men for himself and look over their shoulders as they were working, as it were. But he was so absorbed by his quest to define these many centuries-old acquaintances of his that he neglected the present. His contemporaries were too close to him for him to give himself the time to consider them. He never asked anyone how they were today. Instead, he could trace back various versions of the same paragraph in different manuscripts and talk about their evolution from the perspective of the personal characteristics of each scribe. But he was incapable of relating to the circumstances of his fellow travelers in space and time. He just assumed that if anyone had any issue to raise with him they would step forward and say so. Body language and gestures were simply beyond his understanding. The mundane faded into insignificance when he was struggling to analyze and understand a seven-hundred-year-old margin label on a torn vellum manuscript. He accumulated enormous knowledge. And he needed an outlet for that. He was a writer of only average ability and compiling reports bored him, but he could stand and talk about his interests for hours on end. And he could speak all the Nordic languages with ease. German came to him quite easily, too. He used his lectures to formulate his opinions and findings, put some order into them, and place them in a logical context. Talking was, therefore, the final phase in the formulation of his theories, and it didn't matter to him whether anyone was listening or not. If the issue was above the heads of the university students who sat with him, then he would just talk to himself or the one listener who was always close by and never flinched, little Jóhanna. And he used the time to explore new angles on his subject matter and could even make original discoveries in the middle of lectures in unknown cities. But as soon as that was all taken away from him, he withdrew into himself. He couldn't find peace anywhere, because he'd lost his outlet in the mundane world. He sank into depression and numbed his pain with alcohol. It could only end in one way."

Fridrik looked at his watch and stood up, but Dagbjartur remained seated. "How do you suppose Björn Snorri reacted when Gaston Lund showed up in Flatey?" he asked.

"To be honest, I haven't the faintest idea," Fridrik shrugged. "He might have treated him with disdain, he could do that, or maybe they were both delighted to have found each other again. I'd say that's more likely."

"Is it possible that Björn Snorri would have wanted to harm Lund in some way?"

Fridrik sat again at stared at Dagbjartur in bewilderment. "What do you mean?"

"Maybe by dispatching Lund to that island."

"Björn Snorri had been too ill to travel over the past years," said Fridrik.

"But his daughter?"

"Are you asking me if Jóhanna Thorvald could have harmed Professor Lund?"

"Yes."

Fridrik suddenly rose to his feet. "Jóhanna was like a daughter to me when she was my son's girlfriend. I won't tolerate that kind of talk about her," he said, walking toward the door.

"Now if you'll excuse me, my wife is waiting," he said.

Dagbjartur stood up and said, "Sorry, I didn't mean to upset you, and I won't delay you any longer. But could you direct me to someone who knew them well?"

"Thorgerdur, my daughter, studied medicine at the same time as Jóhanna. They've been in regular contact ever since. Thorgerdur is a doctor at the National Hospital. Try to find her."

Dagbjartur was on the way out, when he turned at the door and apologetically asked, "But what about the mother of Gaston Lund's child? Any ideas on where I might find some information about her?"

Fridrik looked at him gravely. "Have you spoken to Árni Sakarías about the Flatey enigma?"

"Yes."

"Did you ask him about Gaston Lund?"

"No."

"Then you better."

Question sixteen: Drowned in a deep bog. Second letter. He told her that when she got there, he would give her a wedding with all the honors. Gunnhild liked this arrangement and traveled to Denmark with a fine retinue. But when King Harald heard of her arrival, he sent slaves and guests to her. They grabbed Gunnhild with a lot of commotion and jeering and drowned the wretched queen in a terribly deep bog. This brought an end to the cruelty and crimes of Gunnhild, the king's mother. The answer is "Gunnhild," and the second letter is u.

CHAPTER 33

After the Whitsunday mass, the congregation drank coffee on the slope below the Flatey church. The weather was still fine so everyone sat outside, but otherwise the community center would have been opened for the after-mass coffee. The guests from the various isles took out their picnics, and little clusters of different ages and genders soon formed. District Officer Grímur found himself grouped with the old farmers of the islands. The first topic for discussion was the Dane who had been found out on Ketilsey. One of the inner isle farmers was convinced that foreign pirates had left the man there. And maybe also a treasure. Had anyone looked into that? Grímur confirmed that their investigation had revealed that there was no treasure to be found on Ketilsey. It was then prophesized that the island would be haunted for generations to come and it would yield very little while the curse lasted. Most of them agreed and glanced at the Ystakot clan, Valdi and Jón Ferdinand, who had exclusive rights on that skerry. The two men kept to themselves, drinking coffee and nibbling on the pieces of cake that someone had handed them, but the boy was nowhere to be seen.

Grímur told the farmers that a reporter from Reykjavik had arrived on Flatey and that he was here to dig up a story about it. The district officer asked the men to be careful about what they said to this guest. There was no need to implicate the locals on the islands in this unfortunate event. There had been enough damage done as it was.

The conversation then shifted to farming and forecasts. There was good news on the pricing front. The head of the co-op had heard that they could get eight hundred krónur for a good seal pup fur and at least fourteen hundred krónur for a kilo of cleaned eiderdown. This could be one of the islands' best farming years if the weather stayed good.

Question seventeen: King Harald's meal. Fifth letter. King Ólaf walked out to the pond where the children were playing. Then the king called the boys over and asked Guttormur, "What would you most like to own?"

"Fields," the boy answered.

"How vast would you want the fields to be?"

Guttormur answered, "I would want the ness to be completely sown every summer. There would be ten farms on it."

Next the king asked Hálfdan, "What would you most want to own?"

"Cows," he answered.

"How many?" the king asked.

"So many that it would be tight for them to drink together if they were to stand all round the lake side by side."

The king answered, "That would be a big herd. And what would you want, Harald?"

"Soldiers," he answered.

"How many?"

"I'm not very good at counting," he said, "but I think it would be good if there were enough of them to eat all of my brother Hálfdan's cows in one meal."

The king laughed and said, "You are bringing up a king here, Mother!"

The answer is therefore "Hálfdan's cows," and the fifth letter is d.

CHAPTER 34

Dagbjartur spent the rest of Whitsunday tracking down Árni Sakarías. He wasn't at home in Raudarárstíg, nor at the swimming pool or the diner in Austurbaer. "Try Café Hressó," said the lifeguard at the municipal swimming pool, "or 11 Laugavegur." It was in the café on Laugavegur that Dagbjartur finally found the author in the company of a group of good friends. Árni Sakarías was slightly tipsy and introduced the detective to his buddies.

"This good man here works for the detective division of the police force and is specialized in liaising with poets and writers. Salute him."

Dagbjartur nodded to them and got straight to the point with Árni Sakarías: "Did you know Gaston Lund, and did you know that he was connected to a child in Iceland?"

"Those are big questions," Árni Sakarías answered. "That can't be answered on an empty stomach. Let's just go to Hotel Borg and have some dinner, beef patties and fried eggs, courtesy of the police department."

Dagbjartur wasn't sure he'd be able to get a reimbursement on these bills but didn't want to run the risk of insulting Árni

Sakarías. After all, the man was under no obligation whatsoever to answer these questions, and it was therefore best to keep him happy. One cheap meal wouldn't go to waste if he got some good information out of it in return.

Árni Sakarías wasn't open to questions as they walked down Laugavegur, but instead launched into a lecture on contemporary poetry. It was not until he had received his payment in food at Hotel Borg that he finally came to the detective's question:

"You're asking about events that took place during the royal visit of June 1936, when King Christian the tenth came over. The king was still a bit wary after his previous visit for the celebration of the Althing in 1930. Everywhere he went, conversations seemed to veer toward the Icelandic sagas, as if he was supposed to know them inside out, and he never knew what answers to give. So this time he decided to bring along a Danish scholar who was an absolute expert in the field, Gaston Lund. His job was to follow the king every step of the way and answer on his behalf if the topic of the sagas cropped up. As soon as the Icelandic government got wind of this, they were dead scared that the Danish expert would wipe the floor with the Icelanders, so they called in an Icelandic expert of their own to follow the conversations and join in if the need arose. The person they appointed for the job was me. Already on the banks of the harbor, one could see that Lund had done his homework because the king delivered a short speech in Icelandic. The day after that, we went on this dreadful trip east to the waterfall of Gullfoss and Geysir and stayed in Laugarvatn. Gaston Lund and I were like two roosters in a cock fight, although as in most cock fights, most of the energy went into strutting about and flapping our wings, but there was little actual pecking. Then we started to relax a bit, and it all ended in a wonderful booze-up."

Árni Sakarías pondered the memory wistfully before continuing with the story: "The following day, on the way to Reykjavik, we went to the Sogsvirkjun power plant, and some silly inauguration ceremony took place there. Then there was a dinner party in the evening at Hotel Borg, and that's when the real story begins."

Árni Sakarías leaned over the table toward Dagbjartur and lowered his voice: "I arrived at the hotel early because I had some errand I wanted to discuss with Gaston Lund before the dinner party. I announced my arrival at reception, and a bellboy was sent up to his room with a note from me. I waited patiently because I knew he was preparing for the party and that it could take a while. Foreign guests were gathering in the foyer before going into the hall, and I greeted some of those I knew. Despite the crowd, I couldn't help but notice a young woman who had planted herself on a chair in reception and was obviously waiting for someone. She was very pretty to look at and nicely dressed without being ostentatious. Standing beside the woman, there was a boy who was probably ten years old. He was also well dressed and all spruced up. No one paid them much heed, and I was probably the only one who was giving them any attention. Even though the woman was considerably younger than I was, I nevertheless allowed myself to feast my eyes on her every now and then. She was the best looking woman in the room, and I can never resist eyeing a pretty woman if I get a chance. Meanwhile, it was quite some time before Gaston Lund appeared. I was standing to one side, talking to one of the king's retainers, and I didn't notice straightaway that Gaston had come down the stairs. Then I saw him standing on the bottom step and gaping in horror at the woman and the boy, who were walking toward him across the reception floor. The woman said something to him when they met and offered him her hand. He responded very oddly, by refusing to accept her greeting and slipping his right hand behind his back, as if to avoid her touching it. The woman then slipped her arm around the boy's shoulder, pushing him forward at the same time and saying out loud in Danish, 'Gaston Lund. This boy is your son.' Lund then backed off, moving back up two steps, and glared at him with a gaping jaw, speechless. This was beginning to attract some attention. The woman looked around apologetically on both sides and then at Lund again. She entreated him to speak to them, by all means. Then, it was as if Lund had suddenly snapped out of a trance. He beckoned the doorman over and, pointing at the woman and boy, shouted, 'Out, out!' The boy, who up until that moment had been so polite, started to bawl his eyes out, and so did the woman, yes, the woman, too. I'd never seen such a pitiful sight. All the dignity she possessed vanished with that single wave of his hand. Her back stooped and she stared bleary-eyed and blankly at the floor without uttering a sound. 'Out! Out!' Lund shouted, horror-stricken, and waving his arms. The doorman took the woman by the arm and the boy by the collar and practically dragged them out of the building. Everyone who had been in the foyer witnessed the scene and now stared at Lund. Then he turned on his heel and ran up the stairs. The woman's words echoed in the foyer as people repeated them. 'She said the boy was his son,' they kept on repeating, both in Icelandic and Danish. Those who knew Gaston Lund better than the others recalled that he had come to Iceland in the summer of 1926. Could he have had a relationship with this woman and fathered that boy? Regardless, his behavior was considered as nothing less than shameful, and he never showed himself again for the rest of trip. The story reached Copenhagen and tarnished his reputation. I've never been ashamed to tell this story if I'm asked. I don't think Gaston Lund came to Iceland again until last autumn."

Árni Sakarías had finished his speech and now concentrated on his food. "Who was she, this woman?" Dagbjartur asked.

The writer shook his head as he finished chewing and swallowing. "No one knows. No one who saw her at the hotel knew her by sight, and she was never seen there again. I tried to track her down, but without success. No one in town was familiar with the description I gave of the woman. It was assumed she wasn't from Reykjavik. The Icelanders in Copenhagen tried to recall Gaston Lund's trip to Iceland in the summer of 1926, but no one had any particular memory of any liaison with a woman. It occurred to no one to mention it to Lund himself, and bit by bit the story was forgotten in Copenhagen."

Question eighteen: Earl Hákon's tooth token. First letter. Hákon became so uncontrolled with women that he felt entitled to have his way with all of them, whether they were mothers, sisters, maidens, or married. He also treated his underlings cruelly in many other ways and came to be known as Hákon the Bad. Eventually the yeomen formed an army and took up arms against him. Hákon escaped and hid with his slave, Kark, who had been given to him as a tooth token. Kark then killed the earl in their hideout and delivered his head to Ólaf Tryggvason. The king rewarded Kark by having him beheaded as well. The answer is "Kark," and the first letter is k.

CHAPTER 35

After dinner Kjartan strolled out onto the embankment in front of the district officer's house. He liked feeling the breeze on his face and decided to go on a walk to the east of the island. The village had sunk into tranquility, and he passed no one but a curious calf roaming between the houses. Walking past the island store, he heard a radio through a window. A short while later he had reached Innstibaer. He felt he was being watched from the window of a house, but he avoided looking back. His mind was busy connecting the few threads linked to the disappearance of Gaston Lund. Even the women in Innstibaer. But right now he wanted to forget, and he walked across the island in a determined stride. The track meandered up to a reef that dropped onto the sea, and he saw some puffins perched on top of the rock. He carried on walking and soon stood on the shore on the innermost part of the island. The village had vanished behind him, but to the east of the strait he could make out the houses of the nearby islands in the evening sun. Far behind them the sky had darkened with clouds of rain.

Kjartan enjoyed the view for a brief moment, but then he turned to walk back along the island's southern shore. He spotted eider ducks flying from their nests along the trail here and there and then the arctic terns spiraling over him. He snapped an old twig of northern dock and dangled it over his head as he crossed the densest swarm of terns. It was low tide, and mud flats protruded between the small islets to the south of Flatey. Shorebirds he was unfamiliar with were feeding there. A sheep with two lambs used the opportunity to stroll over the shallows to the grassy isle on the other side of a narrow strait. Kjartan wanted to continue walking out to the little isles to the south of the inhabited island but decided to do so later. It was getting late and rainy.

As he walked along the shore right to the south of the church, he saw a faint light glowing in the library window. Intrigued, he decided to peep in to see if there was someone inside. If it was someone he didn't want to talk to, he could always say that he saw the light and just thought that he'd forgotten to switch it off. Then he could leave.

He walked up the field toward the building and knocked on the door.

"Come in," a female voice answered from within.

The door creaked as he opened it and stepped inside.

Dr. Jóhanna sat by the glass case containing the Munksgaard edition of the manuscript open in front of her. An oil lamp glowed on the wall above her. A small gas heater on the floor generated some cozy warmth.

Kjartan hovered in the doorway and finally said, "I was in the church this morning when they announced that your father passed away. I'm very sorry."

She was slow to answer but finally said, "Thank you. My father was actually very ill, and he'd been longing to die for some time."

"I know, but it's still sad to lose a father," said Kjartan.

"Yes, that's certainly true. It leaves a vacuum, and maybe it's harder than I expected. I came here this evening to take a look at the books he admired the most."

Kjartan looked around. "It's not a big library," he said.

"No, but it's served its purpose for a hundred and thirty years. The building is exactly 11.2 feet wide and 15.4 feet long, I'm told."

She was leafing through the manuscript again.

"Are you reading the *Flatey Book*?" he asked.

"Yes, I'm just perusing through it and jogging old memories. My father knew the original version of this manuscript more than most. The islanders take good care of their book, though, even if it's just an imperfect copy. They normally keep it under this glass, but I've been given permission to browse through it."

Kjartan drew closer and looked at the book. "Can you read that text?" he asked.

"Yes, most of it."

"Where did you learn that?"

"My father taught me, indirectly."

"How do you mean, indirectly?"

"It might strike some people as odd, but it seemed perfectly logical to me at the time. My mother died when I was six, and after that I was brought up by my father on his travels. We lived in Copenhagen when Dad was working on his research at the Arnamagnæan Institute and the Royal Library. He'd just completed his doctorate when my mother was diagnosed with the cancer that killed her within two years. My father and I were very close and couldn't be parted from each other after that. Dad was withdrawn and didn't mix much with other people unless he had to for his work. So we had few friends. I learned very early on that if I could sit quietly and behave, I could follow my father just about anywhere. He, therefore, never tried to find me a foster home. I didn't even go to school until we moved back to Iceland after the war. Dad taught me everything I needed to learn and a lot more besides. It mightn't have been on the national syllabus, but he often allowed me to decide what we read myself."

She smiled at the memory. "I also believe that children should be allowed to choose what they study. The subjects should be introduced to them, and then they should decide. I realize that that would mean that everyone would have to have a private tutor, of course, which wouldn't be very economical."

Jóhanna smiled again and then continued: "My father traveled around the Nordic countries and Germany, delivering lectures about the Icelandic sagas at universities. I tagged along and sat in the corners of the lecture halls. I often read something I brought along with me or drew pictures or allowed myself to daydream about having friends and playmates. Naturally I longed for friends, but I never dared to tell my father that. I was too scared he would send me to boarding school so that I could mix with other girls. He sometimes mentioned that it might be a good idea, but I categorically refused. He was all I had after Mom died, and I didn't dare to let go. I preferred to be with him on his trips and put up with sitting still in stuffy classrooms for hours on end."

Jóhanna mused in silence a moment and then continued: "Sometimes I listened to Dad when he was delivering his lectures. I also accompanied him when he was conducting his research at the library. That was on the same conditions. I was never to disturb him while he was working. The manuscript texts could be difficult to read, and he was used to reading them out loud and skimming the words with his finger. I often stood by his side, listening and following. That's how I learned how to read the Gothic letters and understand the spelling and abbreviations."

Jóhanna stopped talking. Kjartan's question had been answered.

"That must have been an odd life," he said.

"Yes, but they were also very special times. I was only ten when the war broke out, and after that people just became preoccupied with themselves. No one gave much thought to a little foreign toddler of a girl following her dad around everywhere."

"Where were you during the war years?"

"We carried on living in Copenhagen, and Dad continued on his research. After the Germans occupied Denmark, he continued his lecture tours to Germany. He was totally apolitical and completely indifferent to who happened to be in power, so long as he could pursue his studies. Researching the sagas and deciphering their mysteries was his only goal in life. There was a great deal of interest in Germanic philology in Germany at the time."

"Why did you move back here to Iceland?"

"We were forced to. My father hadn't realized that during the German occupation his Danish colleagues resented him traveling around Germany on lecture tours. He had such a poor grasp of what was actually going on around him that he didn't realize that people's attitude toward him was changing. He didn't feel the need for friends. So long as he could find a group of university students who were willing to listen to him for part of the day, he was happy. It didn't matter to him whether he spoke Icelandic, Danish, Swedish, Norwegian, or German. And I tagged along and listened, too. But then the Germans lost the war, and the day they pulled out of Copenhagen my father's world crumbled. He was fired from the Arnamagnæan Institute and was never allowed to set foot on the premises again. The Royal Library was closed to him, too. His greatest treasure, the *Flatey Book*, had been taken away from him forever. He was driven back to Iceland and could count himself lucky that he got a teaching post in a secondary school."

"Did he need to have access to the original manuscript to able to continue his research? Couldn't he have used a copy like this?" Kjartan asked, pointing at the book lying on the table in front of Jóhanna.

"That's a good question. Is this old vellum manuscript of any value? Everything it can say to us in the text has long been copied down, letter by letter, and even photographed, as you can see. The only thing that remains is the object itself, the vessel used to convey texts that have long reached their destinations. Why then are some people so obsessed with this ancient vellum manuscript?"

She peered into Kjartan's eyes, but he seemed unable to offer an answer. She provided one herself: "It's because when we look at this book and pick it up, it brings us into direct contact with people who lived in the fourteenth century. We sense their presence in the manuscript's aura. And that was the presence that my father needed to feel. I think there are very few people who can sense that contact. To other people, this is just manuscript number 1005 folio in the Royal Library."

"Have you seen this vellum manuscript?" Kjartan asked.

"Yes, I have. I read practically every single page over my father's shoulder."

"Did you sense this presence?"

"Not in the way my father could, but it's the most beautiful book I've ever set my eyes on. The glowing black letters on the light brown vellum are like endless strings of pearls. To me these illuminations are on a par with the most beautiful frescoes on the ceilings of majestic palaces. Unfortunately, these photographs are just a pale reflection of what they're really like."

Jóhanna turned the pages in front of her. "When I look at these pages, I get the same feeling I get when I look at photographs of relatives and friends. It gives me some pleasure, but I'd rather meet them in person. Each page in the book is like an old friend you long to see again."

"Tell me about the *Flatey Book*," he asked.

She pondered a moment. "Do you want to hear the long story or the short one?" she finally asked.

"The longer story if you have the time."

She gazed through the window where the sun was setting behind the mountains in the northwest and said in a soft voice, "I've got plenty of time now."

She then started to tell the story, talking relentlessly for hours. Kjartan listened intently, and they both became oblivious to the passage of time.

Finally, the story ended, and Jóhanna silently leafed through the Munksgaard edition. Kjartan was also silent and pensive. Then he took out the sheet that Reverend Hannes had given him with Gaston Lund's answers to the Flatey enigma.

"Do you know the story of the Flatey enigma?" he asked.

Jóhanna nodded. "I've read the questions. My father spent hours grappling with it."

"Was he able to solve the riddle?"

"He'd figured out the key to the solution. I don't know if anyone else got as far as he did, since living here gave him daily access to the clues in the library. He knew that the answers to the first thirty-nine questions were useless until the answer to the fortieth question was found. There was no other way of verifying the answers. He overexerted himself the night he unraveled the clue and collapsed by this table here. I found him really ill on the floor.

Thormódur Krákur helped me to get him home on his cart. My father never got back on his feet to be able to complete the task after that, and he didn't want me to finish it. His notes have been waiting here ever since." Jóhanna pulled a ring binder off one of the shelves.

"I've got a copy of the professor's answers here," Kjartan said. "Can you help me to understand the questions and answers?"

"Yes, probably," she said pensively. "I can try."

Jóhanna leafed through the Munksgaard book until she found the loose sheets with the Flatey enigma. She placed them to the side where she could see them and also took a sheet out of her father's folder. Then she read out the questions one after another, checked the answers that her father had guessed, and looked up the relevant chapters in the Munksgaard book with her nimble fingers. She knew all these pages so well and found the right chapters in the bat of an eyelid. Running her finger over the text, she occasionally read a few lines out loud, but she generally just gave Kjartan an overview of what the chapter was about. Kjartan limited himself to a silent nod whenever Gaston Lund's answers were the same as those of Björn Snorri, but otherwise he read out the alternative answer. In this manner they went though each of the forty questions, one after another…

Question nineteen: Cannot be hidden from. First letter. Thormódur walked up to the cook and grabbed a haggis, broke it in two, and ate half. The cook said, "The king's men have poor manners, and he wouldn't be too happy about this if he knew what you were doing."

Thormódur answered, "We often act against the king's wishes. Sometimes he knows it, sometimes he doesn't."

The cook said, "It cannot be hidden from Christ."

"I guess not," said Thormódur, "but if half a haggis is to be the only thing that stands between me and Christ, we would be quite satisfied."

The answer is "Christ," and the first letter is c.

CHAPTER 36

Monday, June 6, 1960

It was raining. The nocturnal eastern wind had subsided at dawn, but the downpour persisted as the islanders gathered for their morning chores. The sheep had taken shelter under the gables of the houses in the village during the night. Ewes lay about pensively chewing the cud, while the lambs slept off the troublesome night. The farmers examined the sky and forecast more of the same weather.

Grímur had no nets in the sea and therefore took it easy for most of the morning. The nets had all been taken up before the day of the mass, so there was no hurry to go out to sea. The seal pups could play undisturbed on the furious surf by the skerries that day.

Kjartan was upstairs in the loft and seemed to be sleeping. Grímur had gone to bed early the night before and had not heard the guest come in, although he saw his wet overcoat in the hall. *Let him rest*, the district officer thought to himself as he was drinking his morning coffee. He didn't really know where the investigation was supposed to go from here. The most sensible thing was probably to request some assistance from Reykjavik.

Ingibjörg sat in the living room, listening to music on the radio as she knitted a sock out of a ball of coarse wool. Högni popped by and accepted a cup of coffee, but then he headed home when Grímur told him their sea trip was on hold. It looked as if they were in for an uneventful day.

Grímur went into the shed, milked the cows, and led them out to the field. There were three of them, two of which he owned himself and one which he fed for Sigurbjörn. In exchange the Svalbardi farmer housed a few sheep for him.

Thormódur Krákur was busy doing something in front of his old barn. He started the day early and had obviously taken his cattle to the pastures ages ago. Grímur walked over to him and said hello.

"What are you making there, Krákur?" he then asked.

"Can't you see? A new lid for the well. You've been hassling me about it for long enough," Thormódur Krákur answered, brandishing his hammer. He was in a bad mood.

Grímur examined the work. It was true that he'd told Thormódur Krákur several times that the lid to the well needed mending. The wood was starting to rot, and it could be hazardous to step on it. Thormódur Krákur had found material to make the lid from some boat wreckage lying on the southern shore.

"That'll make a great lid, Krákur, my friend," said the district officer, but then he left when he realized that Thormódur Krákur wouldn't be answering him.

Grímur let the cows roam freely in the field while he was shoveling the dung channel, but then he led them to the pastures further out on the island. They were lazy in the wet weather and moved slowly. Little Rósa from Rádagerdi was also out with her father's cows.

"Grímur, Grímur," she said breathlessly when they met. "Svenni says there's a red angel in the churchyard. Do you think that's true?"

"There are certainly many angels in the churchyard, Rósa dear," Grímur answered, "and who knows, some of them might be red."

"Yeah, but you can't see them normally. Svenni says that you can see this one very clearly."

"When did little Svenni see this angel?"

"Earlier on. He slipped into the churchyard to gather some tern eggs. I met him when he came running back. He was so petrified that he ran straight home. Maybe the angel appeared to stop Svenni stealing the eggs from the churchyard."

"Do you really think God would send an angel down to us just because someone was pilfering a few tern eggs in the corner of a garden?" Grímur asked.

"The priest says we're not allowed to take any eggs out of the churchyard. It's sacred. You can't even pick sheep sorrel there," Rósa said gravely.

They ushered the cows through the gate into the outer pastures and then closed it with a sliding hinge bar.

"Off you go now, and eat well," Grímur said to the cattle as he left.

"Shall we go take a look at this angel, Grímur?" Rósa asked.

Grímur smiled at her. "Sure, we can pass the churchyard on the way back, even if it's raining a bit," he said. "It's not every day that you get a chance to meet a real angel."

They sauntered back and turned right along the road to follow a narrow track toward the churchyard. Everything seemed normal. The fences that lined the graves and tombstones were surrounded by dense clusters of tall yellow grass from last fall, and the wet ironwork glistened in the drizzle. There was some commotion among the arctic terns that nested in the southern part of the cemetery. They were screeching noisily over one of the graves, and Grímur thought he spotted something new by the tombstone.

Rósa saw it, too, and stopped. She tugged at Grímur's jacket and whispered, "I think I'll just take a look at the angel later. I've just remembered I was suppose to go straight home."

"Right then, you just go on home," said Grímur, but she hadn't waited for an answer and was already running back the same way they came and swiftly vanished down the slope without looking back.

There was no opening in the fencing on this side of the churchyard, but Grímur had no problems climbing over the low wire netting, even though he was a bit stiff in his hips. Once he had entered, he felt it appropriate to bless himself but then continued walking. The quarrelsome arctic terns then turned on Grímur and dived toward his head, one after another, as he trod the narrow trail between the graves. He waved his arms at them and pushed his cap to the back of his head. His visor was pointing in the air now, so that the most daring terns would knock their beaks against it, while his bald head remained mostly protected. He had dealt with terns like this countless times before and wasn't too bothered by their uproar. His eyes were firmly focused on what lay ahead.

Inching forward, step by step, Grímur approached a mass that initially looked like a red angel, as Svenni had said. But as he drew even closer, he saw that it was a half-naked human body covered in blood and kneeling on the grave. Its arms and head dangled over the white tombstone. On its bare back there was something that in the distance had looked like fiery red wings. Blood had trickled down the body in the rain and dyed it red. The body's coat, jacket, and white shirt had been yanked down over the man's waist.

Grímur froze and swallowed in an attempt to moisten his parched throat. Then he drew closer to see who had met this terrible fate in the night.

Question twenty: Who ate his father's killer? First letter. Sarcastic Halli said, "I don't know of anyone who avenged his father as gruesomely as Thjodolf because he ate his father's killer."

The king said, "Tell us how this is true."

Halli said, "Thorljot, Thjodolf's father, led the calf home on a lead, and when he got to his hayfield wall, he hoisted the calf up the wall. Then he went over the wall, and the calf tumbled off the wall on the other side. But the noose at the end of the lead tightened around Thorljot's neck, and he was unable to touch the ground with his feet. So each hung on his own side of the wall, and they were both dead by the time people arrived. The children dragged the calf home and prepared it for food, and I think that Thjodolf ate his full share of it." The answer is "Thjodolf," and the first letter is t.

CHAPTER 37

Dr. Jóhanna was wearing a green raincoat and held a black umbrella, but Kjartan was in his trench coat and bareheaded. They stood a few feet away from the grave and stared at the man on the tombstone that Grímur had alerted them to. The rain had intensified during the course of the morning.

"That's got to be the reporter from Reykjavik who arrived on the mail boat on Saturday," Grímur uttered in a low voice. "I'm told his name is Bryngeir."

Jóhanna walked up close and then circled the grave. She stooped over the man's back and examined him. "The ribs were chopped on both sides of the spine from the back with two or three big blows and then stretched out," she said. "Both lungs were then pulled out from the chest." She walked another circle around the man and then added, "Those are the only injuries I can see."

Grímur looked at them and asked, "Should we pick him up and carry him into the church?"

"No, no," Kjartan said in a tremulous voice, "absolutely not. We won't move anything here. We'll do nothing. We'll close the churchyard and immediately call the Criminal Investigation Department in Reykjavik."

He clasped his coat around his throat, but the rain streamed down his hair over his ashen face.

"Whoever carved this man up like this had to be strong and knows how to handle a knife," Jóhanna said. "It takes a lot of strength and skill to be able to cut through the bone like that. And the knife was big and sharp."

"Will you call the police in Reykjavik?" Grímur asked Kjartan.

"I would prefer you to do it," Kjartan answered. "This is all so way over my head. I think I'll just take the first trip back to Patreksfjördur. I hope you can deal with communicating with the police."

Grímur scratched the beard under his chin. "But I've got to hang around here and make sure no kids come near this," he said awkwardly.

"I'll phone Reykjavik," Jóhanna said, "and ask them to send an investigator straightaway. I can describe the incident."

Grímur was relieved. "Yeah and find Högni for me and tell him to come up in his sailing overalls. He can take it in shifts with me."

"I'll do that," Kjartan answered, swiftly turning and rushing out of the cemetery.

Question twenty-one: The ugliest foot. First letter. Thórarinn Nefjúlfsson was in Tunsberg staying with King Ólaf. Early one morning the king lay awake while the others were asleep, and the sun was shining so there was a lot of light inside. One of Thórarinn's feet stuck out of his bedclothes. The king stared at the foot for a while and then said, "I've witnessed an invaluable sight; this man's foot has got to be the ugliest in the whole town."

Thórarinn answered, "I'm willing to bet you that I can find an uglier foot."

The king answered, "Whoever wins the bet shall demand a favor of the other."

"So be it," said Thórarinn. He then produced his other foot from under the bedclothes, which was no more beautiful and had a toe missing, too. "And now I have won the bet," said Thórarinn.

The king answered, "The other foot is uglier because it has five ugly toes on it, but this one has only four, so I can ask a favor of you."

The answer is "Thórarinn," and the first letter is t.

CHAPTER 38

The announcement of another death in Flatey did not go down well with Dagbjartur. Now he knew that the peace was over. He'd be required to give an account of his investigation over the past few days and submit a report. The worst part was that he hadn't written anything down yet. This would become a priority case now, some higher-ranking officer would be put in charge, and the department's best men would be dispatched to Flatey. The only positive thing to come out of that morning was the fact he would no longer be required to travel to the island.

Using three fingers, Dagbjartur hammered out the conclusions of his interviews with Fridrik Einarsson and Árni Sakarías on his typewriter. He didn't need to write much to cover the essentials, but it still took him a long time. His chubby fingers were stiff on the keyboard and didn't always hit the right letters.

It didn't take the head of the division long to race over his subordinate's text.

"The Flatey enigma?" he erupted in a rage. "What childish nonsense is that?"

"The magistrate's assistant in the west seemed to feel it was important," Dagbjartur answered defensively.

"Oh yeah? And what's this? A child out of wedlock. That might be worth looking into. Who's this woman?"

"We don't know."

"Don't know! What have you been up to over these past few days?"

"This." Dagbjartur pointed stubbornly at his papers. "But no one knows who this woman is."

"Aren't there any birth records from those years that we can go through?"

"Everywhere's closed on the Whitsunday weekend."

"Right, well, keep going and keep me posted."

For the remainder of the day Dagbjartur tracked down the friends, relatives, and colleagues of the reporter, Bryngeir, to dig up some information about his life and habits. His colleagues at the paper seemed to be mostly relieved to be free of him, although no one had the effrontery to say so straight out.

The list of relatives was a short one. His maternal grandfather was in an old folk's home in Stokkseyri, and he had an uncle on his mother's side who was a farmer in the east in Öræfi. Dagbjartur tried phoning the grandfather but was informed that the old man was deaf and unable to talk on the phone. When he finally reached the uncle in Öræfi, it took the man some time to remember he had a nephew by the name of Bryngeir. He hadn't heard of his death, but betrayed little emotion. He did, however, ask if the man had left any assets behind.

Most of Bryngeir's friends considered themselves to be more acquaintances than close friends and showed no sign of grief. He wouldn't be dearly missed, it seemed.

Collecting a few snippets of information from here and there, Dagbjartur managed to build a reasonable personal profile of Bryngeir and submitted it to his boss that same evening.

Question twenty-two: Who were the soldiers of King John of England? Seventh letter. Earlier that summer, the English king had sent King Sverrir two hundred warriors when he was in Bergen; they were called the Ribbalds. They were as swift on their feet as beasts and were great archers, audacious, and had no qualms about committing bad deeds. The answer is "Ribbalds," and the seventh letter is d.

CHAPTER 39

The women in Innstibaer had not ventured outside because of the weather that morning and hadn't seen anyone. They attended to their chores, but they were surprised that no one had come to pay them a visit. The goodwife from Svalbardi usually popped over to them after the lunchtime radio news and gave them a rundown of the main events in the outside world. They couldn't afford the luxury of a wireless in Innstibaer, so the two ladies relied on other channels for news. Newspapers didn't reach them until they had been through several other readers. District Officer Grímur bought the *Icelandic Times*, and Ásmundur in the island store bought *Morgunbladid*. The *Times* was passed on from Grímur to Gudjón in Rádagerdi, whereas the Svalbardi family bought *Morgunbladid* from Ásmundur the storekeeper at half price when he'd finished reading it. Högni, the teacher, on the other hand, bought the social democratic paper, which he preserved meticulously in folders. The farmers then donated their papers to the library after they had read them, which was when the women could take a look at them with the other islanders. By that time the papers were normally several weeks old and the news had grown stale, but the serialized novels they contained were classics and very popular in Innstibaer. When the papers had been on the paper racks of the library for several months, they were placed in a bin by the gable of the building, after which they were destined to end their days shredded in the privies of some of the poorer families on the island. The little that was not recycled in this manner was given to the Ystakot clan to be used in the fire.

No news came that day, and Högni, who also used to pass by in the afternoon for a cup of coffee, didn't show. They had coffee ready in the flask and had saved a bit of the cookies, which Ingibjörg of Bakki had sent over to them on Whitsunday. They hadn't spotted the district officer going out to sea that day, so the teacher was probably at home. He was bound to pop over to them.

Hallbjörg sat by the kitchen window and peered through the rain falling against the glass. She wanted to be able to see guests when they appeared in front of the house and to be ready to open the door. Contrary to their habits, they had locked the front door. Over the past two days, they had heard many stories about that terrible man from Reykjavik, who had been loitering around like the village drunk and causing trouble everywhere. The two women had, therefore, not dared to leave the house unlocked. But they were somehow restless. Even though they wouldn't admit it to each other, they were quite eager to hear the latest gossip about this troublemaker.

Hallbjörg finished knitting the woolen sock and cast on the new one, but she glanced out the window at regular intervals. Gudrún had put down her knitting and picked up an old copy of *Morgunbladid*. She read out the serialized novel, *A Life* by Guy de Maupassant, part 15. This was their routine. One of them would read out loud while the other continued with her work. It enabled them to use their time more efficiently. But more often than not it was Gudrún who did the reading, because she had better eyesight for it and Hallbjörg got hoarse if she spoke at length.

Finally Hallbjörg became aware of some movement outside the house and saw through the window that the goodwife from Svalbardi was on her way up the steps to them and seemed to be in a hurry. Hallbjörg stiffly hoisted herself to her feet to unlock the door.

Question twenty-three: No horse could carry him. Fourth letter. Rögnvald married Ragnhild, the daughter of Hrolf Nose. Their son was Hrolf, who conquered Normandy. He was so enormous that no horse could carry him. He was dubbed Hrolf Walker, or Ganger Hrolf. It is from him that the Norman earls and English kings descended. The answer is "Hrolf Walker," and the fourth letter is l.

Kjartan said, "The guest's answer to this was 'Ganger Hrolf,' and the letter is g."

CHAPTER 40

Ásmundur, the storekeeper, was on tenterhooks. As soon as he had opened the store in the morning, he had heard news of a terrible mishap in the cemetery. He then contacted Thormódur Krákur, who told him that the reporter from Reykjavik had been found dead there, lying on a grave. Details of the story became clearer as the day progressed. And it was good for business. Islanders popped into the store several times in the day under the pretense of running errands, but above all to hear more news. And naturally they felt compelled to buy something to conceal their blatant curiosity. But no one dared to linger in the store for too long. Instead, they would come back again later and something else would be bought. Customers from the neighboring islands traveled over for the same reasons.

The story that was circulating went as follows: Bryngeir, the reporter from Reykjavik, had been found horrendously mutilated in the churchyard early in the morning. There were mixed opinions as to what had happened to him, and the district officer had banned all access to the cemetery and guarded the gate. Police from Reykjavik were expected to arrive to investigate the case any moment. The magistrate's assistant had been spotted coming out of the churchyard and walking down to the school to Högni. He had then gone home to Bakki and had not come out again. The doctor had been the first person to phone the crime squad in Reykjavik. Then the district officer had phoned several times. The priest offered to hold a prayer meeting in the school at four, since the church was now in the off-limits zone that was being guarded by the district officer.

Ásmundur retold this story countless times as he served the customers, who bought all kinds of unnecessary goods during the course of the day.

Question twenty-four: The wooden man. Third letter. Earl Hákon invoked his guardian spirits, Thorgerd Altar-bride and her sister Irpa, to perform whatever sorcery was required in Iceland to kill Thorleifur. Hákon ordered the figure of a man to be made out of driftwood. Then a man was killed, and his heart was cut out to be placed inside the wooden figure. He was then dressed and given the name of Thorgard. They endowed it with such devilish powers that it could walk and talk with men. He was dispatched on a ship to Iceland and arrived when people were assembling at the Althing. One day Thorleifur stepped out of his booth and saw a man crossing the Öxara river from the west. Thorleifur asked the man for his name. He answered that his name was Thorgard, and at the same moment he thrust the halberd at him and through his middle. As Thorleifur was hit, he struck back at Thorgard, who vanished into the earth so that only the soles of his feet could be seen. Thorleifur wrapped his tunic around himself and walked back to his booth. He told people what had happened, and when he threw off his tunic, his guts spilled out. He died there with a good reputation. The answer is "Thorgard," and the third letter is o.

CHAPTER 41

It was still raining at eleven when two detectives arrived in Flatey. They had left Reykjavik by car, shortly after Jóhanna had phoned the criminal investigation department in the capital and requested assistance on Grímur's behalf. A coast guard ship that happened to be a short distance away in the West Fjords sailed to Stykkishólmur to meet them and then take them to Flatey. The ship was now moored to the new pier and looked gray, wet, and bleak in the evening twilight.

Grímur received the investigators on the pier, and the only other people there apart from him were Thormódur Krákur, holding his handcart and dressed in his black suit, and the three generations of men from Ystakot. Valdi had seen the ship approach from the south and went down to grab the ropes as usual. Kjartan, on the other hand, had asked to be relieved of any further participation in the investigation after the discovery in the churchyard, and said he was ill and had gone to bed.

The chief investigating officer greeted Grímur first. "I'm Thórólfur," he said, before introducing his partner: "Lúkas from forensics. He'll be examining the scene and assisting me in the interrogations."

Thórólfur was a vigorous and slim man in his early sixties. His white hair had started to thin slightly and was combed back. His weather-beaten and clean-shaven face was wrinkled, as if it had been exposed to too much sun. Lúkas, on the other hand, was younger, probably in his thirties, short, and chubby, with thick lips and rugged skin that stretched over a broad face crowned with light brown hair.

Two men were on the deck of the coast guard ship, preparing it for the night at the pier. Figures could be glimpsed through the illuminated windows of the bridge.

The policemen were suitably dressed for walking in the rain, wearing good raincoats and rubber boots. They carried two heavy bags with them and an oblong box, similar to the casket they had used to transport Professor Lund to Reykjavik. The older policeman gratefully accepted Thormódur Krákur's offer to carry their luggage in his cart.

They set off, Thormódur Krákur at the front with the cart and the others behind him. Grímur recounted the events of the past few days to the policemen and the little he knew of Bryngeir's movements over the past twenty-four hours. Thórólfur asked how many people were on the island, including both locals and guests.

"There were fifty-two people here this morning," Grímur answered after some thought.

"How many of them would've had the physical strength to do something like this?" the policeman asked.

"Well, that I couldn't say. Most of the adult men and probably some of the sturdier women."

"We'll question everyone from confirmation age up to their eighties tomorrow. How many would that be?"

Grímur silently counted. "That's probably twenty-two men and fifteen women. There are two old men in their nineties, and the rest of them are kids below confirmation age."

The policeman was silent and pondered. "This shouldn't be difficult to solve," he finally said. "The elimination process should narrow the group down quite rapidly. I just hope that the perpetrator doesn't panic and do something stupid."

The sun was still in the air somewhere behind the dark clouds of rain, but was nevertheless beginning to fade. They walked past the doctor's house, where there was a light on in the window. Grímur didn't lead them up the shortcut to the churchyard, but instead he took the road that was more manageable for the handcart. Finally they reached the church, which was open. Högni stood in the hallway, wearing his sailor's overalls and sea hat, watching the approach of the men. He greeted them with a wave.

The inspectors took their luggage off the cart and carried it into the church. They then thanked Thormódur Krákur for his help and told him he could leave, but that it would be good if they could hold on to the cart. Thormódur Krákur dithered until Grímur said, "Just go to bed, Krákur. I'll take care of your cart."

Thormódur Krákur tilted on his toes. "Very well, District Administrative Officer. I'll be off then, even though I never like to be the first to desert the battlefield."

Grímur turned to Högni. "You can go, too, Högni. You've done your shift now. Drop off by my place and get my Imba to make you a cup of coffee. No one wants to be alone tonight."

Högni was visibly relieved. He took Thormódur Krákur by the arm.

"Come on, pal. Your good clothes are drenched."

They walked down the slope from the church, without looking back.

Lúkas grabbed two large flashlights before the inspectors ventured into the churchyard. Grímur followed them, since he needed to show them the way. The body was clearly visible from the side of the churchyard because there was still some daylight, even though the rainy clouds had darkened the sky. It was close to the summer solstice, and the night would be very short.

Lúkas walked with a stooped back, pointing his beaming flashlight at his feet and the grassy path, while Thórólfur followed behind.

"There's no trail of blood," said Lúkas. "And no discernible footprints either."

When they reached the grave the body lay on, the policemen stopped.

"Someone has been walking around here," said Lúkas, pointing at the crushed grass around the grave.

"Yes, I walked there this morning and then the doctor," said Grímur.

"I'll examine the whole churchyard more closely," Lúkas said to Thórólfur, "but if we don't find any trace of blood, then the man was most likely killed on this spot."

He drew closer to the body and scrutinized its back.

"The man must have been barely conscious when he was carved up. There are no signs of resistance. He seems to have been placed in this position, his clothes were pulled over the top part of his body, and then his back was slashed to pieces."

He examined the hands, feet, and finally the head. "There are no signs of him having been tied up and no visible injuries on the head. He is unlikely to have been unconscious from a blow to the head."

"What about alcohol?" Grímur asked "He was drunk when he arrived on the island, and as far as I know he never sobered up."

"That's something the autopsy will reveal," Thórólfur answered. "We'll finish our examination of the scene, and then we'll send the body off with the ship. They'll take it to Stykkishólmur tonight, and there's a van ready to take it straight to Reykjavik. We should get a preliminary report back within twenty-four hours."

Lúkas fetched a camera with a big flash. He took several pictures of the body, changing bulbs after each shot. Grímur was blinded by the light when he made the mistake of looking into the flash, and the whole cemetery seemed to completely darken between shots.

"It's hard to believe the summer solstice is coming soon," he said, looking up at the overcast sky.

When Lúkas had finished taking the pictures, Thórólfur bent over the body and loosened the coat around the waist. Holding the tip of the coat up in the air with the index of his left hand, he searched through the pockets with the other. The only thing he found was an almost empty bottle of rum. The drenched coat and bottle were placed in a large paper bag. Next, Thórólfur loosened the jacket and searched through its pockets in the same way. There was a plastic wallet in one of the inner pockets. Seizing it, Lúkas shone his flashlight on its soaked contents. A bus ticket from Reykjavik to Stykkishólmur, a press card with a photo of Bryngeir, and a checkbook with two checks left. From the other pocket he took out a wad that was held together by a thick rubber band. Lúkas carefully loosened it. A Danish passport, wallet, and Danish notebook appeared. He opened the wet passport with great caution. The photograph was indistinguishable, but the name of its owner was still legible: Gaston Lund.

Grímur was dumbfounded. "That's the man who died in Ketilsey. What on earth was this man doing with his belongings?" he finally asked.

"He seems to have made more progress in his investigation into Lund's fate than you did, District Officer," said Thórólfur.

"Do you really believe there could be a connection between this deed and the death of the Dane?" Grímur asked.

Thórólfur silently pondered the question before answering: "If there is a connection, it's strange that these papers should still be in the reporter's pocket. If he'd been killed because he knew too much about the Dane's death, the papers would probably have been removed from his pocket. At the same time, it's unlikely that two events of this kind could have occurred in a small community like this without them being connected to each other in some way or the perpetrator being the same person."

Grímur shook his head dejectedly. "I thought I knew all my people."

Lúkas finished his job and then fetched the casket from the church. The policemen then lifted the body between them and carefully placed it in the casket. The paper bags with the clothes were also placed in the box. The body no longer looked like a red angel, and Grímur felt it now looked like a giant squashed bluebottle fly at the bottom of the box. He was relieved when the lid had been placed over the casket and screwed down. He felt he ought to say something appropriate, but the best he could come up with was the fragment of an old psalm:

"I lit my candles by the cross of the holy tree," he muttered softly, but then he couldn't remember the rest and just muttered a silent, "Amen."

The policemen carried the box out of the churchyard and placed it on the handcart. They then set off across the island toward the coast guard ship.

It was almost three in the morning by now, and there were no lights on inside the houses, except for the doctor's residence. Another corpse lay within those walls, and the daughter was alone in the house, so it wasn't surprising that the light was on. Reverend Hannes had told Grímur that she wanted her father to be buried in Flatey. Gudjón in Rádagerdi was bound to have started making the casket. The body would be transported to the church after the closing of the casket.

The only lights that glowed on the coast guard ship were those on the bridge where four men were on watch. Two of them stepped on shore, lifted the casket between them, and carried it on board the ship. The inspectors followed them to collect small suitcases containing their personal belongings. Then they stepped back on shore again. The disembarkation bridge was pulled back on board and the moorings untied. The ship slipped away from the pier and smoothly backed out of the strait. It was only when it was far out in the open sea that it finally veered south and advanced at full speed.

The ship had been ordered to go straight to Stykkishólmur to deliver the casket and then return to Flatey. The crew would then remain on standby to assist the inspectors whenever needed in the days ahead. The ship would also to be used as a communications center. Everyone on the island could eavesdrop on conversations that went through the regular radio channels, but the coast guard could send messages that the general public were unable to decipher, and the policemen therefore needed it to be able to communicate with their colleagues in Reykjavik where the investigation was also still being pursued.

Grímur and the policemen watched the coast guard ship sail off and then walked toward the village. Accommodation had been set up for the guests in the school.

Question twenty-five: What did Ívar lack? Second letter. Ívar the Boneless was king in England for a long time. He had no children because it was said that he lacked carnal desires, but he wasn't short of cunning and cruelty. He died of old age in England and was buried there. The answer is "desires," and the second letter is e.

CHAPTER 42

Tuesday, June 7, 1960

District Officer Grímur woke up early, despite the night watch, and was dressed by eight. Kjartan also descended from the loft and said good morning.

"Feeling better now, my friend?" Grímur asked.

"Yeah. I'm over it now, thanks. I'm sorry for dropping out like that."

"It was a perfectly natural reaction. You're a young man and you're not used to that kind of horror."

"Yeah, it's also being in this position of authority. It doesn't suit me. I should have turned down this job straightaway when the district magistrate sent me here. This isn't the kind of job I moved west to do. It'll turn me into a depressive because my nerves can't take it."

"What doesn't kill a man makes him stronger."

"I'm not so sure about that," Kjartan answered.

It was still raining, and the eastern winds had started to pick up again.

Grímur checked the weather. "The forecast is for more of the same," he said dejectedly as Ingibjörg put on her rain clothes to go out to the shed. The district officer had to assist the policemen, so someone else had to take care of the cows.

At around eight, Grímur and Kjartan set off for the school with morning coffee in a flask and freshly baked bread for the overnight guests. On their way they picked up Benny in Rádagerdi, gave him time to quickly dress, and took him along to the school. It was best to get started straightaway if they wanted to question all the adults on the island. Benny was undoubtedly the person who would have the most to say. He had followed the reporter around for almost two days.

The policemen were up. Högni had heated up some shaving water in a washbasin on a primus stove, and they were finishing washing. Kjartan greeted them, introduced himself, and asked if they needed his help.

Thórólfur eyed the magistrate's envoy with an inquisitive, slightly intrigued air. "No," he said finally, "we'll finish the questioning ourselves today, and the district officer can bring the people in for us. You can just take it easy until we call you in."

"Call me in?" Kjartan asked, surprised.

"Yes. We'll be taking statements from everyone who was on the island last night. Even the district administrative officer will have to account for his movements."

"Yes, of course. I'm ready whenever," said Kjartan, nodding good-bye before he disappeared outside.

The policemen sat down for a coffee and offered Benny a seat. Grímur and Högni waited for further developments by the door, feeling uncertain about their exact role in these proceedings.

Four school desks had been pushed together, and the policemen sat on two sides, Thórólfur facing Benny. There was a long silence while the guests devoured several slices of bread. Benny lit himself a cigarette, and Högni handed him an old saucer as an ashtray.

Thórólfur finally signaled Högni to leave the room but invited Grímur to sit beside them. When the door closed, he turned to Benny and asked him for his name and age. The young man answered in a slightly tremulous voice.

The policeman peered into his eyes at length. "When did you see Bryngeir for the last time?" he abruptly asked.

Benny was quick to answer: "Sunday evening, at around eight."

"Where?"

"In the shed at Thormódur Krákur's place."

"What did you do on Sunday, where did you go, whom did you talk with?"

This time Benny had to think a moment. "I met him twice. First at lunchtime. He came home to Rádagerdi and scrounged a meal because Sigurbjörn in Svalbard threw him out in the middle of the night."

"Why was he thrown out?"

"This Bryngeir guy was a bit of a stupid asshole. He told me there'd been some kind of misunderstanding. But then I heard that he'd tried to slip into bed with Hafdís when everyone was asleep. If I'd known he was like that, I would have just let him be and had nothing more to do with him. Hafdís is a good girl, and she'd never have allowed a guy like that to go near her."

"What did you do at lunchtime?"

"I gave him the leftovers of some puffin soup at home in the kitchen and walked down to Eyjólfur's pier with him to look at the people from the other islands who'd come over for the mass.

I had other things to do then, so I didn't see him again until the afternoon."

"What did you have to do?" Thórólfur snapped.

Benny blushed. He inhaled his cigarette and exhaled through his nose. "I had to go to the church," he said. "I sing in the choir. They needed a tenor this winter and Högni asked me to join."

"Where did you meet Bryngeir again?"

"In the island store after mass. He was talking to the store-keeper, Ásmundur."

"Wasn't the store closed?"

Benny blushed and averted his gaze. "Ásmundur keeps hooch in the store, which he's willing lend to people for the same plus a half when they're in need. District Officer Grímur doesn't allow it, though. Bryngeir was trying to get Ásmundur to lend him a bottle of hooch."

"The same plus a half? What does that mean?"

"It means you pay him back a bottle and a half when it's delivered to the post office."

"Did he get a bottle from Ásmundur?"

"Yeah, he got a bottle of rum, but not before I'd promised to cover the cost myself if Bryngeir failed to pay for it."

"So you trusted him then?"

"Yes, I thought so. Or at least, he said he was expecting loads of money. I don't know how that'll work now that he's dead. Maybe I'll have to pay. I have to talk to Ásmundur about it. I have a good seal fur that should be enough to cover the debt."

"How come Bryngeir was expecting money?"

"When we got the bottle from Ásmundur, we walked up to Thormódur Krákur's yard. Bryngeir kept his stuff there. Then he told me that he had solved the mystery about that Danish guy. He was going to write about it in his paper, and no one was supposed to know how the case was solved until the paper came out. Not even the police. He said the paper would sell like hotcakes and that he'd get a percentage. I promised I wouldn't tell anyone about it. He was going to visit someone and then try to get someone to take him to Stykkishólmur in the evening."

"Who was he going to get to take him to Stykkishólmur?"

"Just someone with a boat."

"Who was he going to visit?"

"He just said some friend. He was a bit secretive sometimes."

"Did he know anyone on the island from before?"

"No...yeah, at least he knew who the magistrate's assistant was, yeah, and Doctor Jóhanna. But I don't know if he knew them really."

"When did you leave him?"

"Around eight. I had to go home to dinner. I was hungry."

"Was he alone then?"

"No, Thormódur Krákur came into the shed and they chatted a bit. I think Krákur was telling him old dreams. The old man likes to do that, if he can find a willing listener."

"Did you tell anyone that Bryngeir believed he'd solved the case of that Danish man?"

"No, no. Just Mom and Dad. My sister Rósa heard it, too, but I didn't tell anyone else, I swear."

Thórólfur chewed on a slice of bread and drank coffee during the questioning. Occasionally he jotted something down on a lined sheet of paper.

Now Lúkas started asking questions: "You're sure you didn't see him after eight?"

"Yeah, I'd thought of going out again and trying to find him. Even to go along with him, if someone was willing to take him to

Stykkishólmur. But then it started to rain and I couldn't be bothered. I just listened to the news on the radio."

"Were your parents home?"

"Mom went down to Stína at the telephone exchange when she'd finished washing up, but Dad was at home reading a book to my sister Rósa."

"He can therefore confirm that you were at home all evening?"

"That I have an alibi, you mean?"

"Yeah."

"Do I need that?"

"It's good to be able to eliminate as many people as possible."

"I think Dad fell asleep when he'd finished reading to Rósa, and then Mom came home."

"So you could have left the house without anyone knowing?"

Benny stubbed out his cigarette. "I don't think so. I don't think I can ever leave the house without Mom realizing it. She told me that Bryngeir had been hassling Hafdís when she got back. Stína at the telephone exchange had heard it from the people at Svalbardi after mass."

Thórólfur took over the interrogation again: "What did you two do on Saturday?"

"I met him on the pier when he arrived with the boat and then took him to Svalbardi so that he could ask if he could stay. We spent some time with Sigurbjörn, chatting and drinking rum. Although I got very little rum. He was incredibly miserly, even though he had two and a half bottles. Then we went outside and spied when they were carrying that Danish guy in the casket down to the pier."

"What do you mean, 'spied'?"

"Just, not letting anyone see us. Bryngeir didn't want anyone to see that we were watching. I don't know why. Then we went to Ystakot and spoke to Valdi for a bit."

"What about?"

"Bryngeir was trying to find out if Valdi would be willing to take people to Stykkishólmur if he was well paid for it."

"What did Valdi say about that?"

"Maybe if the pay was good enough."

"What did you do then?"

"We walked back and looked into the church. Bryngeir started trying to play the organ, but he couldn't play a note. Högni, the teacher, then came in and was about to rehearse for the mass. He's our organist. He was really mad at Bryngeir for messing with the organ and was going to throw us out. But Bryngeir wouldn't leave and just talked crap. I think he just liked winding people up. He was such a darn asshole. I didn't want to hang around with him anymore and just went home. I think he just went into Svalbardi to have a snooze when he got bored arguing with Högni." Benny shut up and waited for the next question. Thórólfur kept him waiting and stared at him with searching eyes.

"Have you any knowledge of how Bryngeir died?" he finally asked.

"No, I swear," Benny said hastily. "I've already told you."

"Right then. That's enough for now. Talk to you again later."

Question twenty-six: Left his guts on the roof of a church. First letter. They went to Folskn unexpectedly and immediately killed Gunnar and some of his men. Ívar Korni was in the loft and escaped through a window, dressed only in his underwear. He tried to get into the church but it was locked. A ladder leaned against the church wall, so he climbed up to the roof and stayed there for the night. In the morning they found him, almost dead from the cold. He begged for mercy but did not get any. A man climbed the ladder and pierced him with a spear. Ívar fell, leaving his blood and guts behind him on *the church roof. The answer is "Ívar," and the first letter is* i.

CHAPTER 43

Högni's task was to call in the people on the established list of names, and Sigurbjörn of Svalbardi had arrived by the time Benny stepped out of the classroom with Grímur after his questioning.

"Those guys are real cops," Benny said, excited. Grímur told him to go home and ushered Sigurbjörn in to take a seat opposite the two detectives. He himself sat by the door.

Thórólfur kicked off with: "I'm told the deceased Bryngeir stayed with you on Saturday, is that correct?"

"You'd hardly call it stayed," Sigurbjörn answered. "He came on Saturday and asked to stay the night. We have a spare bed that we sometimes lend to travelers, and he was welcome to it. He also got some food from us when he arrived and then again in the evening. But he was cheeky and incredibly tiring when he was drunk. I threw him out at three in the morning. I'm told he crawled into Krákur's barn and slept there in some old hay until late on Sunday morning."

"Why did you throw him out?"

"He turned out to be such a darned scoundrel. We all went to bed at around midnight, and he was supposed to do the same.

But there was something restless about him, and in the middle of the night he sneaked into my daughter's bedroom stark naked and tried to slip into her bed. He wanted to seduce her, the bloody lech!"

"What happened then?"

"Well, her granny sleeps in the next bed and had her wits about her. She caught him at the side of the bed and shooed him away. I think she emptied her potty over him. In any case, he was all wet on top when I found him in the corridor and kicked him out. Then I grabbed all his stuff and dumped it on the steps."

"Didn't you see him again?"

"No, and I didn't go looking for him either. It didn't surprise me that the man was doomed."

"Oh?"

"Yeah. When I looked into his bag to see if he'd stolen anything from the house, I found sheets from the Flatey enigma that are meant to be kept in the library and not taken away. He'd stolen them the bloody night before. I went straight to Hallbjörg in Innstibaer and got the library key from her to be able to put the sheets back where they belonged. She told me the magistrate's assistant had been the last one to go to the library and that he'd probably forgotten to lock it. They don't know how to handle these precious things, those cultivated people from Reykjavik."

"Is that the only key to the library?"

"Yeah, apart from the key that the late Björn Snorri got a loan of. He went to the library so often."

"You're sure you didn't meet Bryngeir again on Sunday evening?"

"Yes, of course I didn't meet him again," Sigurbjörn snapped angrily. "Do you think I'm lying? Do you really think I dragged that scoundrel up to the churchyard, placed him on a grave, and carved a blood eagle out of his back just because he'd abused my hospitality?"

"Carved a blood eagle out of his back?" Thórólfur asked.

"Yes."

"What does that mean?"

"It's perfectly obvious. Someone carved a blood eagle out of his back. Haven't you read the *Flatey Book*?"

"No."

Sigurbjörn shook his head and said, "Don't they require you to have any education to join the police force these days?"

"The *Flatey Book* isn't exactly on the police syllabus," Thórólfur answered sourly.

Sigurbjörn grinned. "Isn't it now? Well it should be. I'll try to remember it for you. Sigurdur, Fáfnir's killer, fought Lyngvi Hundingsson in Friesland and captured him. Then they had a discussion about how Lyngvi should die. Regin suggested they carve a blood eagle on his back, and that's what they did. Regin cut through Lyngvi's back with his sword, broke his ribs to make them look like wings, and then he pulled out his lungs. So Lyngvi died with great valor. There are also accounts of blood eagles in the Orkneys saga and in the tale of Ormur Stórólfsson, if I remember correctly. If you ask me, that's exactly what was done to that wretch in the churchyard."

The policemen glanced at each other, but Sigurbjörn continued: "And then there's that Danish fellow. You can find parallels with his fate in the *Flatey Book*, too, but I guess you don't know that story either, do you?"

Thórólfur shook his head. "How did that one go?" he asked.

"It's in the saga of Ólaf Tryggvason. Eyvindur Kelda went to Ögvaldsnes with the intention of killing King Ólaf. Using magic he summoned a dark mist so that the king wouldn't be able to see them, but it blinded them, too, and made them walk around in circles. The king's protectors spotted the men and arrested them. The king then invited them to abandon their evil ways and to believe in the true God. But when Eyvindur and his men categorically refused to do so, they were taken to a skerry in the sea and left there to die of exposure. Since then it's been called the Devil's Skerry. That's how it went. I think you'll have to start reading the *Flatey Book* before you try solving the Breidafjördur mysteries."

"Is it long, this book?" Thórólfur asked.

"Not really. Thormódur Krákur has an edition that came out straight after the war. It's four volumes of about six hundred pages each. You could finish reading it by the fall if you really put your head down."

Thórólfur looked at Grímur. "Can you get us a copy of this work?"

Question twenty-seven: The most cunning chieftain. Second letter. The Norsemen who were on the rampage in Constantinople were known as the Varangians. Their chieftain was Harald, who was called Nordbrigt... They besieged another town that was both bigger and harder to overtake. There were lush and open fields close to the town with beautiful trees in blossom. The birds always flew there from the town during the day and then flew back to their nests on the rooftops of the houses in the evening. Nordbrigt addressed his men: "There is some clay here just outside the town, which we shall collect and knead until it turns into a kind of mortar. Then we will rub this wet mortar on the trees outside the town." The birds then stuck to the trees when they came looking for food, and many small birds were caught in this manner. Then Nordbrigt said, "Now let's collect dry and highly flammable wood and ignite a little fire in it by adding sulfur and enveloping it with wax. Then we will attach this load to each of the birds' backs so that they can fly with it. When night falls we will release them all together, and my guess is that they will fly back to their nests in the town, as is their habit." This was done, and the birds flew back to their nests and young ones. All the houses on which the birds had made their nests were thatched, and it did not take long for the birds' feathers to catch fire and then the rooftops, with one thing igniting another. At the same time, the besiegers armed themselves and attacked the town. The townspeople then had to fend off both the fire and the fierce attack, and they were unable to cope with both. The answer is "Harald," and the second letter is a.

Kjartan said, "Here Lund wrote the name 'Nordbrigt.'"

"Then the answer is either a *or* o.*"*

CHAPTER 44

Högni went off to collect Thormódur Krákur, who, as was to be expected, arrived for the questioning in his Sunday suit, and with his walking stick and medal of honor pinned to his chest. His clothes were still damp after the night, although he had made a worthy attempt at drying them over the stove that morning. He had brought along his copies of the printed version of the *Flatey Book*, at Grímur's request, and clutched them firmly in his arms.

Thórólfur contemplated the deacon at length from head to toe before starting the interrogation.

"Did you meet the deceased Bryngeir on Sunday?" he asked.

"Bryngeir came to my cowshed at around dinnertime on Sunday," Thormódur Krákur haughtily replied. "He offered me a sip of rum, and I gave him a cup of milk and some dried fish instead. I sometimes have some stockfish hanging in the corner of the barn to nibble at between meals, and it came in handy that evening. Then we sat there and chatted a little."

"What did you chat about?"

"We spoke about dreams and the extrasensory powers of some thinking beings. The late Bryngeir was knowledgeable on the subject, and it then transpired that he was very apt at deciphering unusual dreams. He'd also studied spiritism at night school with some famous medium in Reykjavik. Unfortunately, one doesn't often meet evolved souls of this kind on the island. He was slightly psychic when he was sober. That's why he drank so much, he told me. Some people can't handle the power and try to suppress their talents. They need help. But he was willing and capable of reading dreams. He was able to solve the calf dream I'd been grappling with for so long. The dream is as follows: I sense I'm inside this church and then..."

"Thanks, that's enough," Thórólfur interrupted. "Where did he go after he left you?"

"He said he was going to find some way of getting to Stykkishólmur but that he was going to see the doctor first."

"Was Bryngeir ill in some way?"

"No, it wasn't a medical visit. I told him the old man's body was in the house. He told me was going to offer his condolences to Jóhanna. I asked him to show some respect when he got there."

"Did you expect him not to?"

"Naturally, he was a bit tipsy, but easy enough to handle, although in between he could be quite mischievous."

"Did he ever mention the Dane?"

"No, not to me."

"Do you know how he was going to get to Stykkishólmur?"

"Well, he was going to talk to the islanders who have boats or the small boat fishermen, but I doubt anyone would have been foolish enough to take him that night. The weather was getting worse."

"Did he talk about where he would stay on Flatey if he didn't get to Stykkishólmur?"

"No. I couldn't put him up at my place because I don't have an extra bed in the house, but I told him he could sleep in my barn if he wanted to. I just asked him to be careful with fire."

"Do you think he stayed in the barn?"

"His things were still there when I walked into the barn yesterday morning."

"What time did he leave your place?"

Thormódur Krákur thought a moment. "Let me see…I took the milk over to Reverend Hannes at around eight and went home for dinner. Then I went back up to the shed at around ten to give water to the cows and prepare for the night. He was gone by then."

"Didn't you see him again?"

"No, not alive."

Question twenty-eight: Augurs a lucky journey. First letter. King Magnús and Earl Erling's fleet anchored near Brottueyri, outside Skipacrook, and the men landed there. As the earl leaped on shore, he fell on his knees. Thrusting both hands into the ground, he said, "A fall augurs a lucky journey." The answer is "fall," and the first letter is f.

CHAPTER 45

Dagbjartur arrived early at the National Hospital in Reykjavik and asked for Dr. Thorgerdur Fridriksdóttir. After a number of enquiries, it transpired that she was in the operating room.

"I'll wait," said Dagbjartur, smiling patiently.

He had been waiting for three hours when a young woman approached him.

"I was told you were looking for me," she said.

She was wearing a white coat with large splatters of blood on the front.

"I was just removing some tonsils. There can be a lot of bleeding sometimes," she added when she noticed he was staring at the stains.

Dagbjartur smiled awkwardly. "Sorry to disturb you. This won't take long."

"OK. What's it about?"

"I believe you know Jóhanna Thorvaldsdóttir?"

"Yes, we're friends."

"Have you seen her recently?"

"No. Not this year. She's been busy taking care of her father. I hear he's finally passed away now."

"How did you meet?"

"Why are you asking me about Jóhanna?"

"There was a terrible incident on Flatey and we're trying to form a picture of the people who live there. It's a relatively small number of people, so we can get a pretty good idea of each individual."

"I see. I've got nothing but good things to say about Jóhanna, so I hope none of this will harm her. We met in Copenhagen at the end of the war when we were teenagers and became good friends when she became engaged to my brother."

"What kind of a teenager was she?"

"She was a strange kid because she had been brought up by her father on the move across northern Europe. It took our family many months to break through the shell. Once we had, though, I realized she was an extremely gifted, tender, and fun girl. At first she sounded too much like an adult when she spoke, and her Icelandic was quite funny. Sometimes it was as if she were talking straight from the Icelandic sagas. She wasn't used to speaking this language with kids her own age. We actually spoke Danish together to begin with because that's what I was used to when I spoke to my friends in Copenhagen. We sometimes still do that for fun."

"Have you stayed in contact with her since then?"

"On and off. After my brother died, she vanished from our family life. She got into a doomed relationship with some guy for a couple of years. She was a year ahead of me in med school, and we caught up a bit once the relationship ended. She was very unhappy during those years but did very well in her studies. I think she saw a shrink for a while."

A nurse came running down the corridor. "Thorgerdur, come straight back," she called. "The boy is starting to bleed again!"

Question twenty-nine: What cracked with such a loud noise? First letter. Then the earl said to Finn Eyvindarson, "Shoot that man by the mast."

Finn answered, "The man cannot be shot if he is not fey. I can break his bow, though." Finn then shot his arrow, which struck the middle of Einar's bow just as he was drawing it for a third time, and the bow split in two.

Then King Ólaf said, "What cracked with such a loud noise?"

Einar answered, "Norway out of your hands, sire."

The first letter is n.

CHAPTER 46

Back at the vicarage, Frída was filled with indignation at being summoned for an interrogation by the Reykjavik inspectors like this without notice. Högni had been sent over to the priest and his wife with the request, but the lady had taken it badly. She stood fuming in the hall, clutching her hat between her hands, as Reverend Hannes tried to appease her.

"Frída dear. This is a perfectly natural request for the authorities to make," he said pleadingly.

"Request! We're clergy, for God's sake!"

"Yes, yes, it's only a formality. They want to talk to everyone on the island."

"Couldn't these officers just show us a little bit of respect and come here in person so that we wouldn't have to walk over there with everyone gawking at us as if we were common criminals?"

"These are busy people, dear," Reverend Hannes tried to explain. "They're investigating a most hideous crime, you know."

Frída's eyes were beginning to well with tears. "Yes, precisely. So how should we know anything about it?"

"Now, now, Frída dear," said the priest, slipping his arm around his wife's shoulder. "Tell the men we'll be there at eleven," he said to Högni.

"Eleven thirty, not a second earlier," said Frída with a sobbing gasp.

Högni took this message down to the school, and Grímur changed the order of the interviews to accommodate the priest's wife's request. The questioning was running smoothly, and there were no visible signs of the policemen tiring. Most of the people questioned were in with them for ten to fifteen minutes. The islanders accounted for their movements between Sunday night and Monday morning and also provided the names of those who could confirm their testimonies. It all proceeded rapidly and efficiently, and there seemed to be no contradictions in the accounts. The overall picture of how Bryngeir had spent the last two days of his life on the island was beginning to sharpen. It was only on that hour while the mass was going on in the middle of the day that no one could comment on his whereabouts. Everyone had been in the church, except for Dr. Jóhanna and two visiting fishermen who were lying hungover and asleep in an old house they had rented with others.

Jón Ferdinand only spent two minutes with the inspectors. Thórólfur simply wrote "senile" across the page and sent him away. Little Nonni was the next to enter and corroborated everything Valdi had said about their movements. They had spent the whole evening at home boiling sea stew.

The priest and his wife then arrived at the school at eleven thirty on the dot.

Högni knocked on the door of the school, stuck his nose inside, and announced their arrival. Stína from the telephone exchange was finishing her statement and had nothing new to add, much to her regret. She remembered that the goodwife from Rádagerdi had confidentially told her that the Reykjavik reporter had bragged that he'd solved the Ketilsey mystery. It could also be that she had confided the story to someone else later that evening, she couldn't quite remember.

"Let the priest's wife come in first," Thórólfur said to Grímur, once Stína had left the room. It was clear to him that most of the inhabitants of Flatey had been privy to the reporter's secret by Sunday evening.

Grímur vanished out of the room and then reappeared in the doorway again.

"The priest's wife refuses to talk to you without her husband being present," he said. "I wouldn't argue with her if I were you. She's quite adamant," he added.

Thórólfur smiled. "Bring them both in."

An extra chair was placed in front of the desk.

"I'm sorry for troubling you," said Thórólfur with a smile. "We felt we needed to question all the islanders. We feel it's particularly important for us to talk to the more educated and intelligent members of this community, since you obviously have a clearer perspective on things than some of the local workers around here."

Frída seemed thrown by this flattering welcome and decided to remain silent and allow Reverend Hannes to answer the questions.

"We're happy to be of any assistance," he said.

"Did you meet the reporter this case revolves around?" Thórólfur asked.

"No, not really. He actually knocked on our door early on Saturday evening, but he'd gone to the wrong house. He was looking for alcohol. I shooed him away. After that we spotted him every now and then, strolling around the village or up the pass. We have such a clear view from our living room window."

"Can you put a time to these movements, particularly on Sunday?"

Reverend Hannes thought a moment. "On Sunday we first saw him at around noon, probably at eleven thirty, when he was coming from Thormódur Krákur's barn. He prowled around the village a bit after that. Then, of course, we were busy preparing the mass and didn't see him again until late that afternoon when Benny in Rádagerdi escorted him up to Krákur's shed. Benny then came back on his own at around eight. Krákur brought us his half pot of milk at eight and told us that he had authorized the reporter to sleep in his barn if he needed to. Krákur is a generous man, and people sometimes take advantage of that. He's also a bit gullible and into spiritism."

Reverend Hannes glanced at his wife. "Wouldn't you say that's true, Frída dear?" he asked. She nodded.

"Was there anyone else walking on the pass that evening?" Thórólfur asked.

This time Frída answered: "Högni, the teacher, came out from the district officer's house after dinner at around eight, and the magistrate's envoy came down at around nine and walked across the village to the interior of the island. Krákur then went back up to the shed at around ten. After that we went to bed and therefore didn't witness anyone else's movements."

Thórólfur jotted down some notes on his sheet and then asked, "Is there anything else you can think of that might be of help to us in this investigation?"

"No," Reverend Hannes said, shaking his head, but Frída nudged him.

"Don't you remember?" she whispered.

"Remember what, Frída dear?"

She took the initiative. "People here on the island have been gossiping about the fact that the Dane had been our guest and that we were the last people to see him. That's simply not true, and I want it to be known."

"Who saw him last then?"

"When he left us he was going to go to Doctor Jóhanna to buy seasickness pills. He was so afraid of being seasick. That's why he left so early. That means that she was the last person to see him, not us, so you can write that down for the record." Frída punctuated this statement by tossing back her head and crossing her arms.

Thórólfur thanked the priest and his wife for the chat, and the couple said good-bye, telling the policemen that they were welcome at the vicarage anytime. They could even stay with them if the school was uncomfortable. Frída had taken a shine to them.

"We need to talk to the doctor," Thórólfur said to his assistant when the priest and his wife had left. "All our leads end with her."

A member of the coast guard crew appeared with an envelope. Thórólfur opened it and read its contents. "Yes, we definitely need to speak to the doctor," he said, folding the paper again.

Question thirty: The greatest sorcerer. First letter. On the eve of Yule, Svasi the dwarf came to King Harald Fairhair and, using sorcery, turned his mind to a Finnish woman by the name of Snæfrid. Harald married her and loved her to distraction, blinded by Svasi's spell, which made her seem like the sweetest woman in the world. They had a son together. When Snæfrid died, a veil made by Svasi was draped over her. It possessed such a powerful spell that King Harald found her corpse so bright and vibrant that he refused to bury her and sat by her side for three winters. Then a wise man suggested the veil should be removed from her body and it was done. The body was rotten and gave off a foul smell. Following this, King Harald was so angry about the spell and all the sorcery that he banned the practice of all magic in his kingdom. The answer is "Svasi," and the first letter is s.

CHAPTER 47

After lunch, Högni was sent down to the doctor's house to summon Jóhanna to an interview. It was still raining and cold. Högni walked swiftly against the wind, tightly clutching the collar of his jacket under his chin. In less than twenty-four hours, everything seemed to have taken a turn for the worse in Flatey, including the weather. And instead of attending to their seal nets and picking eiderdown, farmers sat at home and waited for the inspectors to track down the monster who had started to kill people.

Högni knocked many times on the doctor's hall door and, when no one answered, opened it and stepped into a little hallway. The islanders were not in the habit of locking their houses on Flatey, and it was all right to pop one's head through the door if the matter was urgent.

"Hello?" he called out, hearing nothing but the echo of his own voice in the small, dark hallway in reply. He could smell odors from the infirmary and pharmacy. All kinds of peculiar scents combined to produce that special mysterious hospital aroma that could feel both menacing and comforting, depending on the circumstances.

Högni penetrated deeper inside and saw a patient's room to his right in which there was a hospital bed containing a corpse veiled under a white sheet. Björn Snorri Thorvald was lying there, waiting for his removal and final farewell to the house. A flame glowed on a candlestick by the side of the bed.

Jóhanna wouldn't have left the house like this, Högni thought to himself. *She must be home.*

"Hello?" he called out louder than before.

This time he heard a door open on the floor above, and Jóhanna appeared on the stairs.

"What is it, Högni? Are you sick?" she asked.

"No, no, no one is sick. But the inspectors from Reykjavik would like to talk to you. They're talking to everyone."

"Yes, I know. Is it my turn then? I won't be a minute."

"I'll wait," said Högni. "We can go together."

Jóhanna vanished for a moment before reappearing at the bottom of the stairs in her coat. She walked over to her father's bed, blew out the candle, and locked the room behind her. In the hallway she grabbed an umbrella off a hook.

"It's not often that you see one of those in Flatey," Högni said as they set off and Jóhanna opened the umbrella.

"No, people around here are so used to having their faces pelted by the rain it doesn't bother them. I'm more delicate," Jóhanna answered. Then they walked in silence.

Högni wasn't sure, but he thought he might have spotted Kjartan's—the magistrate's assistant's—coat in the hallway of the doctor's house.

Question thirty-one: The cause of the death of King Harald Gormsson. Fifth letter. The Jomsvikings saga tells of a man called Pálnatók, who was a Viking, lived in Fjón, and was one of the most powerful men in Denmark, apart from King Harald Gormsson. There were feuds between these leaders, which culminated with Pálnatók coming to a place where the king was resting by a fire in the evening after a battle. The king was stooped over the fire with his chest leaning forward and his ass in the air. Pálnatók heard the king talking, armed his bow with an arrow, and fired. It is said that the arrow shot up straight up the king's ass and out his mouth. He dropped dead, as was to be expected. The cause of his death was the "arrow up his ass," and the fifth letter in the answer is w.

CHAPTER 48

Inspector Thórólfur scrutinized the woman who sat facing him, bolt upright, on the other side of the school desk. She seemed calm and reflective and had been waiting in silence since they had shook hands and sat down. District Officer Grímur awaited further instructions by the door.

"Should we call in more people?" he asked.

Thórólfur shook his head. "No, let's wait a bit. This will be a long interview."

He turned to Jóhanna. "Let's start by talking about Professor Gaston Lund. Do you remember him coming to you last autumn to obtain some seasickness tablets?"

"Yes, I remember that."

"Did he get the tablets?"

"Yes. They're kept in the pharmacy."

"What happened then?"

"He went off to catch his boat."

"Are you sure he caught that boat?"

"No, I don't know anything about that. I didn't follow him."

"Did he stay with you longer than he needed to when he bought the seasickness tablets?"

"Yes, he stayed on a bit with me and my father."

"Why was that?"

"We knew each other from the days when my father and I lived in Copenhagen."

"So it was, in fact, a reunion?"

"Professor Lund and my father were happy to have the opportunity to meet again."

Thórólfur unfolded a sheet of paper on his desk. "As you can appreciate, there are many people working on this investigation. Both in Copenhagen and Reykjavik. They've been talking to people to try and understand what kind of lives Gaston Lund and Bryngeir led. Is there anything in particular you would like to say before we continue with this interview?"

Jóhanna gave Thórólfur a long stare, and then she shook her head with a numb smile. "Let's just assume your colleagues are doing their job right and you, yours and just see what happens."

"Very well, if that's the way you want it." Thórólfur picked up the sheet. "Here's the first telegram with information on this case. We asked people in Copenhagen if they knew of anyone in Iceland who might bear a particular grudge against the professor. People could only think of one name."

"Really, and what name was that?"

"Björn Snorri Thorvald. Isn't that your father's name?"

"Yes."

"Professor Lund, therefore, wasn't exactly welcomed with open arms when he visited your home last autumn?"

"Yes, as a matter of fact he was. My father and Lund were actually very good friends and colleagues at the Arnamagnæan Institute for many years. The friendship then became increasingly strained during the German occupation of Denmark and turned to hostility at the end of the war. But when Professor Lund came into our home by sheer coincidence last autumn, they chatted for a while and were fully reconciled again. I think they both felt better after that."

"Is there someone who can bear witness to what you're saying?"

"No, my father's dead, as you probably know."

"What fueled this hostility in the first place?"

"My father was fired from his post at the Arnamagnæan Institute and he partly blamed the professor for it."

"Why was your father fired?"

"I'm sure your men in Copenhagen will dig up a plausible explanation for that. It only happened fifteen years ago, and somebody should be able to remember the story."

Thórólfur clenched his fists and leaned over the desk. "It would speed up our interview here if you would be willing to collaborate with us," he said.

Jóhanna smiled coldly. "Yes, that's probably true. Maybe I should explain it to you, since I doubt that your men will either have the ability or the will to get to the bottom of what really happened."

Jóhanna told the inspectors how she had been brought up traveling with her father across the Nordic countries and Germany. How her father continued to travel to Germany after Denmark was occupied, and how he stirred up animosity among his colleagues at the Arnamagnæan Institute and the Royal Library. Finally the war ended and the Germans abandoned Copenhagen.

"I accompanied my father to the institute as usual that morning, but just as he was about to enter they blocked him. Then some superior came to tell him that his post had been abolished and that he no longer had access to the manuscript collection. He was given no explanation, and he was escorted out of the building when he started to raise his voice. A number of employees witnessed the scene, including Professor Lund. I don't know how it would have ended if Fridrik Einarsson, his Icelandic friend, hadn't been there to break it up. Fridrik then took us to his home and offered us some refreshments. He could tell my father that his lecture tours around Germany had probably been the cause of this animosity. He suggested we go to Iceland with him and his family a few weeks later and suggested we stay there until the turmoil had blown over."

"Did you move to Iceland then?"

"Yes."

"But did you never go back to Copenhagen?"

"No."

"Why not?"

"My father desperately tried to get his post back from Iceland, but failed. I'd also grown opposed to the idea of moving away from Iceland because I got to know Einar, Fridrik's son, when we stayed with them in Copenhagen and when we traveled on the ship together. He was the first friend of my own age I'd ever had, and he then became my boyfriend. He was a great guy and I couldn't think of leaving him. We were together for the first few years of high school, and then he died in an accident."

Thórólfur scribbled down a note and then asked, "You were called upon to examine the bodily remains of Gaston Lund when he was found and transported here last week, were you not?"

"Yes."

"And you didn't recognize him?"

Jóhanna smiled numbly. "It would be easy for me to say I didn't. No one could doubt me, considering the state of the body. And it would be easier for me if I stuck to that version, but I don't want to lie. I recognized him as soon as I opened the casket."

"Why didn't you say so?"

"I was in such a terrible state of shock. And I thought of my father. The cancer had progressed so far and he only had a few days to live. He wasn't suffering, though, because I'd managed to treat the pain quite effectively. At that moment I couldn't bear the thought of him spending his last hours agonizing over the fate of his friend. So I decided to postpone any revelations, while I was still catching my bearings. It wouldn't really have greatly changed the outcome of the investigation, since the man had been dead for several months anyway. It was just a twenty-four-hour reprieve, and that was all I needed. My father died without ever knowing about this incident."

Lúkas coughed several times to attract Jóhanna's attention. It was his turn now. "That's quite a story," he said, moistening his lips. "But I think the reality is slightly different. What if it went something like this, for example: Lund came to you as a doctor and pharmacist. What kind of initial exchange you had I don't know, but he asked you for some seasick tablets. You gave him some drug and advised him to take one pill straightaway, maybe two. He did as he was told, but soon felt drowsy and then fell asleep. You keep some strong sleeping pills, I take it, don't you? We can easily check that."

Jóhanna looked at him, aghast. "That's correct, there's an ample supply in the pharmacy, but your suggestion is preposterous."

"Well, let's see. Lund is asleep in your living room. Maybe you needed to give him an injection or something to keep him as unconscious as possible? Then you took him out on a boat to the most forsaken island you knew of in Breidafjördur. We know that considerable fuel vanished from one of the boats on the island at that time. You know how to handle a motorboat, don't you? You know I can easily check on this."

"Yes, I can handle a boat all right. But I haven't a clue of where Ketilsey is in the fjord. And I don't have the physical strength to carry a sleeping man on my own, let alone onto a boat and then off it again."

"Perhaps your late father gave you a hand moving him? Maybe he was in better shape last autumn than he was lately. And happy to avenge himself. The man could also have been transported on a handcart. There are several of those on the island."

"This is in very poor taste."

"Yes, well you can't really prettify an atrocity like this. The retribution was clearly meant to be memorable and final. How do you think that man felt when he woke up and realized where he was?"

Jóhanna gave Lúkas a long stare before answering: "How do I think he felt? I'll tell you. For the first few hours he was angry. Then very angry. He yelled and yelled and shouted and shouted. Then he was cold, and when night fell he was scared. Then he got very cold and even more terrified, and he cried. When the sun rose in the morning, he was thirsty and hungry and very tired. He gathered some driftwood and built himself some shelter by placing the wood against a crag. He packed some gravel and seaweed around the sticks and then crawled inside and lay down. Maybe he slept for one or two hours, and then woke up again shivering from the cold. Then it started to rain. He found an old plastic flask drifting on the shore and was able to collect some of the water that was running down the rocks. He drank and drank, but he got badly drenched in the rain. He crawled into the shelter and it didn't rain on him. But he was already wet, and when night fell again, he was colder than ever before. He lay there shivering for many hours until he couldn't take it anymore, and he crawled out and ran to try and get some warmth into his bones. It helped a bit, but it hadn't stopped raining, so he got even wetter and colder. The day after the rain stopped and the sun appeared. He managed to sleep a few hours. Then he went down to the shore in search of something edible. He turned over stones, picked some copepods, and dug up some lugworm. He found shellfish. He shoved it into his mouth and washed it down with the water without chewing. He couldn't bear the thought of biting into those bugs. He arranged the stones in the grass so that they would form a big SOS. Four days later he had a cold, a day after that a bad cough, and then he contracted pneumonia. Then he arranged some little pebbles on a flat rock and tried to write some kind of message. He coughed and coughed until he threw up and developed a high fever. And then he died."

Lúkas was dumbstruck. Eventually it was Thórólfur who asked, "How do you know all this?"

"This isn't something I know," Jóhanna answered, "but I can imagine it, and I can tell you that I've thought about him every single hour since I saw him in that casket, and felt a great deal for him. I've tried to place myself in his footsteps, tried to convince myself that it went swiftly and that the pain wasn't unbearable. But everything you've said here is pure supposition. I'm in no way responsible for this nightmare Gaston Lund got himself into. The events in my house were exactly as I described them to you."

Thórólfur peered at her skeptically. "Yeah sure, give it to me all again then, in every detail."

"Professor Lund knocked on our door and told me what he'd come for. I welcomed him in and immediately recognized him. He obviously didn't recognize me because I had only been a child when I had been with my father in Copenhagen. I was just about to give him his seasickness tablets when he saw my father through the door. It took them both a moment to decide how they were going to take this reunion, but then they embraced and it was all just like the good old days. They had so much to talk about, and time was precious. Lund told my father that he'd been to the library to try and solve the Flatey enigma. He had the answers to all the questions but couldn't test them by getting them to fit with the final key. He couldn't figure out the methodology. My father had spent endless hours at the library poring over the string of letters that constitute the final key. He discovered that if the letters were placed in a certain order, they formed a sentence. If the letters in the answers were placed in the correct order, following the same pattern, they formed the last two lines of the poem and thereby the solution to the whole riddle, the Aenigma Flateyensis. Lund was very taken by all this and decided to go back to the library to test his answers using this method. My father could lend him the key to the library. We could already see the mail boat heading south on its way from Brjánslækur, so he didn't have much time. We never saw him after that, so we presumed he'd caught the boat. I later walked up to the library and it wasn't locked and the key was on the table."

"But he didn't catch the mail boat?" said Thórólfur.

"No, it seems not. He must have run to the library, sat down, and started to arrange the letters. The mail boat was steadily approaching, and he finally didn't dare to wait there any longer. The last thing he did was to write down the key on a piece of paper so that he could continue later. We found that note in his pocket. But that was against the rules of the game."

"So he was doomed to some mishap, according to folk belief," said Thórólfur.

"So they say, but I don't believe in that stuff. In fact, I think it's just a perfectly honorable and innocent game. But when people start connecting it with accidents and deaths, I think that's going too far."

Question thirty-two: Who made Earl Hákon's crotch itch? Third letter. Thorleifur visited the earl in Hladir on Christmas Eve, disguised as a beggar. The earl had him brought before him and asked him for his name. "My name is an unusual one," the man answered. "I'm Nídung, the son of Gjallandi, and I come from Syrgisdalir in cold Sweden. I have traveled widely and visited many chieftains. I've heard a lot about your nobility."

The earl said, "Is there something you excel at, old man, to enable you to mix with chieftains?"

Nídung wanted to recite a poem he had composed to the earl. But as the poem was being recited, the earl was puzzled to feel a terrible itch spread all over his body and particularly around his thighs so that he could barely sit still. He had himself scratched with combs wherever they could reach, and three knots were made in a coarse cloth so that two men could pull it between his thighs. The earl started to take a dislike to the poem. The answer is "Thorleifur Ásgeirsson," and the third letter is o.

Kjartan said, "Here the guest writes 'Nídung.' So the answer is either o *or* d."

CHAPTER 49

The coroner's preliminary report on Bryngeir's body, which had been transported by van from Stykkishólmur earlier that day, was expected in the afternoon. Dagbjartur was sent over to collect the results firsthand because it was sometimes difficult to decipher these documents. If there was something in it that was difficult to understand, it was always best to have it explained on the spot. Sometimes it was possible to get the coroner to talk off the record about certain aspects that he would never have put down on paper except until maybe several weeks into the investigation. There seemed to be little doubt about the cause of the reporter's death, but it needed to be confirmed. Further data might have come to light, such as some indication of the perpetrator's physical strength, or whether he was left- or right-handed, etc.

Dagbjartur met coroner Magnús Hansen in the examination room. Two humanoid shapes covered with sheets lay on separate slabs in the center of the room. Dagbjartur was relieved to see that the examination seemed to be over. He had witnessed plenty of autopsies over the years and never found them enticing. If at all possible, he preferred to avoid being present.

"You're certainly keeping us busy these days," said Magnús. He was a tall man in his sixties, big boned with a big aquiline nose. He made quite an imposing figure as he towered over Dagbjartur in his long white coat, rubber apron, and white hat. A white surgical mask dangled loosely from his throat over his apron. Poised on the tip of his nose were glasses that he never seemed to look through, and he was holding copious sheets of notes in his hands.

Dagbjartur nodded and backed off a step. He was fearfully respectful of Magnús, who was famous for the pleasure he took in winding up investigators he considered to be too cocky.

"Do you have anything for us?" he humbly asked.

Magnús peered at him over his glasses and came to the conclusion that this little soul wasn't worth teasing. "There's not much to say about the first one," he said. "He's too far gone to be able to draw any conclusions about the cause of his death. There's actually little more than a skeleton and shreds of skin around the legs that are held together by the clothing. Some wasted muscle and soft tissue around the bones. Except for the spots the birds got at, of course. There's only bone left there. There's almost nothing left of his internal organs, except for some remains of his heart and his enlarged prostate gland, which tells me little about the cause of his death but the fact that he probably had difficulties urinating. All the bones are intact, so they weren't damaged by any attack. I examined the skull particularly well and saw no sign of any damage to it. There is, therefore, nothing to add to the local doctor's report, which suggests the man died of exposure. The cause of death is therefore most likely to be hypothermia, unless he had some other underlying condition that kicked in once his resistance was weakened."

Magnús stopped talking and peered over his glasses at Dagbjartur again.

"What about the other guy?" Dagbjartur asked, feeling the onus was now on him to say something.

"The other guy is another kettle of fish altogether," said Magnús, perking up. He lifted his papers up to his nose and this time looked through his glasses.

"This is a very interesting case," he said. "I first examined the many wounds on the subject's back."

He read from the sheets: "Paravertebral, contiguous to the spine on both sides, bilateral stab wounds piercing subcutaneous tissues and ribs, from the third to the eleventh rib on the right-hand side and the third to the tenth rib on the left-hand side at the intersection with the columna vertebralis."

"The columna what?" Dagbjartur asked.

"Spinal column."

"Right."

"This was done with two powerful thrusts of a knife on the left side and three on the right side. I'd call these blows more than stabbings, because it takes a lot of power to tear the ribs apart like that. The perpetrator is probably right-handed and used both hands to hold the weapon, which was a very big sharp knife, sword, or even an axe. The lungs were then pulled out through the wounds. There are some scattered shallow fissures on them, probably caused by the friction with the broken ribs. Also fissures on the veins to the lungs for the same reasons."

Magnús stopped talking and continued to read in silence.

"Do you think he died instantly?" Dagbjartur asked.

Magnús peered at him over his glasses. "What do you think?"

"Probably, I would imagine."

"Yes, he probably would have died quickly if he hadn't already been dead for a long time."

"Huh?"

"Anyone with an ounce of brains would have been able to see that on the scene, but I guess brains are in short supply in your department."

Dagbjartur remained silent. He realized Magnús was launching into one of his rants and that it was best to just let it wash over.

"There's no inflammation around the rims of the wounds. Any fool should be able to see that."

"That's true," said Dagbjartur in a total bluff. He couldn't think of any colleague of his who would have been capable of recognizing a clue of that kind.

"The edges of the wounds are a yellowish brown and dry. No bleeding in the adjacent tissue. This is a clear sign that the man was not alive when the wounds were inflicted."

"So how did he die then?" Dagbjartur asked.

"I found a bruise on the back of his head that indicated bleeding in the scalp. This suggested he was subjected to a blow to the head of some kind, which wasn't fatal, however. But he probably passed out. The cause of death was therefore probably drowning."

"Drowning?"

"Yes. Drowning is difficult to diagnose, especially when the lungs have been messed with like they have in this case. But all the symptoms of drowning are there when you look for them." Magnús read: "Foam in the larynx, trachea, and bronchi."

He stopped reading and gazed at Dagbjartur over his glasses. "Those could also be symptoms of heart failure or carbon poisoning, so I had to exclude that using other methods. But then I looked for other symptoms of drowning."

Dagbjartur nodded to show interest.

Magnús continued to read: "Hyper-inflated lungs, hyperinflatio pulmonum, with indentations on the surface, under the ribs, pulmonary edema. Liquid in both pleural cavities, bilateral hydrothoraces. Liquid in the cranial cavities and ethmoidal and sphenoidal sinuses. Blood congestion in the bones around the auditory canal. These aren't all equally reliable indicators, of course, but when you add them all up I'm pretty certain."

Dagbjartur was baffled and, after some thought, asked, "So was the man knocked out first, then drowned, and then carved up?"

"That I don't know. I just got the results of tests that show that the man was very drunk. The ethanol level in his blood was 3.02 per mil and 2.56 in the urine. He could also have fallen and gotten that head wound before he drowned."

Dagbjartur was still ruminating on these results. "Did the man drown at sea?" he asked.

Magnús pondered. "Is that possible?" he asked.

"Yes, probably," Dagbjartur answered. "This happened on a small island surrounded by water."

Magnús turned and took two steps toward one of the slabs. He carefully lifted the sheet off the body's face and beckoned Dagbjartur to approach. The policeman was now seeing Bryngeir for the first time. His white eyebrow was very conspicuous. Magnús stooped over the corpse and examined its eyes. "No, he's unlikely to have drowned at sea," he said. "Salty water is a strong irritant of the mucous membrane of the eyes, so if he had, they'd be redder than that. The man probably drowned in clean freshwater."

Magnús pulled the sheet back over the body and said, "It should be added that the man had a damaged liver and that he would have died within a few years if he hadn't stopped drinking."

"There's just one thing I don't get," said Dagbjartur. "The report that my colleagues who went to the island sent said that the body was covered in blood on the scene. But if he'd been dead when he was carved up, there shouldn't have been any bleeding, isn't that right?"

"Exactly," said Magnús with a tinge of recognition in his voice. "Everything therefore indicates that he died lying on his back and even with his legs in the air. The blood accumulated in the back and the cuts then released it. The arteries were also severed, so one could expect to see a lot of blood on the outside of the body."

"Can you imagine how he might have drowned in such a position?" Dagbjartur asked.

"I don't have any explanation that I could put down on paper with a clear conscience."

"But could you hazard an off-the-record guess?"

Magnús glanced at the detective over his glasses and reflected a moment. Finally, he said, "I once read about a case in a specialized magazine about a man who murdered his three wives at various intervals of a period of some years. He approached them all when they were lying in the bathtub, grabbed them by the calves, and hoisted their legs in the air. That way their heads hit the bottom and they drowned without being able to save themselves. There were no wounds on the body, so it was always considered to be an accident. This happened in three different cities, so no one knew of the previous wife when the next one died. Finally someone recognized a pattern between them and the case was investigated. The police tested the method, so a woman who was a good swimmer was asked to lie in the bathtub and then her legs were hoisted in the same way. The woman almost died in the experiment. Don't quote me on this, but that's what could have happened, and the man could have been lying with his legs in the air like that for quite some time. The bruise on the head could have been caused by the brim of the bathtub."

Question thirty-three: Búi's response to losing his chin. Fifth letter. In the battle between the Jomsvikings and Earl Hákon, Thorkel jumped from his ship on board Búi's with a sword in his hand and cut off Búi's chin and lip, causing a row of his teeth to drop onto the deck. After Bui received the wound, he said, "That Danish woman in Borgundarholm won't be as keen to kiss me now, if I ever get home." Búi then struck Thorkel, striking him in the middle and slicing him in two.

"My father thinks the answer is in the words 'that Danish woman.' The fifth letter is d.*"*

Kjartan looked at the note containing the list of answers and said, "The guest's answer was 'sliced Thorkel in two.'"

"That means there are two possible answers to this question, the letters d *and* e.*"*

CHAPTER 50

Thórólfur took a short break from the questioning when a member of the crew from the coast guard ship appeared with a big envelope, which he handed to him. Jóhanna stood up and stepped outside to breathe in some fresh air. Both inspectors were smoking, and the classroom was getting very stuffy. Grímur stood up from his seat in the school corridor and walked outside with her. Högni had gone over to Gudjón in Rádagerdi to help him build the casket for Björn Snorri.

"Still raining," she said.

Grímur looked at the weather. "Someone once said don't wish for rainfall if you don't like getting your feet wet. The fields were getting pretty dry and the wells were low."

"I still need to learn that all weather serves its purpose," said Jóhanna.

They stood there in silence until Thórólfur came out and told Jóhanna that the interview could resume. She took a deep breath and walked back in.

Thórólfur asked Grímur to look for Kjartan, the magistrate's assistant, and to summon him for the final interview. Then he went back into the classroom and sat opposite Jóhanna.

"We just got a message from Reykjavik," he said. "We sent them a list of all the people who were on the island and compared it with a list of all the names that cropped up in their investigation into Bryngeir down south, and it turns out that your name pops up."

"That's not unlikely."

"When did you first meet Bryngeir?"

"In my second year at high school."

"How did you meet?"

Jóhanna thought a moment and finally said, "I wrote an essay about the Tale of Sarcastic Halli in the *Flatey Book*. I sometimes used the *Flatey Book* as assignment material in high school when I was lazy. I knew the material so well, having listened to my father's countless lectures about it in five different languages over the years, so I could write pretty good essays on the subject quite fast. I got good grades for this assignment, and it appeared in the school magazine. Bryngeir was taking his finals that year and was really into Icelandic philology. He was reading the printed edition of the *Flatey Book* every night at the time and felt the urge to meet me after reading my essay. I wasn't enthusiastic about it because I was engaged to Einar Fridriksson, whom I mentioned earlier. I'd met Einar in Copenhagen when I was fifteen years old and he was seventeen. We were good friends back then and later developed a crush on each other when we got a bit older. His parents were studying and working in Denmark. As I told you, they moved back to Iceland at the same time as my dad and I did. At that time Einar was in his last year at the high school, in the same class as Bryngeir."

"You mentioned he died?"

"Yes, he died in a horrible accident."

"What happened?"

"Einar was invited to join a weird students' cultural club called the Jomsviking Society. It was a semi-secret club for snobby, vain young men. New members were initiated into the society through some ridiculous ritual, and there was a terrible accident at it and Einar died."

"What kind of accident?"

"The initiation involved a reenactment of the execution of the Jomsvikings after their defeat in battle against Earl Hákon. The members acted out the scene from the saga, reciting the dialogue between the Jomsvikings and the earl's men like in a play. The initiate had to kneel under a sword, which was then dropped. Naturally, he was supposed to move his head out of the way at the last second, just like Sveinn Búason did in the story. It was a perfectly harmless game, even though the sword was sharp and heavy. On this occasion, however, they were unusually drunk. Something went wrong, and the sword landed on Einar's head."

"Who was it that swung the sword?" Thórólfur asked.

"Don't you know?"

"Yes, but I want to hear it from you."

Jóhanna stared at the policeman for a long moment without betraying any emotion and then finally said, "It was Kjartan, the magistrate's assistant in Patreksfjördur."

Thórólfur broke into a numb smile. "Yes, it was Kjartan, and he was convicted of manslaughter and spent a few years in prison. It must have been a tough experience for him to meet you here again. The man who killed your boyfriend?"

Jóhanna sank into a long silence.

"Yes, it was difficult, but not in the way you imagine," she finally said.

"In what way then?"

"It's a long story."

"I love long stories."

"Very well then, you'll get a long story. I was devastated when Einar died. He was a particularly bright and good young man. I'm not just saying that because of our teenage romance. Now that I'm an adult I can still recall our time together and our nightlong conversations. I've missed him every day since I lost him."

Jóhanna fell into a long silence and didn't continue with her story again until Thórólfur signaled her to do so with a faint nod.

"Anyway, there was a funeral and a police investigation and finally a court case, and Kjartan was convicted. It gave me some outlet to be able to hate him, and I was pleased when he got his prison sentence. Of course, my studies went down the drain during that period, but I still managed to drag myself to school most days. It was then that Bryngeir took it upon himself to console me. I found him to be more considerate than I'd initially expected, and I was vulnerable to someone who seemed to really care for me. I got little support from my father at that time. The only job he could get was teaching in a secondary school, which of course was a total waste of his education and talents, so he got depressed and drank a lot. Bryngeir passed his school exams and started studying literature at university in the fall. I continued in the high school and we became an item that winter. Then we rented a small basement apartment in the west of Reykjavik and started living together. It lasted for four years and almost finished me off before it ended."

"How's that?" Thórólfur asked.

"After I moved in with Bryngeir, he soon started to control my life every minute of the day. I had to be at school during school hours and focus on nothing else but my homework and domestic chores when he didn't need me for sex or whatever else popped into his mind. I wasn't allowed to meet anyone else unless he was present. I wasn't allowed to hold any opinions unless he approved them. I couldn't make any decision regarding my life without him having the last word on it. When I got my high school exams, he decided I should study medicine because I was good at studying and it would be a good source of income for the home once I'd become a brain surgeon. He never laid a finger on me, but he could play me like a musical instrument with his words. With just a few sentences he could make me feel like I was the best thing that had ever happened to him, and then with a few extra words he sent me crashing into hell again. The latter tended to be the norm, because he drank a lot, made a mess of our finances, and blamed me for every misfortune. All of a sudden the strings of the instrument snapped, and I had a nervous breakdown in the middle of a class in my second year at med school. I was taken to hospital and put into the psychiatric ward. An unusually perceptive psychologist realized what the situation was in our very first session and made me realize the relationship was life-threatening. I went straight home to Dad from the hospital. He shook himself out of his self-pity and started to take care of me. Bryngeir tried everything to win me back again, but I had regained my senses after four years of unconsciousness. Finally, after many weeks, he seemed to accept that our relationship was over and allowed me into the house to collect my clothes and textbooks. Naturally, I was slightly wary of him because he had threatened me with all kinds of awful things, but I was sure he wouldn't lay a finger on me and thought that I was by now immune to him hurting me with his words, after my therapy with the psychologist. I therefore went to the meeting on my own. That was a big mistake."

Jóhanna picked up a glass of water, lifted it to her lips, and held it there for a long moment without drinking. Finally, she took a small sip and carefully put the glass down again.

"When I'd finished packing my things into the case and was on my way out, Bryngeir asked me to hang on a moment and talk to him. He said he wanted to tell me about when he saw me for the first time. He'd read my article about the ambiguous Sarcastic Halli in the school magazine, as I've already mentioned. It was some kind of sexual turn-on for him to think that an eighteen-year-old high school girl could have written a text like that. He tracked me down at the school and decided on first sight that I had to be his. The fact that I had a boyfriend spoiled his plans a bit, but he found a way around it. He saw to it that Einar was invited to join the Jomsviking Society, and when the initiation meeting came up, he gave out loads of alcohol. So the kids were all extremely drunk by the time it was Einar's turn to kneel under the sword. Bryngeir waited, prepared, behind his back, and just as Einar was about to dodge the swing of Kjartan's sword, as was the tradition, Bryngeir kneed him and pushed him back under the blow. Einar died instantly, and the second half of the plan with me was easy once the boyfriend was no longer in the way. This is something Bryngeir just wanted to tell me for the fun of it, as a farewell gift, and even though I thought I was ready for anything, I couldn't handle it. I tried going to the police, but I was just being hysterical in their opinion, and Bryngeir convinced them that I was just trying to wreak revenge on him for having broken up our relationship. It was his word against mine, and he was always very persuasive with everyone he was talking to. I should probably count myself lucky that I wasn't charged and convicted for perjury. I can't describe how I felt after that. Every single memory of our four-year relationship felt like a hideous rape. I went back to the psychologist again, and through years of therapy, he managed to teach me a way to free myself of the torment. The wound is obviously still there, but I don't allow it to take a grip on me anymore and ruin my life."

Jóhanna sank into a brief silence, took another sip of water, and then continued without looking at the policemen: "The strange thing is that I continued studying medicine. Bryngeir was right about one thing. It was easy for me to learn this profession, and one of the ways I found for clearing my mind was to totally immerse myself in my studies. But I was no longer studying to be a brain surgeon and studied psychiatry instead."

Jóhanna was quiet again and stooped over the table. Finally she continued: "A few years after I broke up with Bryngeir, my father applied for a post at the university. When they decided to give him the job and notified him, the devil spotted yet one more opportunity. Bryngeir had been kicked out of university early on and fancied himself as some kind of journalist. I had, of course, told him everything about my father when we lived together, and he wrote a very twisted article about Dad's abrupt departure from the Arnamagnæan Institute. It was then felt that it was undesirable for an old Nazi sympathizer to be teaching at the university, and the offer of the post was withdrawn. My father saw the last opportunity of a lifetime vanish into thin air. He drank relentlessly for half a year and eventually ended up in an asylum for the chronically medically ill."

Jóhanna signaled that her story was over.

"But what's a psychiatrist doing working as a local doctor all the way out here?" Lúkas asked.

"By the time I'd finished my postgrad, my father had been diagnosed with incurable cancer. I wanted to nurse him myself, but also had to work to cover our living expenses. I therefore decided to apply for the first easygoing local doctor post that became available. By sheer coincidence it happened to be here in Flatey, and that suited us down to the ground. I'd never been here before and never imagined that this place would somehow be connected to my life through the *Flatey Book*. We've been comfortable here. I'm good at my job, and I was able to give my father the medication that kept him in a reasonable mental balance. As the cancer spread, he also had to follow a precise palliative treatment. He welcomed death in the end."

"How did you react when you met Bryngeir here?"

"I didn't meet him and had no idea that he was here until District Officer Grímur asked me to come to the churchyard to examine the body. I was quite surprised."

"Quite surprised?"

"Yes. Bryngeir had always been fascinated by this ancient tradition of carving blood eagles on the backs of one's enemies. I thought it was an odd coincidence to see him in that state."

"So you were familiar with wounds of this kind?"

"I'd never seen them before, but the descriptions in the *Flatey Book* stood out in my memory. It was pretty clear what had happened."

"A witness claims that Bryngeir intended to visit you the night before he was murdered."

"He didn't. I actually wasn't at home, so I don't know if he tried to get into the house."

"Where were you that night?"

"I went out for a walk and went to the library to read."

"Did you meet anyone there?"

"Kjartan came by."

"How long were you in there?"

"Quite a long time. Until the early hours of the morning, actually."

"That long? What were you both doing?"

"I told Kjartan about the *Flatey Book*."

Grímur stuck his head into the classroom.

"Sorry, Thórólfur, but I can't find the magistrate's envoy."

"You can't find the magistrate's envoy?" Thórólfur snapped in a temper.

"No, he seems to have vanished," Grímur answered, bewildered. "I've been to most of the houses and sent messages to the others."

"Did you go into the doctor's house?" Thórólfur asked.

"Yes, but there was no one there."

Thórólfur turned to Jóhanna. "Do you know anything about Kjartan?"

"Yes, he visited me this morning and I invited him to take a hot bath. There's a bathtub in the house, the only one on the island. He then had a lie-down. This whole case has become a bit too much for him and he had problems sleeping. He managed to fall asleep, and he was still asleep when Högni collected me earlier. I couldn't bring myself to wake him up. He must have woken up and gone somewhere."

Thórólfur eyed her with suspicion. "I hope you haven't done anything to him."

She suddenly stood up. "Is this how this is going to continue? Do you think I tied him to a pole, maybe, and ripped out his intestines or something like that?"

She marched to the door.

Thórólfur signaled Lúkas to follow her and then looked at Grímur. "What did she mean?"

Grímur shrugged. "She might be referring to the killing of Ásbjörn Prúdi."

"The killing of who?"

"It's in the *Flatey Book*."

"That bloody book again? How is this murder described?"

Grímur thought about it. "I don't know the whole book off by heart like my friend Sigurbjörn does, but let me see. I browsed through it not so long ago. Ásbjörn, Virfill's good son, ended up in the hands of Brúsi the giant. Brúsi opened Ásbjörn's belly, grabbed his intestines, and tied them to an iron pole. Then he led Ásbjörn in circles around the pole until all his guts were wrapped around it. While this was going on, Ásbjörn recited many long poems. Finally he died with great honor and valiance. Later Ormur Stórólfsson killed Brúsi the giant and carved a blood eagle on his back, but you know all about that now."

Grímur ended his speech and shrugged again. Thórólfur shook his head. "I just hope the magistrate's envoy still has all his intestines inside him."

Question thirty-four: The most mutilated but healed. Second letter. Following the death of holy King Ólaf, there were many stories of miracles that were attributed to him being invoked, and the priests who wrote the Flatey Book *conscientiously collected them. The most mutilated man was Richard the priest. Einar and his servant broke his legs and dragged him into the woods. Then they wrapped some rope around his head and tightly tied his head and torso to a board. Einar then took a wedge and placed it on the priest's eye, and the servant who stood beside him struck upon it with an axe, causing the eye to fly out of its socket and land on the board. He then placed a pin on the other eye and struck it so that the wedge sprang off the eyeballs and tore the eyelid loose. They then opened his mouth, grabbed his tongue, and sliced it off, and then untied his hands and head. As soon as the priest regained consciousness, he slipped the eyeballs back into their place under the eyelids and pressed them with both hands as hard as he could. The men then asked the priest if he could talk. The priest made a noise and attempted to speak. Then Einar said to his brother, "If he recovers and the stump of his tongue starts to grow, I'm afraid he will get his speech back again." Thereupon they seized the stump with a pair of tongs, drew it out, cut it twice, and the third time to the very roots, and left him lying there half dead. It had taken a lot of power to heal those wounds, but thanks to the intercession of the good King Ólaf, the priest was restored to full health, even though he had been so badly mutilated. The answer is "Richard the priest," and the second letter is* i.

CHAPTER 51

At four o'clock that afternoon, Gudjón and Högni finished making a casket for Björn Snorri Thorvald. It lay on two trestles in the small workshop behind the Radagerdi farm, ready to be transported to the doctor's house. The two carpenters scrutinized their work as they brushed the sawdust and shavings off their clothing. Högni snorted some snuff, and Gudjón lit a cigarette. It was a fairly rudimentary casket made of smoothened unpainted pine planks with a brass cross on the lid, precisely as the deceased had prescribed. Björn Snorri had talked it over with Gudjón several months earlier and, in fact, had asked him to get working on it straightaway, but Gudjón wouldn't hear of it. He could make a decent casket for his neighbor if it was needed, but it would be out of the question to start making it before the person in question was definitely dead. Anything else would have been inappropriate and disrespectful to the Lord.

It was still raining, but it was warm when Thormódur Krákur arrived in his Sunday attire, towing his handcart. The three men carried the casket out of the workshop and placed it on the cart. Then they walked across the island pulling the cart behind them.

Inspector Lúkas and a crew member from the ship stood outside the doctor's house.

"Jóhanna is obviously under house arrest," Högni whispered heavyheartedly.

They carried the casket into the house and all the way into the living room where Björn Snorri's corpse had been laid out on the bed, newly washed and dressed in a white tunic. A white linen ribbon had been wrapped around his head to lock his jaw into place and keep his mouth closed. Three white candles flickered on a bedside table. Jóhanna Thorvald and Reverend Hannes were in the room as they arrived, and received them.

The casket was placed on the floor by the side of the body, and Jóhanna placed a white quilt inside it and a pillow at the head. The three men then helped to lift the twisted body and place it in the casket.

Reverend Hannes stepped forward and said a farewell prayer to the house, after which the gathering recited an "Our Father" and sang a short psalm. Finally, they all drew a cross over the body, the quilt was drawn over the deceased's face, and the lid was placed on the casket. Gudjón took a hammer and firmly sealed the lid with some nails.

Högni and Gudjón carried the casket between them out of the house and placed it on the cart. Thormódur Krákur lifted the handles of the cart and started to pull it away. Jóhanna and Reverend Hannes walked behind him, followed by Högni and Gudjón and finally, at a considerable distance, Lúkas, the police inspector, and his assistant from the coast guard ship.

As they walked, Högni pondered the deceased. He and his daughter had lived in the house for about two years. Last year Björn Snorri had been mobile enough to take walks around the island and speak to people. Everyone knew he had come to Flatey to die, and that made some of the islanders slightly awkward with him. But everyone could see that he was a very intelligent and educated man with an insatiable eagerness for knowledge. He asked people exhaustive questions about their professions and deeds and kept notes in a little diary. Eventually, though, he came out less and less, until finally he just stayed indoors, confined to his medical bed. From then on it was the islanders who visited him at the doctor's house and told him stories. Mostly they were tales about accidents and losses at sea from the past decades and centuries, which had been preserved in people's memories, and Björn Snorri lapped it all up with a smile on his lips and a grateful glow in his eyes. And now Högni started to wonder if these stories could be found in writing somewhere. Some of these incidents were probably recorded in the annals, but who knew if any written record had been kept of the actual stories that lay behind them and had been orally passed down from generation to generation. Perhaps this invaluable knowledge was dying with every individual who passed away on the islands, including Björn Snorri himself. He had undoubtedly written countless pieces about his area of research, but didn't the main bulk of knowledge always go unrecorded? Or was it just that the dead hadn't disappeared, but simply moved on, slightly ahead of us? Would he himself one day get a chance to learn something from Björn Snorri in some other place?

They arrived at the church, and Högni and Gudjón lifted the casket as Thormódur Krákur opened the door. They carried the coffin inside and placed it on trestles in the middle of the floor. Then they walked outside again.

Jóhanna said good-bye and immediately headed back to her house, accompanied by Inspector Lúkas and his assistant, while the others lingered in front of the church, enjoying the mild weather and the view.

"Is that what I think it is? Do I see a man waving from the islet of Kerlingarhólmur?" said Thormódur Krákur, peering south across the strait where it was now high tide. Högni looked in the direction the deacon was pointing and saw a man standing on the edge of the shore waving with both hands.

"That wouldn't be the magistrate's envoy roaming on the skerry?" Högni asked. "They were looking for him earlier today."

Gudjón grinned. "He's worse than the sheep. What's he doing roaming over there?"

"I'll go get him," said Högni. "Sigurbjörn's old boat is down there on the shore. You can give me a hand pushing her into the sea."

Question thirty-five: The price of the king's axe. Sixth letter. The king held an axe that was inlaid in gold and had a shaft that was enveloped in silver with a large silver band embedded with a precious stone. Halli kept staring at the axe. The king noticed this immediately and asked Halli if he liked it. He answered that he did.

"Have you ever seen a finer axe?"

"I don't think so," said Halli.

"Would you submit yourself to sodomy for this axe?" asked the king.

"No," said Halli, "but I can understand why you want to sell it for the same price that you paid for it."

"So it shall be, Halli," said the king. "Take it and make the best use of it; it was given to me as a gift and therefore I shall give it you." Halli thanked the king.

The answer is "sodomy," and the sixth letter is y.

CHAPTER 52

Högni, Gudjón, and Thormódur Krákur found the little boat lying overturned on a patch of grass above the shore to the south of the church. Carefully turning it over, they discovered two oars underneath it. Grabbing the boat, the men then gently eased it into the sea and pushed it. Högni climbed on board with the oars and ensured that the boat was not leaking. Then he rowed vigorously across the strait, while his companions remained on the shore.

A shamefaced young man stood on a rock at sea level as Högni approached. Kjartan stepped onto the boat when Högni reached him, and they immediately turned back.

"Thank you for fetching me. I'm so lucky you spotted me out here," said Kjartan.

"You probably would have survived," Högni answered, unable to suppress a smile. "The tide will be going down again pretty soon, so you could have walked back the same way you came."

"You're probably right. I was a bit taken aback when I realized how high the tide had grown in the strait. The strip was almost dry when I walked out there. I just wanted to take a look at the birdlife. Then, when I was going to turn back, I saw the tide was coming in and I didn't have the guts to waddle across. I didn't know how deep it was."

"You did the right thing to wait," Högni answered. "There's quicksand around here and some steep drops on the way."

"I just hope no one was starting to worry about me."

"The police were asking for you. They'll certainly be relieved to see you again."

Question thirty-six: Killed by a serpent. First letter. King Ólaf Tryggvason went with his men to Raud the Strong's farm and broke in. Raud was seized and tied up, and his men were killed or arrested. The king offered to have Raud baptized, but Raud answered that he would never believe in Christ and uttered many blasphemies. Raud was then tied to an iron bar and a round pin of wood was shoved between his teeth to force his mouth open. The king then ordered a snake to be placed in Raud's mouth, but the snake refused to enter it. A red-hot iron was then used to force the serpent in. The snake slid into Raud's mouth and down his throat to his heart and then gnawed its way out his left side. Raud then died. The answer is "Raud," and the first letter is r.

CHAPTER 53

District Officer Grímur and Inspector Thórólfur were alone in the school when Kjartan arrived, breathless after rushing there. Högni came in right behind him.

"I'm sorry," said Kjartan. "I seem to have gotten lost."

Grímur appeared to be relieved to see him again in one piece, but Thórólfur had a sullen air.

"Högni's promised to call off the search," Kjartan continued.

"Where've you been all day?" Thórólfur asked.

"When I left here," Kjartan answered, "I got my bag and walked across the island to visit Jóhanna, the doctor. She invited me to take a bath in her house. After that I lay down for a bit and I must have fallen fast asleep, because when I woke up she was gone. I found it a bit uncomfortable lying there in a deserted house with the corpse of an old man, so I went out for a walk on the southern shore just to look at the birds and think. I walked quite far out from the island and didn't think of the rising tide."

Thórólfur shook his head with a skeptical air. "What was it that you needed so badly to think about?" he asked.

"I needed to catch my bearings a bit."

"Have you gone astray?"

"No, but a lot has happened over the past days, and I'm not used to dealing with this kind of stress. I normally try to avoid situations I can't mentally handle. It takes very little to knock me out of kilter, and then I get depressed."

Thórólfur waited a moment before asking, "Is there anything special you'd like to tell me before I put my first questions to you?"

"Anything special?"

"Yeah. Something that you feel could clarify this case?"

"No. I don't think so."

"Very well. We've been informed that you knew the late Bryngeir and, moreover, that you served a prison sentence for manslaughter."

Kjartan looked apologetically at Grímur before answering. "Yes. Both of those assertions are correct. I knew Bryngeir, and I did time in prison. But I still maintain that the killing was an accident."

"Bryngeir was connected to this manslaughter case," said Thórólfur.

"Yes."

"Tell me about that."

"Do you want to hear the whole story from the beginning?"

"Yes."

"It's a long story."

"I've heard many long stories today, so one more won't make a difference."

Kjartan loosened his collar. "Very well then. The story starts when I was in my final year at high school and I joined a club called the Jomsviking Society."

"Jomsviking Society? Who are they?" Thórólfur asked.

"The Jomsvikings were a pack of young swashbucklers from the ancient town of Jómsborg at the end of the tenth century. Their story ended when they were defeated in a battle against Earl Hákon in Norway."

"Tell me about this club."

"There were about thirty boys in it, who were either finishing high school or in their first or second year at university. A bunch of lively, intelligent young men, most of them from well-off families. I was an exception, since I had very little money and was withdrawn."

"What was the purpose of this club?"

"Officially, it was meant to be a reading or cultural club, but at the same time it was a semi-secret society. It had been running for several decades. New members were selected from pupils in their final years, and normally people left the club when they were well into their university studies. There was, therefore, a constant turnover of fresh blood in the club. When I joined they held meetings once a month, often in little halls or on the premises of a company that the father of one of the members managed. For the fun of it, we'd have readings of racy limericks that members had dug up or composed themselves. Sometimes up-and-coming authors were asked to read something or deliver a lecture. We held debates, and on some occasions music or even plays were performed. There was a touch of cultural snobbery about it all. There was a fair bit of drinking involved, too, and sometimes the gatherings degenerated into semi riots as the evening progressed."

"What drew you to this club?"

"Vanity."

"Oh?"

"I was pretty well read in various foreign authors. My uncle, who was a sailor, used to bring me back quite a few books from abroad, which I loosely translated for the meetings. I was therefore able to supply some pretty good reading material. I thought it would give me some kudos when I was invited to join, and I enjoyed having a drink or two."

"What happened then?"

"When new members were taken in, they had to kneel under the sword, as they called it. The club owned an old Viking-style sword. It was a good replica they had gotten some skilled blacksmith to make for them many decades earlier. And the sword was both heavy and sharp. One of the members held the sword up in the air over the block, and the new member was supposed to kneel under it. Part of the Jomsviking saga was read out during the ceremony, and at some point in the text, the sword would be swung down. The patter went something like this in the end: 'A hirdman took hold of the hair and twisted it round his hands and held Sveinn's head on the block with both hands, as Thorkell prepared to slam down his sword.' That was the cue, when the words 'slam down his sword' were spoken, the sword was supposed to be swung. The new member could always see the executioner's shadow and get his head out of the way in time. The longer you could hold your head on the block for before the sword dropped, the braver you were considered to be. In the story the hirdman's hands are cut off when Sveinn pulls his head off the block, so everyone at the meeting would shout out in unison, 'Whose hands are in my hair?' and that was it, the new member had been initiated."

"Why were you holding the sword on this occasion?"

"There was a certain prestige to it. When you'd been a member of the society for a while and created a niche for yourself, then you got to draw the sword once and that elevated you to a higher status. Bryngeir suggested I be given the role that night."

"But there was an accident?"

"Yes, there was an accident—or it looked like an accident. I swung the sword down on cue and could see that Einar had pulled his head away from the block under me. But then it was like he'd hit a wall because he bounced right back just as the sword was coming down. It struck him in the back of the head and he died instantly."

"It must have been a shock for you?"

"Yes, of course, horrific. When the sword hit the obstacle, it seemed hard at first, the way you'd expect the block to be, but then it was strangely soft. When I realized what had happened it was as if I'd been hit by a train, and I collapsed with my head hitting the edge of a table."

Kjartan lifted his hand and stroked the scar on his forehead.

"So it was an accident, then, or what?"

"Yes, of course, a horrendous accident. But then someone said I'd swung the sword too soon. And instead of backing me in the police investigation, my companions testified that I had swung the sword faster and harder than normal. They said that this was normally a harmless prank that put no one in danger."

"Was that true?"

"No, it was part of the ritual to ensure that the sword remained firmly planted in the block after the strike."

"According to my information, you blamed Bryngeir for the accident."

"Yes. When I was over the initial shock a few days later, I was able to recall the scene. I'm sure that Bryngeir was standing behind Einar and kicked him back onto the block."

"Weren't you believed?"

"No, and someone even testified that Bryngeir wasn't in the room. It was used against me to give me a heavier sentence when the verdict was reached. They said I was making false accusations. I spent five years in jail, as you undoubtedly know."

Thórólfur nodded. "So you just came here and took the law into your own hands!"

Kjartan shook his head. "I never asked to come here. I expected to be doing other things when I accepted this summer job."

"How did you react when you met Bryngeir here?"

"I didn't know who the reporter was until I saw Bryngeir dead in the churchyard. It was a terrible shock for me."

"Where were you on Sunday evening?"

"I went for a walk across the island and popped into the library on the way back. Doctor Jóhanna was there."

"Did you know that she'd been the late Einar's girlfriend?"

"I didn't know that then, but I do now."

"How did you first find out?"

"She told me late that night after a long conversation."

"Did she tell you that Bryngeir had confessed to her that he had caused Einar's death?"

"Yes."

"How did you respond to that?"

"I was greatly relieved to hear it."

"Oh?"

"Yes. Even though I believed the accident hadn't been my fault, it was good to hear it confirmed. Not that it could take away all those years of hell I had to go through."

"You perhaps wanted to reap vengeance on Bryngeir?"

"I've been struggling to find peace with myself and start a new life. Bryngeir wasn't supposed to come into the picture."

"But he did come into the picture?"

"Yes. He was like a resuscitated ghost there in the churchyard. I thought I'd had a nervous breakdown when I saw him there yesterday morning."

"Do you feel better today?"

"Yes. I went to Jóhanna yesterday afternoon to ask her for something to help me. She gave me some tranquilizers, and I managed to recover."

"It was pretty handy finding a shrink on the island you could go to." That last comment came from Lúkas, who had just entered the room and joined in the interview. "But I find these coincidences a bit odd," he continued. "A notorious boozehound of a hack arrives here from Reykjavik. Within twenty-four hours he's pranced all over the island, creating a racket and offending people left, right, and center, and yet you two innocent lambs hadn't the faintest idea that he was here! Isn't that just a little bit too incredible?"

"I knew about the reporter, but I didn't know who he was. I later came to the conclusion that he'd tried to avoid me and Jóhanna. I guess that's hardly surprising."

"Yeah, sure, that's what he did, but then he decided to pop in to see Jóhanna on Sunday night," said Lúkas.

A crew member from the coast guard ship stuck his head through the door and handed Thórólfur an envelope.

"We were both in the library that night," Kjartan continued. "So he must have found the door locked when he arrived."

"But what if he bumped into the two of you together?" said Lúkas. "With no other witnesses around, and you with a newly purchased penknife in your hands. Wouldn't it have been tempting to even the score with that monster?"

Kjartan gave a start and groped his trouser pockets.

"You did buy a penknife in the store, didn't you?"

"Yes, but I think I've lost it. There's a hole in my pocket."

"Right. But I think the story went like this: Bryngeir went to see Jóhanna. He entered the doctor's house, which was unlocked, and poked around when no one answered. Jóhanna was, yes, in the library chatting to you. Being the scoundrel that he was, Bryngeir, of course, took the opportunity to look around the doctor's house, even though there was a dead body lying in there. And what do you know? He found Professor Gaston Lund's papers, which Jóhanna had put aside last fall, after she'd taken the sleeping old man to Ketilsey. Something must have put Bryngeir on the right track in the Lund case, according to what witnesses say. Anyway. Then Bryngeir staggers outside and decides to walk across the churchyard when who should he meet in the middle of it but you and Jóhanna. And you hadn't lost your penknife then yet, had you? So after saying good evening to him, you both pin the punk to the ground with his face pressed into the ground to smother his cries and start carving up his back and pulling his lungs out through the cuts. Or was it maybe the doctor who did that bit? Anyway, when you were done you draped him over a tombstone and went home to celebrate a job well done. You just didn't have the good sense to look through his pockets, where you would have found the papers he'd stolen a few moments earlier."

Kjartan answered none of this, but stuck his hand into his pocket and pulled out a bottle of pills.

"What's that?" Thórólfur asked.

"This is the medication I got from Jóhanna. I think I need one. These are outrageous accusations."

Thórólfur snatched the bottle of pills from him, read the label, and stuck it into his pocket.

"Not just yet. My colleague's hypothesis is not improbable, but it needs to be completed somehow. I've just received the preliminary postmortem report, according to which Bryngeir drowned and had been dead for a long time before he was carved up."

This time it was Lúkas's turn to be baffled. "Drowned at sea?" he asked.

"No, in freshwater," Thórólfur answered.

"In freshwater? But are there any ponds or streams on this island?" Lúkas was addressing his question to District Officer Grímur.

"No, just the swamp, but that's almost completely dry after the long spell of warm weather we've had," Grímur answered.

Thórólfur read the sheet again and then looked at Kjartan. "Our colleague in Reykjavik seems to think it's possible that Bryngeir drowned in a bathtub, and there's one of those in the doctor's house, I believe. Maybe the man was dragged into the bath before he was carved up. So you must have found him in the doctor's house and taken care of him there. Isn't that possible?"

Kjartan seemed to have stopped listening, but his shoulders were trembling. Thórólfur pulled the bottle of pills out of his pocket and slammed it on the table in front of him.

"Here, take your pills and tell us the truth!"

Kjartan looked at Grímur. "Could I have a glass of water?"

Grímur rushed into the corridor and swiftly returned with a cup full of water.

Kjartan slipped two pills into his mouth and took a sip. Finally he said, "There is just no other truth to tell you."

Thórólfur shook his head. "We've checked everyone's movements here on Sunday night and the early hours of Monday morning. There was nothing unusual. You and Jóhanna, on the other hand, were up and about into the early hours and had every motive to want to see the reporter dead. You're going to have to tell me a hell of a lot more if you want me to start believing you."

"I didn't go near Bryngeir," Kjartan repeated.

"Go over the evening for me," said Thórólfur.

"Jóhanna and I were at the library until the early hours of the morning, and then I walked her home and left her outside her house. It had started to rain, so I rushed home to the district officer's house and crept up to my bedroom in the loft. I didn't know anything about Bryngeir before Grímur sent for me in the morning." Kjartan wiped the sweat off his brow with the palm of his hand.

"What the hell were you doing in the library all night?" Thórólfur asked.

"Jóhanna was telling me about the *Flatey Book*."

"Is that something you could talk about all night?"

"Yes."

"What time was it when you went to bed?"

"I wasn't keeping track of time, but it was daylight. I would guess six in the morning."

Thórólfur pondered a moment and then said, "You'll accompany us on board the ship. There's a cabin reserved for you there. Jóhanna will be kept under observation at the doctor's house. Both of you will be asked to write a full account of every single moment of that night. It'll be interesting to see how your details match up."

Question thirty-seven: The place where a man's laughter is located. First letter. A man's rage is located in his gall, life in his heart, memory in his brain, ambition in his lungs, laughter in his spleen, and desire in his liver. The answer is "spleen," and the first letter is s.

CHAPTER 54

A cloud of gloom hung over the district officer's dining table that night. Grímur, Högni, and Ingibjörg sat in the kitchen eating fried kittiwake eggs, puffin breast, and sugar-browned potatoes. There was plenty of food to go around because Ingibjörg had expected both policemen and Kjartan to join them for dinner. But they were on board the coast guard ship and would be there all evening. Probably overnight, too. Björn Snorri Thorvald's funeral was scheduled for eleven the next morning, after which the coast guard ship was supposed to depart in the afternoon. Jóhanna and Kjartan were to go with them for further questioning. The detectives were now convinced that they were responsible for Bryngeir's death and that Jóhanna had also played some role in Professor Lund's fate.

"There's no way that Kjartan and Jóhanna had anything to do with this nonsense," Ingibjörg said decisively. "I know people, and I can see it in their eyes when they're speaking the truth."

Grímur looked bewildered. "It is very strange, though. All the islanders have been able to account for their movements that night. And they were the only two people who were up. Not that

I bring myself to believe that there's anything bad about Jóhanna. And Kjartan seems like such a decent guy, too, even if he had that stroke of bad luck in his youth."

Högni's mouth was full of food. He liked it.

"Mmm, maybe they found him dead and just did those things to mock him," he said.

"No, no, no," said Ingibjörg. "Not my Jóhanna."

They finished the meal and drank coffee afterwards. The sky had cleared, and the evening sun now appeared in the west. Grímur felt somehow restless. "Come on a walk with me," he finally said to Högni. "I find it easier to think in the evening air. We can collect the cattle for the night while we're at it."

The men stepped outside and walked over the eastern slope. Thormódur Krákur was carrying water to his shed. He didn't answer when they said good evening to them and just vanished behind the shed door with his buckets of water.

"Everyone seems to be in a somber mood this evening," said Grímur. He looked around. "This is where Bryngeir was last seen alive," he said, puzzled. "And it's from here that he was going to walk across the island to visit Jóhanna. What route could he have taken?"

"Well," Högni answered, "he must have taken the road and followed it down. I walked that way with Inspector Lúkas today. He was timing it and measuring the distance. It's six hundred strides."

One of Thormódur Krákur's cows bellowed loudly from within the shed.

"Yes, that's a short walk," Grímur said. "But what did the man do when he realized Doctor Jóhanna wasn't in her house?"

Högni thought about it. "Krákur says he was trying to get someone to take him to Stykkishólmur."

"But none of the boat owners could remember him asking to be taken over that night."

Högni thought again. "Maybe he went out to Ystakot and asked Valdi. He'd done it once before," he said.

Grímur started walking. "But don't forget the poor man drowned before he was carved," he said. "In unsalted water. There isn't a single drop of water in the rocks around Ystakot."

"No, except in the barrel in Valdi's yard."

"Do you think Valdi might have dragged the rascal by the scruff of the neck and drowned him in the barrel of water like a kitten?"

"Nah." Högni was baffled. "But Valdi can be hot tempered."

"And why should he have dragged the body to the churchyard?"

"I don't know," Högni answered, feeling uneasy about taking on the role of the accuser in this reasoning.

"Let's walk across the island and see what the Ystakot clan have to say for themselves this evening," said Grímur. They walked down the road below the church in silence, each lost in his own thoughts. No lights shone in the doctor's house, but when they reached the pier they saw the coast guard ship was lit up.

"Those Reykjavik people obviously don't go to bed early," said Grímur, but then he suddenly halted when he saw that the Ystakot boat wasn't anchored in its place at the pier.

"Damn, they're out at sea," he said. "We can't talk to them then."

Högni looked at the coast guard ship. "Should we step on board and talk to the police about Valdi?" he asked hesitantly.

Grímur thought it over. "No. It's just pure conjecture on our part, and we have no proof. I want to talk to Valdi myself when he gets back."

Högni seemed relieved. "Then we should just go to bed," he said.

They walked the same way back and fell into an even deeper silence. At the crossroads, Högni said good night and walked on home to the school.

Question thirty-eight: How did Erlingur Hákonarson die? Sixth letter. Erlingur was a promising seven-year-old boy when his father Earl Hákon was fighting off an invasion from the Jomsvikings in Norway. The earl was faring very badly in the battle and eventually invoked Thorgerd Hördabrúd, vowing to make a human sacrifice, offering Erlingur for this purpose. This brought about a great transformation because clouds erupted and the Jomsvikings had to struggle against a violent hailstorm that broke out over the ships. The hailstones weighed two ounces each and pelted the Jomsvikings' faces so fiercely that they almost blinded them. They had pulled off some of their clothes during the day because of the heat, but now it grew much colder. They then realized that Thorgerd was on the earl's side, and arrows shot out from all her fingers. Every single arrow killed someone. The answer is "sacrifice." The sixth letter is f.

CHAPTER 55

Wednesday, June 8, 1960

It was past midnight by the time Grímur started to undress in the small bedroom of his house. Ingibjörg seemed to be asleep, but she stirred as he slipped under the quilt.

"Did you remember to give water to the cows, Grímur dear?" she asked sleepily.

Grímur sat up on the edge of the bed again. "No, of course not. I've been so preoccupied, or maybe I'm just going senile," he said, stretching out for his clothes.

"These are bad times. I haven't been myself these days, goddamn it," he said as he walked to the cowshed. He fetched some buckets from the shed and lowered them into the well. The water level was reasonably high after the rainfall, so it was easy to fill them. He took two trips, but as he was passing the shed door, he noticed that Thormódur Krákur was also fetching water in the well by his shed.

Grímur walked across the field to him. "Are you still up, Krákur?"

"Yeah, got to take care of the animals," he answered heavily.

Grímur was silent a moment. Finally, he said, "These are bad times for us on the island."

Thormódur Krákur silently nodded.

Grímur continued: "The inspectors think that Kjartan, the magistrate's assistant, and Doctor Jóhanna killed the reporter and dragged him up to the churchyard."

Again, Thormódur Krákur silently shook his head.

"Then they got news from Reykjavik that the reporter drowned," Grímur added, "not at sea, but in freshwater."

"Oh, in that case the police must realize they're innocent," said Thormódur Krákur eagerly.

"No, they say that Kjartan and Jóhanna drowned the man in the bathtub in the doctor's house," said Grímur.

Thormódur Krákur shook his head again. "Bullshit. They haven't harmed anyone," he said.

"I happen to agree with you, but who did it then?" Grímur asked.

Thormódur Krákur didn't answer.

"Högni and I were wondering if Valdi in Ystakot might have lost control of himself. Do you think that's possible?"

Thormódur Krákur looked at Grímur and suddenly started to cry, the silent, tearless weeping of an old man.

Grímur stared at the broken man in astonishment.

"It's all my fault," the old man yelled into the night in a cracking voice, as if he wanted the whole island to hear his confession.

Grímur struggled to understand. "Your fault?" he asked.

"Yes, it was me, it was me," Thormódur Krákur uttered through his heavy sobs.

"How do you mean, Krákur?"

"It was me, and now everyone else is being blamed for it."

"Did you murder that man, Krákur?"

"Murder? No, not at all. He drowned helplessly, but then it was me who did those things to him."

"Did you place him in the churchyard?"

"Yes. I had to do it because of the dream."

Grímur patted Thormódur Krákur on the shoulder. "Come on, pal. Tell me the whole story."

Thormódur Krákur got a hold of himself, wiped his eyes with his sleeve, and then started to talk: "The reporter came up to me in the shed on Sunday evening and asked me for some milk to drink. Then he offered me a sip of rum and we started chatting."

Thormódur Krákur pulled out a handkerchief and blew his nose before continuing: "The man wanted to hear some good stories, so I told him stories, old dreams, deciphered and undeciphered, as I usually do. Then I told him about the calf dream, which is about the three eagles over the church and the eagle that sits in the churchyard and has blood on its wings and the distinguished-looking men leading the calves up the pass. D'you remember?"

Grímur nodded. He had often heard Thormódur Krákur describe that dream.

"The man said he could decipher the dream. He said that when a blood eagle perches in the Flatey churchyard, it would be a sign that the *Flatey Book* was on its way back home out of its exile."

"Huh?" Grímur wasn't quite following.

"Yes, the distinguished figures are the ancient Norwegian kings and the calves symbolize the 113 vellum sheets of the manuscript. Then the reporter said these exact words to me: 'If you ever have to kill anyone or stumble on anyone who's already dead, take him up to the churchyard, place him on a grave there, and carve a blood eagle on his back. Then see what happens.' That's what he said, and that's what I did. Obviously the bird with the bloody feathers meant a man cut into a blood eagle, as described in the *Flatey Book*. Bryngeir could see that, but I was so blind that I never made the connection, even though I'd read about blood eagles many times. It was the most ingenious decoding of a dream I'd ever heard. Then, after we'd been chatting for a while, I had to take the milk to the priest, and the reporter was going to visit Doctor Jóhanna."

"Yes, I know." Grímur nodded.

"From the vicarage I went home for dinner and then up to the shed again in the evening to give water to the cows for the night. But as I was fetching the water, I saw the man there at the bottom of the well. He was lying on his back at the bottom with his legs sticking out of the water."

"How the hell did he end up in there?" Grímur was aghast.

Thormódur Krákur shook his head. "I don't know. The old lid was smashed, and pieces of wood were floating around the man in the water."

Grímur looked at the path that led from the shed to the well. It pointed to the southwest of the island in a direct line to the doctor's house. "Maybe he intended to take the shortcut across the island from the shed," said Grímur, "and the path just led him across the field to the well. Then he stepped on the old lid of the well and broke it."

Thormódur Krákur nodded and shook his head alternately. "The man was stone dead when I finally managed to hoist up him with my long hook. My first thought was to go and get you, Grímur, but then I remembered what he'd said. 'If you ever have to kill anyone or stumble on someone who who's already dead, take him up to the churchyard, place him on a grave there, and carve a blood eagle on his back.' That was his final wish, and I couldn't deny him that. The man had said it to me in all seriousness, and I didn't dare to disobey. He could have started to haunt the shed here, and the *Flatey Book* was at stake. I grabbed my slaughtering knife in the shed and took the man up to the churchyard on the cart. I placed him on a grave there as I'd been instructed to do and carved his back. Then I dug my hands into the wounds and pulled his lungs out and all this blood came out. Then I just left him there and went home to sleep. The man didn't mention how long he'd have to stand there like that for the prediction to come true."

"Didn't anyone see you doing this?" Grímur asked.

"No, no. It was so late."

Grímur peered into Thormódur Krákur's eyes. "You're not just saying this to save Jóhanna and Kjartan and get them out of this mess they're in, are you?"

"No, no. God forbid. I'm telling you the truth."

"Very well," Grímur gasped. "I remember you were making a new lid for your well on Monday. So the old lid was destroyed by the reporter?"

"Yeah, it was smashed to pieces."

Grímur shook his head. "I'm not sure you did the right thing in all of this, even if the man did say those things to you."

Thormódur stood dejectedly, fiddling with some wool between his fingers. "I guess I better tell the police about this. I just can't bear stepping on that pier," he added.

Question thirty-nine: A smaller steak than the king. First letter. Ali Hallvardsson was dressed just like the king. He rode into the woods with just a few men. The yeomen swiftly came to him and killed him. They stripped off his armor and loudly exclaimed that the king was dead. But when the king heard of this, he ordered a battle horn to be blown and defiantly rode on, and the yeomen realized that they had a smaller steak on their spit than they had imagined. The answer is "Ali," and the first letter is a.

CHAPTER 56

It was almost five in the morning when Grímur and Kjartan clambered down the debarkation bridge on the side of the coast guard ship. Thormódur Krákur had come on board with Grímur after midnight and told the policemen his story. First orally, twice, and then he was asked to describe the events in writing and to sign his statement in the presence of witnesses. The policemen were very suspicious. They couldn't imagine how anyone could commit such an atrocity on the mere basis of a dream. Finally, Thormódur Krákur was allowed to go home for the night. Inspector Lúkas went with him to confiscate the slaughtering knife. The matter was then to be investigated in greater detail in the morning, when the well and broken lid would be examined. Thórólfur reluctantly agreed to release Kjartan from custody since he was lying awake in his cabin. Jóhanna, on the other hand, was to remain in custody. The case of the Danish professor still loomed over her.

The district officer and the magistrate's envoy both walked off the pier in silence. The morning sun had risen in the east and was beginning to draw long shadows. An icy nocturnal breeze played on their cheeks, and ice crystals glistened on the pier. Temperatures had dropped to freezing point in the heart of the night.

Some seagulls that had spent the night on the edge of the jetty silently scattered into the sky, disturbed by the men's approach. An ewe with two lambs lay by the corner of the fish factory and obstinately stood up when they almost stepped on them. Kjartan gazed at the lambs running up the slope toward Ystakot. There were two huts at the end of the shore, and he thought he could make out someone peeping at him from behind one of them. He halted and tapped Grímur's arm without saying anything. The little head popped out again and now realized it had been spotted and decided to recoil. The small human figure swiftly headed up the slope toward Ystakot.

"Isn't that little Nonni?" Grímur said. "What's he doing up so early?"

"Or late," said Kjartan.

Grímur glanced back at the boats anchored at the pier. "His father's boat isn't back yet. Could they still be out at sea and the boy alone at home?"

"Maybe it's not all as it seems," Kjartan said softly.

They walked up the slope after the boy. When they reached the croft, they saw the boy in the doorway but then vanishing inside.

Grímur called through the door: "Nonni, come out and talk to us, my friend. We want to help you if there's something wrong."

There was no answer, so Grímur stooped to step into the dark cottage. Kjartan followed. They first came into a small, smelly, dirty kitchen. Beyond that there was a small bedroom with four beds, two on either side. Daylight filtered through a small window at the top of the gable, and a half-full potty lay on the floor. Kjartan felt nauseous, turned around, and rushed outside to deeply inhale the clear morning air several times.

"Nonni, my friend," Grímur called inside. "We only want to ask you about your dad and your grandpa. Have they been away for long?"

Some noise was heard from within, and soon the district officer reappeared with the boy by his side.

"The boy was all alone in there," Grímur said to Kjartan.

The boy stood beside them, downcast.

"Are your dad and grandpa at sea?" Grímur asked.

"Yeah, but they've been gone such a long time," the boy answered. "They left really early this morning."

"You mean yesterday morning. Did you get any sleep last night?"

"No, I was waiting for them all day."

"Where did they go?"

"Out to Ketilsey to pull in the seal net and check on the eiderdown. They weren't going to be gone this long."

"Maybe the engine broke down. I'll go out looking for them. I'm sure they're in no danger. The weather's so good. Why didn't you go with them?"

"I wasn't allowed to. Dad was punishing me for taking a crap on the island last time, and then I sneaked out of church during the mass on Sunday and he saw me."

Kjartan had an idea and gently asked him, "Do you have a camera, Nonni?"

The boy looked at him in surprise but didn't answer.

Kjartan repeated his question: "Don't you have a camera, my friend?"

Nonni was about to say something, but the words got stuck in his throat.

"I think you have a camera and maybe also some nice binoculars," said Kjartan.

"How do you know?" said the boy.

"Can I see them?" Kjartan asked.

The boy looked at them with trepidation but then walked away from the croft. Grímur and Kjartan followed him. Nonni walked past the potato patch toward a shed built into the earth of the slope. He entered it through a low doorway and swiftly returned, holding a small bag.

"The foreigner left this bag in the boat when Granddad took him to Stykkishólmur," he said. "I found it myself and kept it."

Kjartan took the bag and examined it. Inside it he found a camera, pair of binoculars, a toiletries bag, and underwear that had grown musty from damp storage.

"The camera's broken," said the boy. "I've tried everything you're supposed to do, but there's no picture in the box."

"Tell us about when your grandpa took the foreigner out," said Kjartan.

The boy looked up and said, "Dad went to the mainland with the mail boat to get Mom. Me and Grandpa went down when the boat was coming back to grab the ropes. We were then going to go out in the strait to fish some small cod for dinner."

He grew silent and stared at his treasures. He was trembling from the cold and fatigue.

"What happened then?" Grímur asked.

"We were still on the pier when everyone else had left, and we were going to go out on our boat, *Raven*. Then the foreigner came running over and calling. He was far too late because the mail boat had left ages ago. Then he ordered Grandpa to take him to Stykkishólmur, but it was really difficult to understand him."

"Did your grandpa agree to sail with him?" Grímur asked.

"Yeah, the man showed us the loads of money he was going to give us when they got to Stykkishólmur."

"So they went then?"

"Yeah, but the foreigner didn't want me to come along."

"Was your grandpa away for long?"

"Yeah, he didn't come back until the next day. The motor was completely out of fuel, so he came in using the sail when the southern winds started blowing. Grandpa then went to sleep, but I found the bag in the boat and hid it. I would've given it back to the foreigner, but he never came back to ask for it."

"Didn't your dad know about this?"

"No. He was so angry when he got back from the mainland because Mom wouldn't come back with him from her roadworks job. He complained about everything and got really mad when he saw the boat was out of fuel. Grandpa couldn't remember anything about his trip with the foreigner, and I didn't dare to tell Dad about it. Grandpa has started to forget so many things. I think the foreigner also forgot to pay him the way he'd promised because Grandpa didn't have any money on him when he got home. I peeped into his pockets when he was asleep."

"But what about that man from Reykjavik, the reporter? Did he know you were keeping the bag?" Kjartan asked.

Nonni averted his gaze. "Yeah, when I sneaked out of mass, I went home to have a little look through the binoculars. Normally I hardly ever dare to use it because no one's allowed to see me. I was sure that District Officer Grímur would take it away from me if anyone saw me."

The boy looked shamefacedly at the district officer.

"Did the reporter see you?" Kjartan asked.

"Yeah, I thought that everyone was still in the church, but then he was suddenly there standing beside me."

"What did he say to you?"

"He asked me if I owned the binoculars. Then he looked into the bag and saw the little books. Then he asked me if Dad had taken the foreigner to Stykkishólmur. I told him that Grandpa had, but he'd run out of fuel. Then he asked me if he could keep the little books if he promised not to tell anyone about the binoculars and the camera. I said yes, if he wouldn't tell anyone. He promised and said that then I wasn't to tell anyone either."

The boy started whimpering. "And now the reporter is dead and I'm breaking my promise."

"Do you remember the dead man you saw in Ketilsey?" Kjartan asked.

"Yeah," the boy answered.

"Had you seen him before?"

"No, I don't think so. You couldn't see his face."

Grímur had listened to the whole story in silence and now spoke: "Right, my friend. Let's go to my house, Nonni, and we'll get my Imba out of bed. She'll give you some milk and something good to eat. Then maybe you'll get a slice of cake and go to bed. Me and Kjartan here will go looking for your dad and grandpa."

Question forty: The final question has now been reached. It is the key to all the other answers and goes as follows: "Who spoke the wisest?" The answers can vary greatly, according to personal taste and wisdom. There are many wise sayings in this book, but the key here is composed of the following letters:

O S L E O Y I A R N R Y L
E M H O N E A E N W T L B
A U R M L E Q W T R O N E

"My father went through the entire book, page by page, trying out all the sentences that felt reasonably sensible to him and contained some ounce of wisdom. He played around with them, rearranging the letters to see whether they could make up a complete sentence. The spelling was supposed to be in line with what was used in the latter half of the nineteenth century, as far as he knew, and the sentence had to contain exactly thirty-nine letters. He created little tables with these letters and shuffled them over and over again, but still couldn't find the text to unlock the riddle, and he eventually gave up. Many weeks later, he started thinking about the enigma again. He realized something else was needed to find the right key sentence. Some letters appeared more than once in the rows of key letters, and it was impossible to say how the rows were connected. There had to be some other way of decoding the answer. Then he focused his attention on the drawing that accompanied the clues and had come to be known as the magic rune. Personally, he didn't believe in that kind of stuff, but he was sure that the author had placed the picture beside the riddle for a reason. He noted that on each side of the picture there were thirteen lines that crossed the picture and reemerged on the other side of it in a different place. Thirteen multiplied by three is thirty-nine, which is the number of letters in the key. He drew a copy of the picture, reproducing it three times in a vertical row. Then he wrote out the key letters downwards in the vertical column and moved them across to the other side of the grid, following each line. The following sentence emerged: 'Rarely is only one to blame when two men quarrel.' This is the second part of a sentence that reads as follows and can be considered wise: 'Remember, though, that rarely is only one to blame when two men quarrel.' It's a line from the old saga of Hákon. My father was so fervent in his quest that he overdid it that night. He was extremely ill when I found him in the library, but I had never seen him in such

ecstasy. Now all he needed to do was to go over his answers to the thirty-nine questions and see whether they formed the end of the key poem. It should only have taken him part of the day, but he was too ill now and never got out of the house again. He knew he could only do this by strictly abiding by the rules. A short while later Gaston Lund arrived on his fateful visit. My father told him how the 'magic rune' was to be used to unlock the solution to the riddle and fortieth question. Lund got very excited about it and was lent the library key to rush up there and try out his answers. But he ran out of time. He didn't manage to finish the test and later probably missed the mail boat. What happened next is difficult to imagine."

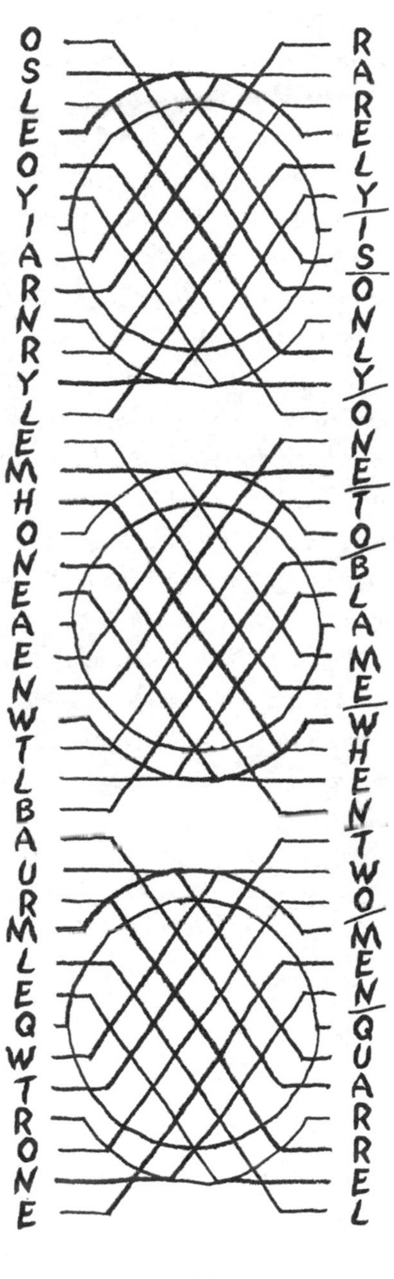
OSLEOYIARNRYLEMHONEAENWTLBAURMLEQWTRONE
RARELY IS ONLY ONE TO BLAME WHEN TWO MEN QUARREL

"My father spent the whole winter trying to muster up enough energy to return to the library and try out his solution. I often offered to do it for him, but he didn't want me to. He wanted to see the solution appear before his own eyes. Then finally, yesterday, he asked me to go up and try out his solution. He felt death was approaching and wanted to hear the end of the poem before he passed away. I was going to ask Ingibjörg to watch over him and sent for her, but he lost consciousness as I was waiting for her to arrive. He steadily deteriorated during the day and died that evening. He'd solved the code but never knew if he'd found the right solution to the entire enigma. But now we'll see what happens."

Jóhanna wrote down the thirty-nine letters in a single column, following her father's diagram, and numbered them at the same time. Then, starting on each letter, she followed each line across the grid to where it ended on the other side of the picture and wrote the letter out again. Wherever Björn Snorri and Gaston Lund's answers differed, she wrote down both possibilities. Then she scrutinized the solution for a moment. She crossed out three letters in her father's answers and three letters in Gaston Lund's and inserted dashes between the words. She said, "The solution is:

t h e f e y i s d o o m e d t o d i e
t h e l u c k y i s s a f e f o r n o w

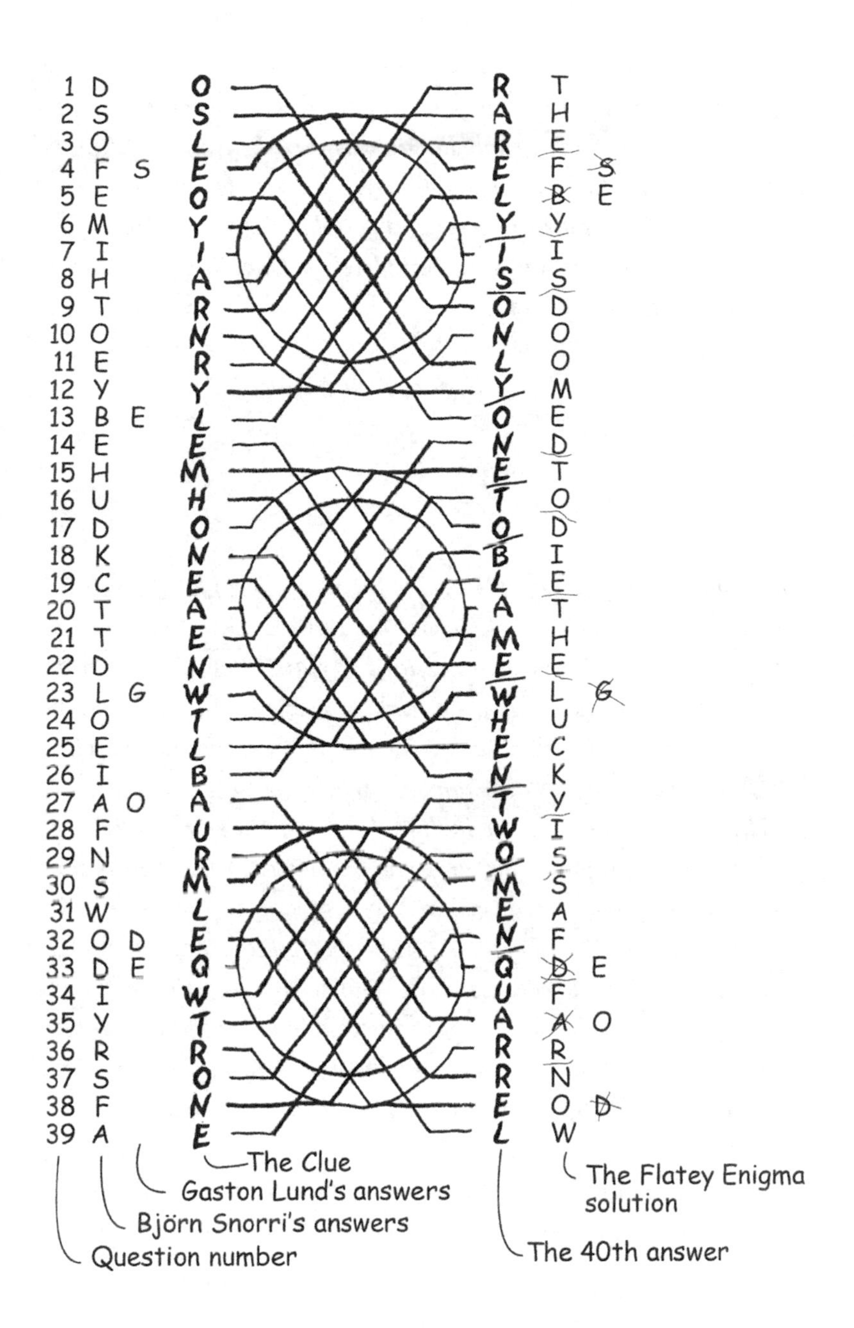
1 D O R T
2 S S A H
3 O L R E
4 F S E E F S
5 E O L B E
6 M Y Y Y
7 I I I I
8 H A S S
9 T R O D
10 O N N O
11 E R L O
12 Y Y Y M
13 B E L O E
14 E E N D
15 H M E T
16 U H T O
17 D O O D
18 K N B I
19 C E L E
20 T A A T
21 T E M H
22 D N E E
23 L G W W L G
24 O T H U
25 E L E C
26 I B N K
27 A O A T Y
28 F U W I
29 N R O S
30 S M M S
31 W L E A
32 O D E N F
33 D E Q Q D E
34 I W U F
35 Y T A A O
36 R R R R
37 S O R N
38 F N E O D
39 A E L W
The Clue
Gaston Lund's answers
Björn Snorri's answers
Question number
The Flatey Enigma solution
The 40th answer

"There are, therefore, errors in my father's answers to questions seventeen, twenty-six, and thirty. Lund got those answers right. There were three errors in Gaston Lund's answers. But once he'd found the solution to the key, it should have been easy for him to correct his answer. The guess someone had scribbled at the bottom of the sheet sometime was somehow completely wrong. The final lines of the poem were as follows:

Heavy gray clouds of eerie pelting hail
Demanding the magic words
The fey is doomed to die
The lucky is safe for now."

Jóhanna looked up Sverrir's saga. "This is an account of a yeoman who followed his son to the warships and gave him some advice, urging him to be bold and audacious in battle. Reputation is what survives a man the longest, he said. In every battle you're in, remember that you will either die or survive. Be valiant, therefore, since everything is predetermined. 'The fey is doomed to die, the lucky is safe for now. To die in flight is the worst death of all.'"

Kjartan pondered this wisdom. It reflected a belief in predestination that might have been be useful to resort to when your life was turned upside down, but he still preferred to live by other laws. He pulled out his pocket notebook and scrutinized the picture he had drawn in Ketilsey. "Lund had probably managed to complete the solution on Ketilsey, and since he had nothing else to write with, he used the pebbles to form the missing word from the poem. Lucky *wasn't the name of a boat.*

"I feel slightly ashamed because I almost caused an uproar today by connecting Sigurbjörn in Svalbardi's boat to Gaston Lund's

death. And then I was going to claim that Gudrún in Innstibaer was the mother of Lund's child and that their son had been involved in this case. It was a good job District Officer Grímur brought me to my senses and made me hold my tongue."

"Yes, a good job he did. Gudrún's son is not Gaston Lund's son. The child that Gaston Lund did his best to disown is another man altogether," said Jóhanna.

CHAPTER 57

Grímur, Kjartan, and little Nonni walked across the village together, and Grímur woke up his wife. She got up to prepare some food and also fetched a snack from an old cake box. The boy then stayed in the district officer's house with Ingibjörg, while Grímur and Kjartan continued on down to the moored boats.

Both men were silent, lost in separate thoughts. They boarded the boat, and Grímur started the engine. The sound of the motor seemed abnormally loud as it broke the stillness of the morning. Even the birds in Hafnarey were silent just before dawn.

Grímur headed to the west of the island, passing the new pier and the coast guard ship and skerries.

Finally Grímur spoke: "How did it occur to you to ask the boy if he had any binoculars?"

Kjartan hesitated a moment before answering. "It was a hunch. On Thursday when we went to collect the body in Ketilsey, we spotted the boy on the shore below the croft. I saw he was holding something up to his eyes that glistened. It occurred to me that they might be binoculars. Then I remembered that Lund had been carrying some binoculars and a camera in his luggage that were never found. I knew there could be a connection there somewhere. That's why I asked the boy."

Grímur nodded. "I think it's becoming quite clear then. Professor Lund delayed for too long at the doctor's house and lost track of time. He thought he had enough time to go to the library, but when he finally got down to the pier the mail boat had already left. He could probably still see it sailing south. He now badly needed to get to Stykkishólmur and from there south to Reykjavik because he had a flight to catch to Copenhagen. Old Jón Ferdinand and the kid were on the pier with the boat, and Lund managed to communicate to them that he needed to get to Stykkishólmur. He must have insisted and been pushy enough to make the old man sail off with him. But I think it had been many years since Jón Ferdinand had sailed all the way to Stykkishólmur. He must have forgotten himself on the way and headed for Ketilsey, since that was the route he was most used to sailing. Lund saw nothing strange about this, because Ketilsey is to the southeast, which could have been the sailing route to Stykkishólmur, as far as a stranger was concerned. The boat then ran out of fuel close to Ketilsey and they rowed to the landing slip. Lund must have gone on land to look for inhabitants and get some help, while Jón Ferdinand waited on the boat. After a while, Jón Ferdinand completely forgot that he had a passenger. All he can think of is that he's out of fuel in Ketilsey and has to get home. Then a southerly breeze picks up and there's no time to waste, so he hoists the sail and heads home for Flatey. Lund is left stranded on the island, and we know how the story ends."

Kjartan said nothing but nodded. This was also how he had imagined the course of events.

The rocks of Ketilsey glistened in the morning sun as they approached. Then they saw a black boat drifting about a kilometer west of the island. As they drew closer to it, they saw Jón Ferdinand standing by the engine bay, staring vacantly at the sea and shivering in the cold. A dark stain ran from the crotch of his trousers down his thigh.

"He's soiled himself," Grímur uttered in a low voice. The old man sat down on the thwart as they arrived and seemed to be totally oblivious to their presence. Grímur stretched out to grab the hawser on the other boat and tied it to the back of his own. Then he continued to sail on to Ketilsey at full speed. They spotted Valdi long before they reached the island. He was standing on its highest point, waving his sweater. Then he came running down to the slip. He was crying with rage.

"What the fuck were you doing, Dad, leaving me like that?" he yelled as soon as they were within earshot.

"Take it easy, Valdi. Your father is incapable of answering that question," said Grímur as he let his boat drift toward the slip. "Just hop on board and tell us what happened."

Valdi clambered on board, and Grímur carefully backed the boat away from the shore. As soon as they had reached a short distance from the island, he turned on the motor again and dragged the Ystakot boat up by their side. Grímur held a hand out to Jón Ferdinand and helped him to step between boats. He sat the old man on the thwart and draped his jacket over his shoulders. Grímur then headed toward home at full speed, towing the *Raven* behind them. Jón Ferdinand sat transfixed on the thwart, staring blankly at the backwash. Every now and then he called out in his raucous old voice: "Where are the nets, lads?"

Valdi struggled to recover and said in a tremulous voice, "The stupid old fool just abandoned me on the island."

Grímur silently nodded, as Valdi continued in his quivering tone: "We were checking out the eider duck's nests and collecting down, and then I suddenly noticed that he was back on the boat. I thought he was just putting down some eggs or a bag of down so I wasn't really watching him, but then I heard him turn on the motor. I ran down then, but he'd already untied the moorings and gone off by the time I got to the slip. He didn't even look back. No matter how loudly I cried out, he just stared into empty space, as if he were the only person in the world. Then I heard the motor die, and since then the boat's been drifting back and forth here for almost twenty-four hours. No matter how much I yelled, he didn't seem to hear me."

Grímur took out the picnic box and gave the father and son something to eat, and little else was said on their journey back to Flatey.

As they approached the island toward noon, they saw a flag flying at half-mast in front of the church and people on their way to the cemetery.

"They're burying the late Björn Snorri," said Grímur. "It was supposed to be a quiet affair before the coast guard ship sailed south with the inspectors and the prisoners, but that's all changed now, thank God."

The district officer steered his boat past the coast guard ship and over to the end of the pier. Little Nonni was standing on it all alone, and every now and then he ran back and forth a few steps. They tied the boat to the pier and climbed the steps.

"Take your father home, Valdi," said Grímur, "and try to all have a bit of a rest."

Grímur and Kjartan watched the three generations of men walking up the slope without glancing back, and then Grímur turned his gaze to the coast guard ship.

"I need to talk to the inspectors," he said wearily.

"Gaston Lund's visit to Iceland last fall was not his first visit to this country. He came here in the summer of 1926 with a few of his buddies from the University of Copenhagen. They were young and lively men and got up to all kinds of things during their two-week stay in Iceland. They followed the Njál saga's trail in the south, and the upshot of it all was a pretty young country girl from Rangárthing ended up pregnant, and Gaston, who was still just a student at the time, was the father. A boy was born, and the mother moved with him to Hafnarfjördur. The child was registered as 'Gestsson,' or guest's son, which wasn't an unusual name in those days for children whose fathers hadn't stuck around with their mothers for long. But there was more behind this name, because the professor's Christian name, Gaston, was also the German word for guest: 'gast.' This young boy grew up with his mother, without any reproaches to his father. His mother told him his father was a cultured man from a respectable family and highly regarded by the Danish king. The boy was proud of him and became a big fan of all things Danish and anything connected to the king. Then, in the summer of 1936, Professor Lund came to Iceland again, as part of the delegation that accompanied King Christian X, and his name appeared in the Icelandic press. The mother took the boy to go and meet Gaston Lund where he was staying at Hotel Borg with the intention of introducing them to each other. That was the sole purpose of her visit and nothing more. But Lund took it very badly, claimed the woman was mentally unstable, and categorically denied any knowledge of the boy. He had the mother and son forcibly and shamefully thrown out of the hotel. It was a terrible shock for a young and impressionable soul, and it marked the boy for life. He had always been brought up

with the myth of a father who mixed with kings and queens abroad and held far too important a post to be able to spend time with him and his mother. The boy's self-esteem had been shattered in an instant, and the mother changed from being a proud, independent, driven woman to a grumpy bundle of nerves who had been deprived of the only recognition she needed in life. Ten years later she died of TB. Her son's name was Bryngeir Gestsson. We lived together as a couple for a while, and I know he also had a vast impact on your life, too. But Lund didn't dare to come back to Iceland until last summer, and he tried to avoid any further encounters with the mother of his child and the boy by concealing his identity."

CHAPTER 58

Kjartan tried to lie down after his return from Ketilsey, but he was unable to sleep. He tossed and turned until he eventually gave up and decided to take a walk to calm his mind. As he walked up the steps toward the church, he saw Thormódur Krákur standing by the flagpole, propping himself up with his walking stick. He was wearing his Sunday suit, which after its repeated use over the past few days was by now beginning to look pretty crumpled and smudgy. An old sea bag lay at his feet.

"Good day to you, Assistant Magistrate," said Thormódur Krákur when he noticed Kjartan.

"Hello, Krákur," Kjartan answered. "The weather is clearing up."

"Yes, good weather for traveling now," said Thormódur Krákur, and they both fell silent a moment.

"Are you going on a journey then?" Kjartan asked.

"Yes, they want to take me south on the coast guard ship to have more of a chat about my nocturnal escapade with the reporter's body. They want the doctors at the mental asylum to check out my brain to make sure I'm not mad or something."

"That's understandable, I suppose," said Kjartan.

Thormódur Krákur frowned and then winced. "No, that's true, I guess it might seem weird to an outsider, but I still believe that everything serves a purpose. We'll see. Old Jón Ferdinand has to travel south as well. They're going to be examining him, too."

Kjartan nodded. "They need to find someplace where they can take good care of him. His son Valdi won't be able to look after him if he gets any worse."

Thormódur Krákur grabbed Kjartan's arm and said, "The worst part of it all is that I got you and my Jóhanna into all that trouble. I was totally devastated by it all."

"We'll get over it," said Kjartan.

They were quiet for a brief moment.

"I hear you're not too keen on traveling," Kjartan said finally.

"That is correct," Thormódur Krákur answered.

"But I guess there's no choice now?"

"No, they insist I go."

"When was the last time you left the island?"

"It's been a good while now."

"How long?"

Thormódur Krákur thought a moment before answering: "When I was a youngster, I took several trips out, transporting sheep, and I did some fishing on the islands around here, but that's about as far as I went. Then, when I was nineteen, they played a nasty trick on me, and I developed a kind of loathing for the sea after that. And from then on, I never went out to sea again. Besides, there was never any shortage of things for me to do at home on the island, so I didn't need to really. I'm almost seventy now, so it's been fifty years."

"So you've actually been stuck on Flatey for fifty whole years?"

"Yes, and I can't complain. I feel good here, and there's nothing that draws me to the mainland. Besides, where would I go? To Stykkishólmur maybe or Reykjavik and spend money? No, my friend. Life has been good to me."

Kjartan grew pensive. Fifty years on an island that is about 1.2 miles long and a third of a mile wide. Was that a lot better than being locked up in jail? Maybe, if one didn't make too many demands.

It was as if Thormódur Krákur could read his thoughts. "I hear you spent a few years inside?"

Kjartan gave a start. Of course, this story was bound to have traveled around the island, but no one had mentioned it until now.

"Yes, that's right," he answered.

"That must have been very trying," said Thormódur Krákur. "Even though I've never traveled, I've always been my own boss. I've worked when I wanted to, eaten and slept whenever I wanted to, drank some schnapps whenever I felt inclined to. I imagine prison life must be pure misery and boredom."

Kjartan nodded.

"And I've been able to enjoy nature and all it has to offer," Thormódur Krákur continued.

"To me, the environment here reminds me slightly of the prison," Kjartan answered. "It also happened to be by the sea, so it was the same birds that I hear here that used to wake me up. I've yet to recover from that experience."

Thormódur Krákur was silent, so Kjartan continued: "But have you never longed to see other places than this little island and what you can see from this hillock?"

"No, my boy, and I've probably seen more with my sight than many other people who spend their whole lives wandering across the globe. I've seen worlds and countries that others can't even imagine. And that is perhaps precisely because I have planted firmer roots in the earth than the puffs of cotton that drift with the slightest breeze. An oak tree never complains that it can't leave its land."

"Are you going to tell the doctors in Reykjavik that you see elves and hidden people?" Kjartan asked.

"Not unless they ask me. Although it remains to be seen whether I'll spot any down south," Thormódur Krákur answered.

"Do you see elves now?"

"Yes. I'm kind of saying good-bye to them, my friends."

"Where are they?"

"They're south of the hillock and below the rock on the shore. And they pop up here every now and then."

Kjartan tried to conjure up the vision.

"It must be fun to observe them," he said.

"Yes. It's like watching newborn lambs playing in the spring," said Thormódur Krákur. "Do you long to see them?" he then asked.

"Yes, I can't deny I do," Kjartan answered.

Thormódur Krákur lowered his voice: "I've sometimes helped people to see if that is their sincere wish."

Kjartan looked at him skeptically. "How then?"

"Kneel down beside me here and place your head under my armpit. Let's see what happens."

Kjartan seemed hesitant.

"Yes, come on then, it won't last long," said Thormódur Krákur hastily.

"Well, no harm in trying, I guess," said Kjartan, kneeling down beside Thormódur Krákur, who took his head under his arm and held him tightly. Kjartan inhaled the smell of the wool of

Krákur's jacket mixed with pungent body odors and was on the point of pulling his head away because he had difficulties breathing. But then, all of a sudden, it was if he had entered another dimension. The air that he was breathing was suddenly sweet and refreshing, and he no longer felt Thormódur Krákur's arm. On the slope below by the shore he saw little flashes of light that fleetingly took on small human shapes. It perhaps lasted for just a few seconds, but he felt it had been for much longer. Then Thormódur Krákur finally released his grip, breathless and gasping, as if he had been holding his breath while it lasted. The visions dissipated and the oxygen seemed to vanish again. Kjartan sank languidly to the ground.

Thormódur Krákur didn't ask him if the experiment had yielded any results. He seemed to know that it had. Kjartan sat dazed on the grass and tried to get his head around the experience.

"You will find happiness, my friend," said Thormódur Krákur at last. "Life has been difficult for you, but that's all behind you now. I dreamed last night that I discovered a nest of beautiful eggs. That's always turned out to be a couple close to me. You shall take my Jóhanna as your own, and it will bring you good luck, my friend."

"She might have something to say about that," Kjartan answered.

"Sometimes it's all determined by fate, my friend, and we shouldn't fight it. I've already asked my Jóhanna to take care of you, and she took it quite well. Now you just need to treat her like a gentleman and it'll all happen of its own accord in a few months. I feel a strong connection there between you. I've been known to ask young people to open their hearts in a certain way, and it's always turned out to be for the best."

Thormódur Krákur turned around and looked down at the village. Högni, the teacher, was walking up the pass and holding a small case.

"Well then," said Thormódur Krákur, "time to get on that ship then. They're sailing out at two. Grímur asked Högni to accompany me and Jón Ferdinand on this trip. Högni knows his way around Reykjavik, and he'll be there to lend us a hand on this trip. I really appreciate that."

They walked down the slope and met Högni.

"Won't you be sailing south with us, Kjartan?" Högni asked.

"No, now I need to rest for one night. Grímur will be taking me over to Brjánslækur tomorrow morning. They'll be sending me a car from Patreksfjördur. Hopefully, I'll be able get back to notarizing property deals again."

"Reckon you'll find any more bodies in the district?" Högni asked teasingly.

Kjartan shook his head. He couldn't even bring himself to smile at the remark.

Högni looked at Thormódur Krákur. "Right then, sir. Let's get going. Can't keep the ship waiting."

Morning had broken by the time Jóhanna and Kjartan's conversation finally ended. They spoke about the event that had transformed both their lives so much for the worse many years earlier. They cried together and forgave. They were still young and no longer intended to live in the past.

Before they left the library, they put the Munksgaard edition of the Flatey Book *back into its place, having decided that the Aenigma Flateyensis should revert back to being an unsolved riddle. The story they now knew about how the enigma had been solved was a harrowing one, and they didn't want any of it to be associated with this ancient puzzle. They both wanted these old events to peacefully fade now. Neither Gaston Lund nor Björn Snorri Thorvald had lived to savor the moment when the solution was fully revealed, and it was therefore preferable to allow it to be rediscovered by someone else, under happier circumstances.*

A fog hovered over Flatey, and it was raining as they walked down the path from the church. In the distance one could hear the faint beat of a hammer from Thormódur Krákur, who was making a new lid for his well.

AUTHOR'S POSTSCRIPT

The *Flatey Book* was returned to Iceland on April 21, 1971, and is now exhibited in the Culture House in Reykjavik. Many sources were tapped in the making of this story. The text of the *Flatey Book* was, of course, the most precious mine, but countless other books were also delved into. I would like to thank these authors for the loan of their work.

My grandfather, Viktor Guðnason, was the manager of the post and telephone exchange in Flatey, as well as the church organist. My grandmother, Jónína Ólafsdóttir, was a goodwife in Sólbakki in Flatey and baked cakes that acquired great fame. I got to spend several summers with them, the last of which was in 1964. In the summer of 1960, I was a five-year-old boy staying with them in Flatey, so this period is firmly embedded in my mind. Among other things, I have a vivid memory of the moment when my grandfather showed me the Munksgaard edition of the *Flatey Book* in the library. The Munksgaard edition can now be viewed there under a glass case, as it is described in this book.

The poet Adalsteinn Ásberg Sigurdsson wrote the poem that appears in this book. He is bound by destiny to write poems in every book I write.

Thóra Steffensen, a coroner at National Hospital of Iceland, was very kind to assist me in the technical detail of the postmortems, and I thank her for all her help.

I also thank my wife, Vala, and daughters, Emilía Björt and Margrét Arna, for their patience and forbearance.

ADDENDUM: EXTRACT FROM THE SAGA OF THE JOMSVIKINGS IN THE *FLATEY BOOK*

There are several references to the Jomsvikings saga in this book. The Jomsvikings were a group of semilegendary Viking mercenaries in the tenth century, who were dedicated to the worship of such deities as Odin and Thor. They would reputedly fight for any lord who was willing to pay their substantial fees, and their stronghold was in Jómsborg on the southern shores of the Baltic Sea. Their exploits are recounted in manuscripts from the thirteenth and fourteenth centuries, and for the interest and entertainment of my readers, I've included a brief extract from the *Flatey Book* below, which describes how the Jomsvikings behaved after they were defeated by Earl Hákon in battle.

Jomsvikings Are Tied Up

Earl Hákon saw men on the skerry and ordered his warriors to row out to capture them all and bring them to him so that he could see to their execution. The earl's men boarded the ship and rowed to the skerry. The men that they found there were so badly wounded and cold that they put up very little resistance and were easily seized by the earl's men, who took them to the mainland. In total sixty men had been captured. Vagn and his companions were escorted on land, and their hands were mercilessly tied behind their backs to one rope. The earl and his men were about to eat and planned on executing Vagn and his men later in the day. Before they went to eat, though, the ships of the Jomsvikings were towed to land, and Hákon and his men divided up the loot and weapons. They felt they had won a great victory. They had captured some of the Jomsvikings, chased others away, but killed most of them, and they now boasted about these achievements and spoils. When they were full after their meal, they stepped out of their tents and walked over to the captives. Thorkell intended to execute them all, but they wanted to converse with the Jomsvikings first to see if they really were as tough as people said. He now freed a few men from the rope. As the men who were about to be beheaded were untied, the slaves were ordered to hold on to them and twists wands in their hair. The first three men, who were heavily wounded, were brought forth, and Thorkell Leira walked up to them and promptly chopped their heads off. Then Thorkell asked his men whether they had observed any change in his complexion as he performed this deed. "Because people say that a man's color changes when he swiftly kills three men in a row," he said. But Earl Hákon answered: "We did not see you change color, but a great change seems to have come over you."

A fourth man was then released and, before striking him, Thorkell asked: "How content are you to die?"

"I am very content to die," the man answered. "I shall suffer the same fate as my father." Then Thorkell cut off his head and thus ended his life. The fifth man was then brought forward, and Thorkell asked him how he felt about dying. He answered: "I would be violating the Jomsviking code if I were to be afraid of my own death, since it is fate that none of us can escape." Thorkell cut off his head.

Earl Hákon and Thorkell intended to pose the same question to each of the captives before executing them, to see whether these men really were as brave as they were reputed to be. Apart from anything else, they thought it would be fun to hear what they had to say. Then a sixth man was led forward and a stick was twisted in his hair to prepare him for his decapitation. When this was done, Thorkell asked him how content he was to die.

"I'm content to die with a good reputation," the man answered, "but you, Thorkell, will have to live with shame and deceit." Thorkell had heard more than enough and chopped the man's head off. Then a seventh man was led to be slain and Thorkell asked him how content he was to die.

"I'm very content to die," he said, "but I would be grateful if you could deal me a single swift blow and place a dagger in my hand. We Jomsvikings have often discussed whether a man retains consciousness after he has been decapitated, if it's done swiftly enough. Let's agree on the following signals: I'll hold the dagger up if I'm still conscious; otherwise it will just drop." Thorkell struck him and his head flew off, but the dagger dropped from his hand, as was to be expected.

Another man was untied from the rope, and Thorkell asked: "Tell me the truth, comrade, how content are you to die?"

He answered: "I am quite content to die, as are all our comrades. But I won't allow myself to be slaughtered like a lamb: I would rather face the blow. Strike straight at my face and watch carefully to see if I flinch, for we Jomsvikings have often spoken about this." Thorkell did as he wished. He was allowed to face the blow, and Thorkell approached him head on and hacked into his face. It is said that the man did not flinch until death overtook his eyes and began to shut them, as if often the case when a man dies. Following this a tenth man was led forward and Thorkell put the same question to him.

"I am very content," the man answered, "but will you first allow me to pull down my breeches so that I can relieve myself?"

"I shall grant you this wish," said Thorkell, "although I can't see what difference it will make to you."

The man, who was a handsome muscular figure, did as he wished. Then, holding his member, he started to speak without pulling up his breeches: "It is true," he said, "that things often turn out differently to the way you expected, because I had intended to introduce this member of mine to Thóra Skagadóttir, the earl's wife, and wanted her to nurture it in her bed." He then vigorously shook his member and pulled up his breeches. The earl then said: "Strike him down at once; this man has made it perfectly clear that he has been harboring wicked thoughts for a long time." Thorkell then chopped the man's head off, thus ending his life.

Sveinn Búason's Life Is Spared

Then the next man was untied and led forward. He was a young man with long hair that was as golden as silk and stretched down to his shoulders. Once more Thorkell asked how content he was to die, and he answered: "I've already lived the best part of my life and I've no interest in outliving those who have just fallen, but I don't want to be led to my death by slaves. I would rather be led by a warrior who is of no less account than you are, and it shouldn't be difficult to find someone. And what is more, I am so particular about my hair that I want this man to hold it away from my head and pull it sharply, so that it won't be stained in blood when you chop off my head as swiftly as possible." And it is said that a hirdman stepped forward to the earl and offered to hold him, but felt no need to twist a wand in his hair, since there was so much of it. Instead the hirdman grabbed the hair and twisted it around his hands. Thorkell prepared to slam down his sword, to grant the man his wish of being struck hard and swiftly, but at the very last moment, the young man pulled his head back and Thorkell's sword fell on both of the arms of the hirdman, who was holding the hair, and cut them off at the elbow. The young man then leaped up and said, "Whose hands are in my hair?" and then shook his head slightly.

Then the earl said: "A terrible mischief has been committed; take this man and kill him and all those who are left without delay. These men are just too difficult for us to handle, and their reputation and valor has not been exaggerated."

But, according to the Jomsvikings saga, after some discussion, the lives of Sveinn and his remaining companions were spared.

ABOUT THE AUTHOR

Viktor Arnar Ingolfsson was born in Akureyri in the north of Iceland on April 12, 1955. He finished his B.Sc. degree in civil engineering from the Icelandic College of Engineering and Technology (ICET) in 1983. He has taken courses in script writing run by the Icelandic Film Producers and at the Institute for Continuing Education at the University of Iceland. In 1990 and again in 1995, Ingolfsson attended classes in public relations at George Washington University in Washington, DC. Ingolfsson started working for the Icelandic Road Administration during his summer vacations from school in 1969, and he has worked there full time since 1983. Since 1985, he has supervised the institution's publications and contributed in public relations.

Ingolfsson has published six mysteries, the fifth of them *Afturelding* in 2005, which was the basis for the Icelandic TV series *Hunting Men*, which premiered in 2008. His short stories have appeared in magazines and collections. His third novel, *Engin Spor (House of Evidence)*, was nominated for the Glass Key prize, an award given by Skandinaviska Kriminalselskapet (Crime Writers of Scandinavia), in 2001; and *Flateyjargáta (The Flatey Enigma)* was nominated for the same prize in 2004.

ABOUT THE TRANSLATOR

Photograph © Brooks Walker

As a translator and writer in his own right, Brian FitzGibbon has a particular passion for the translation of fiction. He has translated a vast array of film scripts, treatments, stage plays, and novels, working exclusively into English from Italian, French, and Icelandic. His translation of the Icelandic cult novel *101 Reykjavik* by Hallgrimur Helgason, published by Faber & Faber in the UK and Scribner in the U.S. in 2002, was hailed by the *Guardian* as "dazzling" and the *New York Times* as "lucid." He is also the translator of the acclaimed *The Green House* by Audur Ava Olafsdottir, which was published by AmazonCrossing earlier this year.